THE DEMON'S DECEIT

Andria Carver

Book I of Divine Evolution

Copyright © 2025 by Andria Carver

Cover design by L1Graphics

ISBN-13: 979-8-9994560-1-4 (paperback)
ISBN: 979-8-9994560-0-7 (ebook)

For my babies

1

THE DEMON FOUND me slumped over on a pile of bloated trash bags in the dingy light of a narrow alley. When the idea of consciousness spread into the muffled corners of my mind, its faithful partner—pain—wasn't far behind. A clanging headache throbbed in time with my churning stomach and almost distracted me from a tongue as dry as a desiccated cactus. Before full lucidity could set in, my fingers crawled around my body in a desperate search for something to drink. I winced when they met the sharp edges of a broken malt liquor bottle. Ignoring the blood, I picked it up and poured the rest of its contents into my mouth.

"Uuuuuugghh," I moaned as the last of the warm, flat liquid trickled down my throat and ignited a painful hiccup. Tossing the bottle aside, I patted my pockets until I located the bottle of pills and shook it. Empty. I sighed—a good evening was not in the forecast. Again.

"Pathetic." The word was so crisply enunciated I could picture the mouth from which it came, like a bubble blown through a sneer. I propped myself up on an elbow to peer over the mound of garbage where I'd crashed after my latest bender. After some time spent squinting against the pattern of broken lights peppering my eyelids, I saw her: a dark-haired woman in a crisp, navy-blue suit. Further inspection revealed clean tailoring, expensive shoes, a sleek coiffure, and an expression of lip-curling revulsion so at home on the faces of moneyed elites.

"Just pathetic." Her sharp eyes pierced into my own and confirmed that I was, undeniably, the object of her disgust. I pushed myself up a little farther to help cough out a gob of off-color sputum, which I spat neatly toward her designer pumps. Unperturbed, she approached and stood square in front of me, hands on hips and disdain as clear as day on her face.

"Please, do come in," I croaked and gestured to a torn and greasy bag across from my makeshift bed. "Make yourself at home." I punctuated the sentence with a loaded burp and more painful hiccups. Alarm klaxons went off in my head when I considered sitting up all the way, and I slumped over onto my side again.

"Do you have any brain cells left, or have you killed them all?"

I ignored her while testing whether my head felt better with my eyes open or closed.

"He better be right about you," she muttered to herself. "Though I don't suppose I have any other options at this point." She sighed. "Get up. You're coming with me."

My hand rose in a weak wave of dismissal before the spins began (eyes closed, definitely closed) and I adjusted my body to get more comfortable. "Listen, lady, I'm not interested in doing weird sex things for money right now, okay? Unless maybe you've got a trunkful of opiates and blow?" I tilted my head up and opened a hopeful eye to check her expression before closing it again in disappointment.

"I can offer you something much better." Her voice carried the hint of a sinister smirk.

I snorted. "There's nothing better than oblivion."

"Oh, I don't know about that, but once you've done my bidding, you can have all the oblivion you want."

My face scrunched as I attempted to parse her cryptic words through the haze of my migraine. "So weird sex things and then the starring role in a snuff film?" I shrugged against the slick black bag beneath me. "I'm not opposed to the idea, as long as I can't feel a thing."

I was only partially joking.

A low, mirthless laugh sent shivers across my skin. "Very well," she crooned.

A drizzle of bitter liquid wetted my lips, and I sank into the welcome embrace of darkness.

2

THE SCENE THAT greeted me when I next opened my eyes was high on the list of least expected. My gaze crept from the smooth ceiling down to my hands, which were clasped neatly over a crisp white sheet and blanket. Sunlight streamed through floor-to-ceiling windows and cast shadows of cool gray across the subtly patterned walls. I was calm, mostly. I saw no need to do anything other than dart my gaze around the room as I tried to recall how I ended up there. When my brain finally deigned to check in on its sensory information reports, something suddenly struck me as very odd. My pain was gone. All of it. Not a hint remained of the unwelcome (albeit self-imposed) scourge of the past two years. I froze, worried that lifting even a finger might break the spell.

Rehab? Mental institution? I quickly discounted the ideas. With my absence of money and friends, I'd never end up in a place as nice as this. I hazarded a stretch—still no pain—so I slowly sat up to take in more of my surroundings. The bed and side table were the only furnishings, but despite the minimalism, the room smelled expensive. Especially when I caught sight of the city across the water. I squinted to orient myself and located the too-distant Space Needle. My nose crinkled in disgust. I was in a worse place than I'd thought: Bellevue, Washington.

Groaning, I tossed the covers off and plopped my bare feet onto the heated marble floor. After giving my eyes a good rub, I attempted to scratch my knee, but thick and slippery silk pajamas thwarted my fingernails. I didn't remember putting the pajamas on, not that my memory could be considered a reliable witness, but in all likelihood, someone else had dressed me. The realization didn't upset me as much as it would have two years ago. I sighed and pattered over to the window to confirm my worst suspicions.

I shook my head as I contemplated the cleaner sister city of Seattle. With no port or industrial area, most of its population consists of overpaid tech workers and the ghosts of wealthy real estate investors. Not the type of people I would ever rub elbows with, based on tax brackets alone. I'd not been to Bellevue in years, largely because its police have a preternatural ability to sniff out the poor and drug-addicted and turn them right back around to Seattle, the regional collection point for the socially unwelcome. Not that Seattle wouldn't do the same thing if it had the opportunity. I breathed on the cool glass and drew a hand with a raised middle finger.

I let go of the resentment with a long exhale and ambled over to take a sip from the water glass by the bedside. "Now what?" I muttered. My head snapped around when the door swung open and a slim, elegant woman entered with a stack of clothing in her arms. I eyed her as she set them down on the bed.

"How do you feel?" Her bored tone indicated she didn't care about the answer.

Recognition kicked in. "You're that lady," I said, my brain tumbling back to my previous waking experience.

"Yes, and you're the pathetic shit-heap I scraped out of an alley."

"Oh, thank you," I said with obvious sarcasm. "Let's see, I should have my donation forms around here somewhere for your tax write-off." I patted my pretend pockets. "Although, I'm not worth much as a charity case."

"You're worth more to me than a simple tax write-off. But you bring up a good point, and I'll get my accountant on that immediately." She looked me up and down and her frown deepened with each pass. Her shoulders slumped as she let out a disappointed breath. "To get right to the point, I've made you my new assistant."

"Mmm-kay." I drew the syllables out while trying to figure out what the hell was going on and if I might be on an especially lucid drug trip.

"A simple thank you will suffice."

I slackened my jaw and stared blankly at her for an uncomfortably long period. It was a tactic I used to keep others from engaging with me when I wanted to be left alone. It worked on most people, except for those experiencing a break from reality, or those wanting to take advantage of people experiencing breaks from reality. She was solidly in the second camp because the ruse didn't work on her; she just stared back, unflinching, before pointing at the clothing on the bed.

"Put these on and meet me in the kitchen at the end of the hall. The bathroom is to the right."

She faked a thin smile before stepping out and closing the door behind her.

I stood there for a minute, mostly because it seemed like something one should do when confronted with an unexpected detour in your life's plan. Then I started undressing. The body odor and thin patina of sweat that typically followed an excessive binge session were missing, and I narrowed my eyes at the door. Someone had bathed me. I searched for a sense of outrage but found none. My body and I had not exactly been on the best of terms. It was more like a distant relation I was obligated to check in on from time to time without making any concrete promises or plans for the future.

The woman had given me gray slacks and a short-sleeved button-down blouse. Not my style, but they fit surprisingly well, even the bra and simple black flats. I took a cautious peek down the hall, and the adjacent door beckoned me into the bathroom. Red and gold mosaic tile gleamed on every surface and a colorful painting of a dark-skinned, nude woman hung on the wall. I squinted at it—it was an original Gauguin. Jesus Christ, the lady must be loaded. The subtle scent of jasmine drifted into my nostrils and I breathed it in with pleasure. It had been a long time since I'd been in a bathroom that didn't look and smell like a dive bar urinal. I took care of my business and let out a deep sigh of relief. Nothing like an empty bladder to start feeling human again.

My reflection in the mirror taunted me as I took the conspicuous toothbrush placed in pole position by the sink and brushed my teeth. After avoiding every opportunity of seeing myself, the woman staring back at me was unrecognizable. I looked like the mug shot of a drug addict. I mean, I was one, but still...the dark circles around bloodshot eyes, cracked lips, and sallow complexion added up to the face of a total shitshow. A brief vision of Tom popped into my head, and I squeezed my eyes shut. I knew what he would've said if he saw me. Shame crept in, and I quickly pushed the thought of him behind the mental wall I'd painstakingly built over two long years.

At the end of the hall was an open-floor kitchen and living space with vaulted ceilings and a tall wall of windows. The view from what I assumed to be the penthouse suite of a sky-high condo building showcased a long stretch of the Cascade mountain range, including Mount Rainier, the region's crown jewel. Minimalist leather couches and chairs, silk rugs, and low bronze tables peppered the large living room, while the kitchen was a sparkling study of immaculate white surfaces.

The woman was sitting at an elegant marble table and gestured for me to take the chair opposite her where a plate of eggs and toast and a mug of coffee waited. My stomach produced an impressive rumble when I sat down and the aroma of hot food enveloped me like a favorite blanket. I tore my gaze away from the meal and looked up at her.

With a curled lip akin to a neoliberal's at a welfare office, she motioned to the plate. "Please eat and see that you get the majority into your mouth. I had to give the maid the rest of the week off; she needed time to recover after dealing with your putrid carcass."

"Well, if you insist!" I said cheerfully before tucking the napkin into my shirt front and proceeding to eat with as much lip-smacking, open-mouthed chewing, and utter lack of manners as possible. The pretense soon gave way to earnestness. I couldn't remember when I last had a meal consisting of more than bargain-bin packaged food and a handful of pills. I scarfed the last bites and looked up at her and then longingly toward the kitchen.

Her gaze flicked to me after my fork's final scrapes, and she shook her head at my hopeful face. "No more for the moment; we have many things to discuss. Plus, I don't think my stomach could survive another display of that nauseating spectacle." She stood up, took my plate, and walked it over to the kitchen sink.

"It's not like you have to watch," I mumbled while crushing crumbs onto my fingertip and relaying them to my mouth. After a trip to the fridge, she set a glass of orange juice down in front of me before reseating herself. She clasped her hands on the table and scanned the ceiling. "Hmm, where to start? Ah yes, my name is Ms. Cummings and you are Jeanine Bennett, but go by Jeanie."

I raised an eyebrow. She was right, but I wanted to see where this was going before I said anything.

She waited a beat before continuing. "You're a month and change short of thirty-eight, you have no siblings or children, your father passed away ten years ago, you've been estranged from your mother ever since, and were widowed, let's see, about two years and three months ago. After your husband's death, you withdrew your measly savings and have been slowly bleeding them out by using every illicit substance you can get your hands on while living in various squats, weekly-rate hotels, and low-rent apartments. Is that about right?" Her mocking tone and callous, yet accurate, description of my life thus far kindled a rage I thought had died out two years ago.

My mouth tightened and I fought to keep up my mask of placid neutrality. One of two lessons I'd learned while navigating through the dark creases of the city: don't lose your shit and draw attention to yourself; and mind your own fucking business.

Her smile was smug. "Don't worry, I don't need you to acknowledge any of this. I know exactly who you are, where you've been, and what you've done with yourself. Any curiosity as to why I've bothered to learn all this about you?"

I watched her expectant face through narrowed eyes before standing up and strolling through the living room, taking the opportunity to mess with things as I went. I poked an artsy lampshade and skewed it to the side, casually pushed a throw pillow out of its perfect alignment on the couch, and slid apart the neat stack of magazines on the coffee table. I was giving myself time to mull it over.

"Seems like you wanted to find someone with no close relatives, friends, or advocates. Someone who won't be missed and who also happens to have strong addictions to many, many substances. I can only imagine what kind of benevolent intentions you have in mind for such a person." I picked up a colorful glass vase from an alcove in the wall and pretended to study it while watching her from the corner of my eye.

Her clap was slow and condescending. "Excellent detective work, Ms. Bennett; perhaps you *will* fulfill my needs."

She walked into the kitchen and rummaged around in a drawer, grabbed something, and hid it behind her back. Her steps were nonchalant as she glided over to where I stood.

I watched her with mild curiosity as she stopped within arm's reach before whipping her hand out to reveal a thin paring knife. I had no time to react before she stabbed it through my arm. Blood pooled around the knife's handle, and the vase shattered when it hit the floor.

"Ow!" I shouted, startled.

I snatched my arm away and stepped backwards. It took a moment of staring wide-eyed at the rivulet of blood trickling down my forearm before I realized I felt absolutely nothing: no pain, no internal alerts indicating a knife was currently lodged in my limb. With heavy breaths through clenched teeth, I looked up at her. She was watching me with a cool, calculating stare.

"What the fuck, lady?!"

My hand reflexively reached for the handle when I glanced back down at the knife. With a Category 5 grimace, I squeezed my eyes shut and pulled it out. The metal slid through my arm with a gentle tugging resistance, and my body convulsed with a disgusted shiver. Blood welled up in the knife's wake, and my stomach turned queasy when I took a quick peek. Still no pain. I dropped the knife and turned my arm over to examine the other side. More blood. My ringing ears signaled an incoming fainting spell, so I lowered myself down onto the broken glass, clutching the wound while I glared up at her.

With a casual and unhurried stride, Ms. Cummings strolled back to the kitchen and grabbed a first-aid kit from a cupboard, pulled a roll of gauze out, and tossed it to me. "Wrap it up before you get blood all over the place, please."

I picked up the roll from where it had bounced away from my fumbling hand and, out of shock rather than obedience, wrapped it around my arm and tied it off with a clumsy knot. A small bloom of red appeared through the gauze, and I stared at it, waiting for any kind of sensation to erupt. Still nothing. If it weren't for the blood, I would've assumed it was a clever illusion she'd pulled.

I glared at her. "What have you done to me?" I asked, referencing my painless condition rather than the sudden stabbing attack.

"I have given you a gift." Her mouth was a satisfied smirk as she sauntered over to the tall windows. "No pain and no fear." She gazed at the distant mountains with her hands clasped behind her. "And nothing left to lose..." She turned around, her dark eyes blazing. "Except my gift, that is. I can take that away at any time, and all the pain and paranoia you've ever experienced will return to you tenfold. So, I would advise you to do everything I ask of you in order to maintain your current blissfully numb state." She walked back to me, her patent-leather pumps crunching over the broken glass, and bent forward so her face was inches from mine. "Because I dragged you out of hell and I sure as shit can throw you back." Her eyes flashed red before she straightened and donned a fiendish smile. "Questions?"

I swallowed and pushed down the swirling emotions battling inside me. I honestly didn't know whether I should be angry or grateful. In all my random drug-addled musings over the years,

I'd never imagined myself in anything like this kind of scenario. Telling fortunes in a traveling circus? Sure. Logrolling in a lumberjack competition? Why not. Roller skating with David Bowie in the spirit realm? Absolutely. Getting kidnapped by a lunatic who can take away pain and fear? Nope.

At that point, I was only sure of three things: she was rich; whatever she'd done to me was solely for her own benefit; and, most importantly, she was a psychopath. She probably gave out copies of *Mein Kampf* for Christmas and had a shrine dedicated to Mussolini in her bedroom. Annoyed by her coolly expectant face, I decided to play her game in order to figure out what she was after.

I gestured to the glass on the floor. "If you're forcing me to be your assistant, this better not be coming out of my paycheck."

Her smile widened at the tacit acceptance of my fate. "Good," she crooned and patted my shoulder. "Very good. Now we can get started."

3

MS. CUMMINGS MOTIONED for me to follow her to the foyer and its adjacent staircase. As I climbed the steps behind her, my mind raced to figure out how she'd eliminated two fairly substantial sensations. Ever since she'd mentioned fear and pain, I'd been probing my mind and body for traces of either. I couldn't locate even a twinge of bodily discomfort, and the fact that I was willingly following a stranger who'd kidnapped, stabbed, and possibly lobotomized me into a dark hallway was proof enough the fear was gone, too.

We stopped in front of an imposing black door, and I stared, dumbfounded, as her fingers plucked an ornate key into existence and shimmied it into the keyhole. I was running my hands over my scalp, feeling for stitches or signs of blunt head trauma, when she turned to face me. "This is my office." Her mouth curled into a devious smile at my expression, well aware she was blowing my fragile mind.

The door swung open on silent hinges, and the scent of old leather and dusty paper wafted out. I cast a suspicious glance around the room before following her inside. Heavy black drapes concealed an entire wall of what I assumed to be windows, and shelves crammed full of books ranging from ancient to modern based on the assortment of smooth and crinkled spines covered the remaining walls. My gaze wandered over the collection, but the titles were unreadable in the semidarkness. An enormous desk occupied the center of the room and offered the only source of light: a solitary desk lamp straight out of a film noir detective's office. Ms. Cummings slid into the leather chair behind it.

"Shut the door and take a seat." The door closed with a gentle whump, and I sat down on the smaller and decidedly less comfortable chair across from her. Dim wall sconces flickered to life when she flipped a switch under her desk. Rather than providing additional illumination, they only deepened the shadows and made the room gloomier.

"Uh, lovely place you got here," I said, drumming my fingers against the lumpy arms of the chair before discovering they were skeleton arms with clawed fingers. I put my hands in my lap. "Cool chair. So, you need some cataloging done or something?"

"Not exactly." Another key appeared in her hand, and she unlocked a drawer in the desk, slid a perfectly ordinary manila folder out, and pushed it across to me. I squinted at it before pulling it over and opening it. A large color photo of a handsome man, maybe late-forties, stared back at me.

I shrugged. "I don't know. He might be a bit out of your league." I peeked under the photo and found more pictures of the same man, but they were surveillance shots—definitely not posed, and obviously taken without permission. "Stalker much?"

"Oh no, Jeanie dear, I don't want to date him; I want you to kill him." Her narrowed eyes radiated danger as she watched me for a reaction.

My serious mind was telling me that fear and revulsion would be normal and healthy responses to her demand, but I felt only amused incredulity. I stifled a giggle and hid my unwarranted smile by giving my face a solid rub. Then, I made a show of crossing my legs, tilting my head back, and letting out a deep sigh before meeting her eyes. "What?"

She stared at me, expression unchanged. "As my assistant, eliminating targets is your primary duty."

It was time to give her a good, long bout of serious contemplation. She appeared to be anywhere from mid-forties to mid-sixties, but her mannerisms and poise made me think she was on the older side despite there being no hint of gray at her temples and no visible wrinkles on her flawless olive skin. While I wouldn't have considered her a beautiful woman, her eyes were striking in a way unlike any I'd ever seen. They were large and dark, with no discernible distinction between iris and pupil. A deep-red ruby with an alluring sparkle glinted from a ring on her finger and matched the color of her impeccably tailored suit and flawless lipstick.

She didn't break her expectant stare, and I groaned and slid down into a slouch, my head bouncing against the carving of the skull that served as a headrest. "Are you fucking with me?" The way her black eyes bored into my own told me she most certainly was not. I let out a long breath and shook my head. "Look, lady, I'm not a killer. I'm going to need a lot more details...and a cigarette. Also, probably a lawyer."

Her tight jaw softened a fraction as she pulled a lighter and pack of cigarettes from her desk. "I can help you with the information and cigarette, but fuck lawyers."

She stood up and slid her hand through the heavy drapes to open a sliding door and beckoned for me to follow her outside. The bright sun hit me like a truck. Ms. Cummings had donned a pair of large black shades and placed a cigarette between her lips by the time my eyes adjusted. She handed me the pack and an engraved silver lighter, and I shook out a cigarette before lighting hers and mine. She inhaled deeply and blew out a long stream of billowing white smoke in my face before walking over to the balcony railing. I waved it aside and followed her, puffing away, lazy and content. The sun warmed my shoulders as I stared off at the distant mountains, and my body relaxed into the gentle tobacco high.

After several minutes of easy silence, she turned to me. "You know, I'm not totally evil, Jeanie. I'm just playing the same game as the rest of them. There's a chance we'd make a good team, and if we can get past a few hurdles, then it's smooth sailing. I can give you much more than a life free of pain. If you succeed, I'll ensure you never suffer again. I have the power to make things happen, which I hope you've noticed by now. Anything you want would be yours." She paused and took a drag, face thoughtful. "I'm sorry we started off in such a dramatic manner." She looked almost apologetic as she gestured toward my bandaged arm. "I've learned that actions speak louder than words, and I wanted your full attention before getting into details."

I glanced at her before taking my final puff. As far as I was concerned, the jury was still out on the "not totally evil" claim, but the rest of her speech sounded sincere. Before I could drop the butt beneath my heel, she sighed, exasperated, and pointed to a table and ashtray off to the other side of the sliding door. I shrugged and walked over.

"Why do you want this guy dead?" I asked over my shoulder while stubbing out the last of the embers.

When I walked back, I noticed her cigarette was gone and glanced over the railing to see it smoldering on the patio two floors below. An innocent smile was her response to my raised eyebrow.

"To put it plainly, he's competition. For me to succeed, I need to take what he has."

I squinted at her. "Yeah, that's pretty plain, I guess. But have you ever considered alternatives? You've obviously got money. Why don't you just sue him, buy off politicians, become a majority shareholder? You know, the usual ways rich people fight each other."

"If only it were that simple." She gestured for me to follow her back inside. "It's a lot more difficult to take down one of my people."

"Your people?" My hands fumbled through the drapes, and the sudden darkness blinded me again. "Would it kill you to get more light in here?" I mumbled as I stumbled back to the desk.

She ignored my second question. "I am not human, as you may have surmised, although your drug-addled brain might not have picked up on the *subtle* clues I've given you." She used air quotes for the word "subtle."

"Not human? I suppose that's one way to describe a person who hoards wealth." I settled back down into the uncomfortable chair and watched the pack of cigarettes and lighter disappear from her hand. "So, you're what; a magic bitch demon?"

She clapped her hands slowly. "You do have a few brain cells left in there. I'm very proud of you."

My eyebrows shot up. "Wait, what?"

She sighed. "I spoke too soon."

"Lady..."

"Ms. Cummings," she corrected me.

"Miss Cummings," I enunciated crisply, "demons aren't real. You're just as delusional as I am." Immediately after I said it, the doubt crept in.

"Oh-ho! First off, we prefer the term 'divines,' and since you know so much, explain to me how I've taken your pain and fear away?" She steepled her fingers and stared at me, expectant and amused.

I shrugged. "I don't know, probably a lobotomy or magic, rich-people drugs."

"I guarantee other rich people can't do this." She fondled her large ruby ring and growled out rough syllables of an unrecognizable language.

An explosion of pain shot through my body. Blood-red stars erupted behind my eyelids, and I slid off the chair onto my knees, my hands desperately trying to hold my head together. I wanted to vomit, but my stomach was a vacuum, and I could barely suck in enough air to breathe. After a moment, or an eternity, the agony abruptly ended. The suddenness of relief was more startling than the unexpected eruption of pain. I lifted my head from my hands and blinked to steady myself before crawling back into the chair to glare at her. Her mouth was a pleased smirk as she twisted the ring in absentminded circles around her finger.

"What the fuck?" I tried summoning the nausea back so I could vomit all over her stupid desk, but every trace of discomfort was gone again.

Her face glowed pale in the dim light as she closed her eyes. Ghosts of wrinkles lined her forehead, and her shoulders slumped forward. After a long pause and a deep breath, she opened them again, straightened her spine, and smiled at me. "That was your first lesson, Jeanie. Do what I say, and you'll never have to feel that again. If you don't complete your task, or if you try to hurt me, you'll feel it for the rest of your pathetic life."

I flipped her off below the desk. "I can tell this is the start of a beautiful friendship," I muttered and stood to wander over to a bookshelf, needing time to get my emotions in check.

Kill someone or be tortured. Marvelous.

My eyes squinted against the shadows as I perused the titled spines: *History of the Americas, The Rise of Civilization, Ancient History of the Mesopotamian Valleys*. History books for every place and time period. I glanced back at Ms. Cummings. Her eyes were closed. I moved to another section: *Fairie Magiks, Auld Sorceries, Mystic Beings*. Lots of books in languages and scripts I couldn't read. I pulled out a worn, leather-bound volume and let it fall open. The text was indecipherable, but the figures were what you'd expect to find in a creepy book in a dark library: ink drawings of flayed anatomies, strange cosmic symbols, depictions of various demonic and supernatural beings.

"Huh." I turned the book sideways to make out what looked to be a gruesome ritual involving several women and animals. "I see you're interested in politics." The cover left rusty-red flakes in my hand after I slid it back into place.

She chuckled behind me. "Yes, you might say I have an interest in a great many things. You have to know quite a lot to succeed as a divine. If you have questions that aren't annoyingly stupid, feel free to ask them."

I had so many questions it was difficult to decide which to ask first. "How are you able to give and take pain away?"

"Ah, yes, that does almost get to the heart of it." She steepled her fingers and cast her gaze up and around, searching for the answer. "How to explain it to an inferior human when I have limited time and patience? I'm afraid I'll have to give you the abbreviated version of what should be a long and colorful account. May I assign you some reading? You can read, can't you?"

"Almost to eighth grade level; I could be a senator!"

"Very good." She stood up and selected two books from her shelves and stacked them neatly on the desk before sitting back down and leaning forward on her elbows, hands clasped like a principal discussing punishment for an unruly child. "As I pointed out, I am not human. My kind have been calling themselves 'The Divine People' or 'divines' for ages now. We have what you might call magic and can manipulate objects and humans." She waved a lazy hand toward me. "This is how I am able to give you pain and also take it away."

My mouth had fallen open, and I squinted at her in disbelief. "Okay, so what the hell do you need me for if you're all magical and stuff?"

Her bright air of superiority dimmed. "We can imbue human assistants with special powers we ourselves do not possess and are undetectable to other divines."

I grinned. "That must really chap your ass to need an inferior human to help you."

She rolled her eyes. "You have no fucking idea. Any more asinine questions?"

"Well, a lot, actually. But in the interest of time, can we start with what you are if you're not human?"

She rubbed her eyes. "You're asking the wrong question, Jeanie. Labels are unimportant, *but* in the interest of moving this conversation along, divines are a supernatural species that evolved separately from humans. We think." She tacked the last part on quietly.

I snorted. "You don't know where you came from? That's hilarious."

She let out a long gust of exasperated air. "As I said, *what* we are and *where* we came from isn't important. It's what we *do* that you should be concerned with. Humans have been tangentially aware of us throughout history but, like you, cannot comprehend our true abilities or importance to the world. We have been a guiding force for your pitiful race since homo sapiens conquered their sister species and rose to the top of the food chain. We've influenced political upheavals, societal unrest, famines, wars, etcetera, etcetera." She circled her hand with dismissive disdain as she listed the exploits of her species. "In fact, most religions were created by quote-unquote *prophets* after a mind-blowing interaction with our kind. Quite a few divines are still creating new factions to this day." She chuckled and shook her head. "Humans are so easy to manipulate and will follow anyone who preys on their fears. Perhaps one day I will create my own cult of zealous nitwits." She gazed off with a wistful smile and sighed. "Humans have given us many names throughout the ages, but the most common are along the lines of angels and demons."

"Angels and demons? Seriously?"

"*We* didn't come up with those labels. You're the ones obsessed with good and evil and creators and all that nonsense." She sniffed. "Anyway, the old ones were charmed by the depictions of us in holy books, so we adopted the names they gave us. What humans don't realize is that angels and demons and gods and goblins aren't separate entities. They are just different stages of our evolution. We all begin as goblins then move to incubi, demons, angels, archangels, demigods, seraphim, and finally, gods." She listed them on her fingers. "I am a demon and you will help me ascend to angel rank."

My voice was skeptical. "Huh, okay. Do you change at each stage, like get wings and stuff? Or is it more like getting a new business card? Are there angel resource departments where you apply for promotions?"

She propped her head on her hand with obvious annoyance. "We do change, but not in ways that are very noticeable to humans. We increase in power, live longer, rule over larger domains…grow even more beautiful." She brushed a hand over her smooth and shiny hair. "The way we ascend is by taking the life force of those above us to gain their power."

"Like a reverse Ponzi scheme?"

She almost smiled. "Which is where you come in. I cannot get close to Dram Nguyen," she gestured to the folder on the desk and then pointed at me. "But you can."

I considered her words. "By life force, do you mean kill each other?"

"Yes...well, not technically," she conceded. "We just have to drink the blood of the higher rank."

"Aha! So I don't have to kill this guy." I walked over and tapped my finger on the folder. "I just need to get some of his blood."

She rolled her eyes. "Best of luck with that. Unless he's ready to die or ascend, he'll never let that happen. Taking a divine's blood without killing them is still a death sentence." Ms. Cummings glanced at her watch. "We need to wrap this up; I'm expecting someone." She slid the folder back into the drawer and straightened up, her eyes shining. She was as close to excited as I'd seen her. "He's one of my underlings who owes me a blood sacrifice."

I raised an eyebrow. "A blood sacrifice?"

She flicked her hand in annoyance. "Yes, the way we accumulate power is to drink the blood of the rank beneath ours."

"Like a Ponzi scheme?"

A soft chime from a distant clock sounded the hour, and her annoyed glare brightened in anticipation. On cue, the doorbell rang. "Be a dear and get the door, won't you, Jeanie? Oh, and make sure to check him for weapons."

4

THE MAN AT the door was a head taller and twice as wide as me and blocked the light streaming through the skylights of the small elevator lobby behind him. My eyes traveled up from his shabby trench coat to his face, and I froze in recognition. "Shady Sam?"

"Aye, Jeanie, you're looking well," he said in his faint Irish lilt. In the elegant entry of Ms. Cummings' penthouse, the patchy stubble and ruddy pockmarks on his blocky face were at odds with the cold, smooth surfaces around him. The artsy overhead light cast the deep indent of the white scar that traced from the corner of his gray eye to below his chin in stark relief. With his stony brow and permanent scowl, he was one of the meanest-looking men I'd ever met. Still, he was more presentable than I'd ever seen him: my primary dealer and most reliable source for cheap and questionable substances.

"What are you doing here?" I asked, trying to fit all the weird pieces of my new life in with my old.

"Got an appointment with Cummings." He shot a meaningful glance at the stairs behind me before his gaze flicked down to my bandaged arm. His eyes narrowed.

"Oh." I stepped back to let him in. My mind churned—Sam was a demon, or goblin, or whatever? How many of these things were there? How many did I already know? I shut the door behind him, and he shuffled out of his coat and handed it to me. Underneath, he was wearing a loose dress shirt with no obvious weapons I could see. I glanced down at his coat in my hand before tossing it on the floor and following him up the stairs.

Ms. Cummings had her disgusted but well-bred face on as we entered. "I think you know Mr. O'Brien, don't you, Jeanie?" Her teeth flashed white at my confused expression.

My gaze darted back and forth between the two. The pieces were starting to fit. "Sam helped you find me."

"Very good, Jeanie," she said in an overly patronizing tone.

I turned to Sam. "You son of a bitch!" The venom in my voice surprised me.

He held his hands up in mock defense. "Hey, I've done you a favor. You got money now; I reckon you owe me." His voice was hard, and I could sense he wanted to spit—his standard punctuation when his customers got uppity. He glanced sidelong at Ms. Cummings and swallowed instead. Her nose wrinkled in revulsion.

"Let's get this over with, please, Mr. O'Brien." She gestured for him to sit in the skeleton chair then pulled a golden goblet and dagger from her desk. Both had intricate carvings of twisted demonic forms and grinning skulls set with deep-red stones around the rim and pommel. The lady did have a flair for the macabre; I was impressed by her dedication.

Sam rolled up his sleeve and leaned over so the crook of his elbow hovered above the goblet. With one smooth motion, he pulled the dagger across his skin, and a line of blood appeared, accumulated, and dripped into the waiting cup. I squinted at the thin stream of red. It glowed with a faint light. As the goblet filled, Ms. Cummings used lazy strokes to wipe the blade of the dagger with a silky red cloth, mouth flat and bored. My jaw dropped lower and lower in horrible fascination as the level in the cup rose higher and higher. When Sam's blood was just below the rim, Ms. Cummings handed him the cloth. He took it and pressed it to the cut, bending his arm to hold it in place, and pushed the goblet to her.

Ms. Cummings' smile widened as she took the goblet in both hands and drank it down, eyes closed. As I stared at her in disgust, I spotted movement from the corner of my eye and glanced over to see Sam straightening the books on top of the desk. Face gray and haggard, he caught me watching him and gave a slight shake of his head, his eyes piercing my own. It was the same look he gave his clients when authorities stopped by the nooks and alleys where he was wrapping up deals. It was a very obvious shut-your-mouth-if-you-know-what's-good-for-you look.

Blood trickled from the corners of her mouth when Ms. Cummings lowered the goblet to the desk. Color bloomed in her cheeks, and the thin wrinkles on her forehead disappeared. When she opened her eyes, they glowed a vivid red.

"Thank you for your offering. You may go." She nodded to Sam.

He stood up, swayed on his feet, and staggered to the door. A look from Ms. Cummings indicated I should see him out. When we reached the foyer, he pulled the bloodied cloth from his arm and revealed a thin, red line where the cut had been. He handed me the cloth, and I took it by reflex before recoiling and dropping it. He swept his coat off the floor and opened the door. On the threshold, he paused. "Remember, Jeans, you owe me one." He winked. "See you around."

I closed the door behind him and leaned against it, staring at the square of red fabric on the floor for several solid seconds. The day just kept getting weirder. I decided to bring the cloth back to Ms. Cummings since she seemed to like Sam's blood so much. I stooped and pinched the fabric delicately between two fingers, wondering if divines had the same blood-borne diseases that humans do.

Ms. Cummings had wiped her mouth and put away her occult goods by the time I returned. She fixed me with an annoyed glare when I dropped the bloody cloth on her desk. She sighed, and it disappeared.

"You're looking better," I said. "Who knew that drinking blood had such marvelous restorative properties?"

Her smile was genuine as she gestured for me to sit.

"It is marvelous. Too bad it only works on divines. I could make a killing on the black market if it worked on humans."

She pulled the murder dossier back out and pushed it to me. "Here's the deal, Jeanie. I've set up a bank account in your name and will deposit money in it regularly so you can establish yourself and get to work on your assassination plan. If you complete the job, you'll be rich enough to retire to the Maldives and kill yourself in a swimming pool of cocaine. You have three months to formulate and execute a plan, and I will check in with you in two weeks to review your progress. This task is not a simple one, but I must impress upon you that time is of the essence." She leaned forward, her gaze level and calculating. "A war is stirring in the higher ranks, and the ensuing power struggle will begin soon. When it does, I need to be positioned to ascend before one of my associates does. Do you understand?"

I shrugged. "Sure, you want to take this guy's place or whatever. Gotta climb that blood ladder, amiright?"

I wondered why it mattered so much to her; it was obvious she was doing well in her current position. But then again, privilege often breeds greed, even in non-humans, apparently.

She must have guessed my line of thought because she leaned back, eyes distant, hands rubbing her smooth cheeks. "I'm old, Jeanie. I've been a demon for too long; I can feel my end coming. My powers are waning, and if I don't ascend soon, one of my incubi will kill me and take my place."

My brow wrinkled in confusion. "You're mortal?"

"Indeed, although our life spans are considerably longer than yours. I myself have been alive for one hundred and ninety-nine years. If I ascend, I'll get another hundred, give or take. That's why it is so important I take advantage of the power vacuum that will happen when our god dies."

I raised an eyebrow. "Your god? I wouldn't have guessed you were into monotheism."

She rolled her eyes. "Oh, keep up, Jeanie. I mean the god of the divines, the one at the highest level of our evolution. Rumor has it he is readying himself to die. He's over eight hundred years old—ancient for our kind. Upon his death, a new god will rise, and the struggle to ascend will ripple down through the ranks. It is a rare event; I imagine it will get quite messy. The higher ranks have already begun stoking unrest in their rival's territories. Fascism is on the rise, wars are breaking out, misinformation is widespread." She sighed. "It would be fun to watch if my survival didn't depend on it."

"I'll pop some popcorn." I said.

The corner of her mouth twisted up, and the red gleam was back in her eyes. "Your survival now depends on it as well, sweet Jeanie. If I die, you die too. And I don't think either of us *really* wants that, do we?"

I watched her through narrowed eyes, trying to detect any hint of a lie and finding none. Since Tom's cancer diagnosis, death was a subject I ran from with the fanatical energy of a boisterous child at bedtime. I hadn't even been able to stay through the entirety of his service. Once the phrase "eternal rest" was invoked, I'd stumbled away from his graveside and hidden behind the funeral home to light up a joint with shaking hands. By the time the groups of mourners had dispersed into the parking lot and back to their lives, I'd concluded there were only two directions to take in my life's new chapter: forward into a world with no Tom and no love, or down into the welcoming darkness. With the iffy logic of a bereaved basket case, I decided a descent into my addictions was the perfect solution to an unsolvable problem. I could both disengage from my bleak new reality *and* slowly poison myself into an early grave.

Now that someone had yanked me out of my fog of despair and into a new life free of pain and fear, I realized Ms. Cummings was right. From a clearer vantage point, I could almost picture living again. Of course, with my luck, it was a given that the gift of lucidity came with another duo of shitty choices: become a murderer, or die as the pain-slave of a psycho demon. I shook my head; if I was going to murder anyone, Shady Sam was at the top of my list. Did me a favor, my ass.

"Well, fuck." I said.

"It seems you're beginning to grasp the enormity of your situation."

I leaned forward and banged my forehead on her desk before pushing my face into my palm. "I don't think you grasp the enormity of *your* situation. I'm not a criminal mastermind or a killer; I can barely even injure someone. A friend described my fighting style as 'monkey humping a football meets spastic raccoon.' You should find someone else for the job. You know, like someone with actual assassin skills. Or at least fighting experience. I don't know what Sam told you about me, but I have neither of those things."

Her face was grim. "Too late, Jeanie. I have put a considerable amount of my power into you and would need more time than I have left to accrue enough to replace you. As for your alarming lack of skills, not all successful takedowns require violence. Cunning is just as important, although I *am* concerned that your intellect was vastly oversold to me." She sighed. "Anyway, I trust Sam, as much as it is possible to trust one of my kind. He is quite motivated to help because if I ascend, he will take my place. Also, he is surprisingly good at taking others down." She tilted her head and lifted her eyebrows in acknowledgement, and possibly respect, of Sam's apparent bad-assery. "He's been putting together a plan to kill Dram, and you will work with him as needed but will also come up with your own should his fail. Contingency planning is the backbone of success!" She pushed up from her chair and walked around to tap the books on the desk. "I've given you a children's primer that explains more about our kind and your duties as an assistant, as well as another book you may need. Sam will fill in the gaps. Keep them safe and don't give them to anyone. They can't fall into the wrong hands."

I pulled them to me, and my eyebrows rose when I read the titles out loud. *"In Search of Lost Time* and *Sabermetrics for Beginners?"*

"This is valuable information, so I've hidden it in the covers of books no sane person would want to read."

"Not bad, Cummings," I said.

At the bookcase, she slid out a thin black box with mother-of-pearl inlays and set it on the desk. Inside was a dagger with a silver crossguard and gleaming wood hilt. She picked it up and pulled it free of its brown leather sheath to reveal a shining blade with a subtle, flowing script etched along its side. "This," she said, "is something you will keep with you at all times. You must use it to collect Dram's blood, as it will give me the greatest amount of power from the ascension. You cannot lose this knife under any circumstances. Do you understand?" She stared at me, and I nodded. "If you lose it, prepare yourself for another trip to the land of excruciating pain."

I put my hands up. "I heard you the first time." She slid it back into the sheath and handed it to me. "It's so...average looking," I said. "No cool skeletons for me?"

She rolled her eyes and walked to the door with a beckoning gesture. I grabbed the books, dagger, and manila folder and followed her out of the office and back down the stairs. In the foyer, she opened a closet door and removed a large designer purse and rolling suitcase.

"This suitcase has some basic necessities to help you settle into your new life." She pushed it over to me. "In this purse, you'll find all the necessary IDs and payment methods you'll need. There's also a phone with Sam's contact information, and a calendar where I've added our future meetings. I took the liberty of making appointments for you at the spa and salon; the time and location are in your calendar as well." Her gaze made a pointed pass up and down my figure as she handed me the purse.

I didn't bother acknowledging the slight as I dropped my armload in and hiked the strap over my shoulder. "So, that's it? No training? No strategy sessions? You're just going to release me onto the streets with a knife and some money and expect me to go murder someone?"

She took a deep breath and exhaled it out as a long sigh while avoiding my eyes. "I admit it doesn't quite add up to what might reasonably be called a plan, but it's time I try something different. Despite extensive training, my previous assistants never accomplished the task. Unfortunately for them."

My eyebrow raised at the implication before I let out an involuntary giggle as the ridiculousness of the situation set in. "I'm your hail Mary?"

She ignored me. "As for letting you go, rest assured you will be watched. Closely. And remember, if you stray from your assignment or attempt to run, I am fully capable of finding other ways to motivate you beyond just pain. It's what I excel at." Her eyes flashed red above a predatory grin before they hardened. "Three months, Jeanie. Now, you're on your own and we've never met."

She opened the front door and pushed me through before shutting and locking it behind me.

The elevator opened to reveal a gleaming white marble lobby, and a pleasant doorman escorted me out through large glass doors. I squinted in the sunlight as I stepped onto the warm sidewalk and took in the quiet, tree-lined street. I shuddered; it smelled like HOA fees and a rigid adherence to the boring status quo. My suitcase thumped a steady rhythm over the concrete joints as I pulled it along, stopping occasionally to peek between the tall condos to determine the best escape trajectory. When I was out of sight of Cummings' building, I stepped into a surprisingly clean fire access alley to inventory the accoutrements of my new life.

The wallet contained a fat wad of twenties, a credit card, a debit card, and a driver's license. I pulled the license out of its sleeve and scrutinized it. It was real, as were the credit cards in my name. I blew out an impressed breath. There was no way I could have navigated the collection agency notices and delinquent account flags that had accumulated during my extended truancy from societal obligations. Turns out nature isn't the only thing that abhors a vacuum; bureaucracy is not a huge fan either. Cummings must have pulled major strings in order to get through that tangled mess. I took the cellphone out next and started poking around until I found the banking app keyed to my fingerprint.

Current balance: $50,000. Holy shit. I checked for recurring deposits: $10,000 every two weeks. Even holier shit. It looked like taking the bus to Seattle wouldn't be necessary.

I tapped my lip. The first question was where to go? I considered the cheap motels and low-rent apartments in the sketchier parts of town where I'd shared rooms with other down-and-outs. Staying in those kinds of places would be awkward and uncalled for now that I was moneyed. I did the math. $20,000 a month meant $240,000 a year. For Seattle, it put me solidly in the middle class. I could easily afford to rent a nice apartment, even a house if I wanted. The fact made me uncomfortable. I would have to start off at a hotel, so no point worrying about it now, and no point thinking too hard about the reason I had the money in the first place.

More bland button-ups and slacks in neat stacks greeted me when I tipped the suitcase on its side and unzipped it. Ugh. I rifled through them and decided a trip to a thrift shop was first on my agenda. I shuddered at the mental image of me walking around Seattle looking like a second-rate accountant's receptionist. The toiletries and underthings got stuffed into my purse. Everything else was going straight into the donation pile.

I tapped through my phone's map and found the nearest thrift store and started walking. With every step, my mind filled with more questions and random thoughts than I could handle. Well, handle without drugs anyway. My smile widened into a grin when my hand drifted into my purse and closed around the fat wallet. I could buy *so* much good stuff with all the money I now had in my possession. By the time I made it to the store, I was picturing myself skipping along in a candyland of illicit drugs with rainbows above me and prancing unicorns by my side.

With the suitcase full of Cummings' dull clothes donated, and several weeks' worth of the eclectic colors and styles I enjoyed purchased, I called a car to take me to Seattle. I'd selected a modest three-star hotel where I could lie low and fade into the background as an average citizen just going about their normal, non-sketchy business.

About six hours after waking up at Ms. Cummings' condo, I found myself in a small but clean room overlooking a boring neighborhood of office buildings and overpriced restaurants. Out of habit, I shuffled around, opening drawers, checking the strength of the exhaust fan in the bathroom, and trying to get a feel for my coming days there. I'd taken the room for a full week —plenty of time to ponder the dark question hanging over my life's new chapter. Commit a cardinal sin and retire rich in the Maldives? Or retain a scrap of morality and get tortured to death?

When I found myself stuffing cash into my pockets and turning to the door, I froze. Two years of chemical conditioning demanded I find a dealer, but the space where my aching need typically dwelled was strangely empty. My complete lack of physical pain rendered many of my choice substances obsolete, and pondering my new knowledge and situation was helping to keep the dark thoughts at bay. Still, my brain was annoyingly active. I bit my lip—technically, there was a legal option for stifling the mess of thoughts swirling around in my head. This could be my best chance to get sober. With a deep, decisive breath, I headed out to get a veritable shit-ton of weed instead. After the day I'd had, I was going to smoke myself into oblivion.

5

RAYS OF DUSTY sunshine streaming through the liquor bottle and glass pipe on the nightstand coaxed me awake the next morning. The smell of whiskey and burnt weed drifted into my nostrils, and I braced myself for the headache that typically manifested after a night of overindulgence. None came. Maybe my power from Cummings stopped those, too. I guess I should be grateful. Unfortunately, it did nothing for a queasy stomach. I groaned and dragged myself to the bathroom.

My hand moved back and forth between the shower knob and the bandage on my forearm as I debated whether I should deal with the stab wound now, or leave it for a time when my gut didn't feel like turning itself inside out. When I passed my arm under the hot spray, the skin beneath the bandage broke into a screaming symphony of itches. I bit my lip as I unwrapped it, bracing myself for the carnage. Instead, once I'd rinsed the dried blood off, I found nothing. I examined it from all sides, poking and prodding, but couldn't find the hint of a scratch, never mind evidence that a knife had pierced through my arm. Perhaps another side effect of Cummings' magic? I considered testing my potential quick-healing abilities, but decided it wasn't worth the necessary psychological leaps. I was only adept at self-harm via chemicals; physical self-harm was unfamiliar territory and best left unexplored.

After showering, I settled down with the books and folder spread out on the small table to ponder my next moves. I knew for a fact I wouldn't be able to murder someone, at least not directly. But…what if my target was a horrible person? What if he tortured and killed people on the regular? Would I be justified in taking him out then? The dark side of me made a compelling point about how nothing matters and we're all doomed to die one day, anyway. Plus, getting killed seemed like par for the course for a divine. I sighed and opened the folder.

My target's name was Dram Nguyen, angel of the territory that included Washington State and parts of British Columbia. He'd been in charge of the area for almost thirty years and had fifteen demons below him, including Cummings. The official human records listed his age as forty-nine, but Cummings had added a note stating he was born in 1769 and his actual age was 254. I blew out an amazed breath; Dram must have seen some crazy shit in his lifetime. Next, I pulled up his home address on my phone's map. His house was in a wealthy neighborhood overlooking the water. When I examined it from the street view, it was not the most ostentatious I'd seen in Seattle. Not even close. A scant paragraph about his job and the places he frequented concluded the information in the lean dossier. I looked him up online.

For the past ten years, he'd been the board president of a nonprofit women and children's shelter. He was also active in numerous other local charities and educational groups. As if that weren't enough, his law firm specialized in pro bono work for underserved and vulnerable populations.

"Well, shit," I muttered—so much for any moral high ground I might've had. From the outside, at least, the man was a flawless freaking gem and deserved the title of "angel."

I didn't know what I'd expected. Dram Nguyen of underground orphan death matches and kitten-kicking championships? I assumed there were such things as charities that provided cover for nefarious dealings, but I'd heard of most listed under his name, and they were all legit. I'd even received help from one when I needed a place to land after being hospitalized from an overdose. If I met him in person, maybe I'd be able to tell if he was as saintly as his online profile suggested?

Sighing, I turned to the books. The title of the first one I opened was *Annals of the Divine Lineage and Hierarchy*. It took a moment of flipping pages before I realized something was off. On the first page was a table of contents listing the ranks from demon level and up: Demon, Angel, Archangel, Demigod, Seraph, and God. An index of regions followed. Corresponding tabs lined the side of the book and when I opened it to the Archangel section, it seemed to expand in order to contain all the information therein: an alphabetical list of names followed by date of birth, date of ascension to each rank, territory, and for most, date of death.

I ignored the weirdness for the time being and turned to the section for Gods. Current god: Kublai Khan. No fucking way, *the* Kublai Khan? Grandson of Genghis Khan? I pulled up his Wikipedia page. It listed him as dying in 1294 from obesity-related illnesses. My eyebrows rose as the realization hit. Divines would have to pretend to die at some point, wouldn't they? Must suck for having a family. Or did they have families? I shook my head. Too many irrelevant questions.

I searched for notable people, curious about the extent of the divine's influence over humanity. There were no entries for Hitler, Mussolini or Pol Pot, but I did find Genghis Khan, Vlad the Impaler, and Kim Jong Il. It seemed tyrants were just as likely to be human as not. Un-faith in humanity restored. Although, if Cummings was to be believed, divines had been pulling strings behind the scenes of the despotism show since before time was associated with numerals. As I started looking up members of the rich and famous, a blurring of text caught my eye, and the name I'd just read now had an entry for date of death next to it. I squinted in confusion and then sighed. Of course the first magical item I encountered would be an index of supernatural assholes. Lame.

I opened the second book, *Magia Deorum*, next. A flowing script without a hint of letters from the Roman alphabet filled the pages. Why the hell would Cummings give me a book she knew I couldn't read? Especially after claiming it was for children. It had to be a joke. I tapped my fingers on the table. Maybe I should find a dictionary and translate the stupid thing so the joke would be on her. My gaze drifted over to the pipe next to the bed, and I paused for a long moment before slamming the book shut and standing up. Time to head to the library.

As I stood in front of the massive Seattle Public Library building, I had a flashback of trying to locate the entrance to the warped architectural mesh of steel and glass while high out of my mind. The full reason for the visit eluded me, but had something to do with proving my theory that the owners of the Space Needle had built a secret lair into its concrete ballast where they could ride out the climate uprisings in relative safety.

The library was just as confusing on the inside as it was on the outside. I sidled up to the information desk and explained to the bored librarian how I needed to translate an unknown ancient language from a text no one else was allowed to see for reasons I couldn't get into. She didn't bat an eye at my strange request and pointed to a location on the library map. The woman had clearly worked with the public for a while.

It took several wrong turns and backtracks before I found the languages section. I groaned—it was huge. I wandered through the stacks, peering at the spines of books and hoping to find a script resembling the one in *Magia Deorum*. No luck. Was the script an ancient or stylized version of a modern language? My annoyance was building. Even if I figured out what language it was written in, I'd still have to go through and translate every stupid word just to figure out what kind of bullshit Cummings was trying to pull.

I searched my brain for potential solutions and realized I was avoiding the main issue. How was I going to help Cummings ascend, preferably with no killing involved? As I pondered the problem, a bigger question flew in and knocked the others out of the nest. How does one kill a divine? Seemed like a crucial bit of information to give a hired assassin.

I reached for my phone. Time to call Shady Sam.

After listening to the default voicemail greeting for the third time, I gave up on calling Sam and hit the streets. It took a lot longer to find him than it used to when I was looking to buy. I finally pinned him down in a makeshift camp beneath a freeway overpass. Suspicious glances greeted me as I slid down the escarpment and wandered through the tents. I offered thin smiles and waves, aware of how out of place I was. I might as well have been an evangelical soccer mom at a BLM rally.

A group of people sitting on a stained mattress, smoking cigarettes and passing around a liquor bottle, looked up as I approached. "Shady Sam around?"

Without breaking his stare, a haggard man pointed in the direction of raised and angry voices. I craned my neck to peer over a tent and saw Sam squaring off with a burly, bald man whose face and body were covered in tattoos.

"Thanks," I told him before walking over to join the small group of onlookers.

Sam's voice was a low growl. "I told you; this is my territory, and you're gonna get the fuck outta here."

The tattooed man laughed. "This ain't your territory anymore, Shady. What're you gonna do about it?"

Sam sank into a fighting stance before he noticed me standing off to the side. "Jeanie?" His confusion caused the other man to turn.

I winced as everyone's gaze shifted to me. "Who the fuck is this?" the tattooed man asked before ejecting a wad of spit in my direction.

While Sam considered his answer, I blurted out, "Just looking to score."

My cheerful tone was at maximum odds with the subject matter and present company. I groaned inwardly, and my smile tightened when I took in the hungry stares of those around me. Rookie mistake, drawing attention to the fact that I had money to buy; especially with the fancy name brand purse slung over my shoulder.

"What are you, some kinda narc?" the tattooed man asked. The others drew away, and all but one took off.

"Uhh, no," I said, rooting around in my purse for the dagger.

"What's in there, sweetheart? You gonna shoot me?" His eyes gleamed red above his deranged grin as he started toward me.

Sam barreled into him and knocked him to the ground. While the two of them tussled, I finally pulled the knife out and clumsily freed it from its sheath. After a flurry of violence, the tattooed man got on top of Sam and rained blows down on his face before jumping up to come at me.

With no time to think it through, I thrust the dagger out, and he ran right into it. Our faces wore matching expressions of stunned surprise before he sank down with a wheezing gasp. I stared at my bloody hand and knife, my brain refusing to believe they belonged to me.

Sam walked over, wiping blood from his nose. "Aye, Jeans, look at you go."

The man had collapsed onto his side, his breaths wet and labored.

"Oh no," I whispered. "Holy fucking shit." My hand trembled, and I nearly dropped the dagger. "I killed him."

Sam reached out and put a firm hand on my shoulder to steady me. "Nah, but it looks like you punctured his lung. Lucky shot, getting in between the ribs like that."

"I'll call an ambulance."

"Not for this one." He beckoned to the last remaining onlooker. "Hey Dimitri, time to move up."

A demented gargoyle of a man stepped forward. Instinctively, I stepped back. Sam guided me around and behind him. "You probably don't wanna see this, Jeanie."

He was probably right, but I peeked around him all the same. Dimitri, the man or goblin or whatever, placed a knee on the tattooed man's chest, forcing a loud gurgle out of his throat. Then he pulled a battered shiv from his belt and stabbed the gasping man in his neck. My jaw dropped when Dimitri leaned forward, put his mouth over the fountain of blood, and gulped down several mouthfuls before sitting back up. With one swift motion, he raised his knife above his head and slammed it into the tattooed man's chest. After a final jerk, the man lay still.

My mind told me I should look away, but I couldn't; it was too dreadful and fascinating at the same time. Dimitri roared in triumph, and the sound rang through the concrete underpass. He grabbed the tattooed man's knife and stood up. My eyes barely registered the transformation until it was complete. His twisted features melted and smoothed out, his gorilla-like body straightened, and his eyes glowed a brilliant red. He was still ugly, but it wasn't the kind of ugly that turned heads. My gaze darted to the body of the tattooed man on the ground. It was shrinking in on itself. Bit by bit, it crumbled until there was nothing but dust.

Sam stepped forward and gave Dimitri a congratulatory slap on the back. "Welcome, Dimitri, to the rank of Incubus. Now get the fuck outta my territory."

Dimitri grinned, his eyes red and wild, before he wiped his bloody mouth and hands on his t-shirt. "Alright, Sam." He nodded at me. "And Sam's girl."

As Dimitri stalked away, people turned to gape at him, eyes bulging with terror. I flinched when Sam suddenly spoke a few low, guttural words in a coarse language. Heads drooped as his deep voice echoed through the underpass. After a few seconds, they all came to, their fear and horror replaced by calm neutrality.

My wide eyes met Sam's. He smiled and clapped me on the shoulder. "Don't worry, Jeanie, no one'll remember your violent stabbing attack on a poor, unarmed man."

My gaze drifted down to my hand and knife, still covered in blood.

"Oh, yeah," he said and walked over to a heap of junk and ripped a piece off an abandoned blanket. The scrap was enough to get most of the blood off my hand, but streaks remained on the knife. At a loss, I looked up at him, and he took the cloth. In the blink of an eye, a new scrap appeared where the old one had been.

I squinted at it as he handed it over. "Huh."

While I cleaned the blade, I caught Sam staring at it, eyes wide in shock. He re-schooled his face back to his usual stony expression when he noticed me watching him. He cleared his throat. "You'll wanna keep that where you can get to it easy," he said as I put the knife in its sheath and then back into my purse.

"Like how, though?" I gestured down at my sundress and sandals.

He looked me up and down. "Get a belt and wear a jacket to hide it. This life ain't about fashion."

"Obviously," I said, staring pointedly at his old-school trench coat. "The 1980s movie *Highlander* called; they want their wardrobe back."

He sighed. "What is it you want?"

"Answers," I replied.

"Fine. Buy me lunch."

6

I GLANCED THROUGH the greasy menu in the dark dive bar where Sam and I ended up after he nixed the cheerful cafes and diners we passed on our walk. To be fair, I couldn't picture Sam sitting in a bright and bustling restaurant with normal people and possibly children nearby. Not that he was a creep, but he was definitely the kind of guy who knew where to bury a body. Besides, being tucked against the wall below a grimy neon beer sign was much better suited to our clandestine conversation. Sam ordered a burger and a beer when the surly bartender deigned to stop by. I told him to make it two.

We sat in awkward silence until our beers arrived and then sat slurping foam while facing forward and avoiding eye contact. I'd never had an actual conversation with Sam, at least not while lucid. I knew nothing about him other than he sold drugs, never smiled despite all my attempts to get him to do so, and was, apparently, an incubus. The tattoos on his knuckles drew my eye, and I angled my head to examine them. RIPM on one hand, RIPB on the other. My gaze drifted upwards. Tattooed flames peeked out from his collar and circled around the back of his neck and ears.

He caught me looking. "You bring me here to look or to talk?"

I leaned back and scrutinized the dusty black ceiling, trying to remember all the questions I wanted to ask him. "How do I kill you guys?"

He laughed. It was unexpectedly warm and made his face a bit less...dodgy. I'd certainly never heard him laugh before. I grinned in response. Finally, a reaction beyond a scowl or growl. Two points for me.

"Getting right into it, aren't ya, Jeans?"

I shrugged. "Seems kind of like the most important thing I should know."

He chuckled and shook his head. "Of course Olita didn't tell you."

"Olita?"

"Cummings. It's her first name."

"Oh." I said. "So…?"

"Gotta stab through the heart. You stab elsewhere, and we won't quite bleed out before the healing starts. Decapitation works too."

As Sam said the last bit, the bartender came by with our baskets of greasy food. He narrowed his eyes at Sam as he set them down.

"Another one of these, please." Sam raised his empty glass. The bartender shifted his gaze to me, and I lifted two fingers and gave him a sweet smile.

When he left, Sam leaned in toward me. "A divine gets the most power from an ascension when they use their own knife." He nodded at my purse. "That's why Olita gave you one of hers. It's got some of her power in it, which is how you injured Johnny so easy. The knife of a higher rank does a lot more damage. A regular knife wouldn't've stopped him."

I paused in thought. "Hmm, maybe I should take knife-throwing classes."

He shook his head. "Only a knife held by hand can pierce a divine's heart. No throwing or bullets." I deflated, though the likelihood that my uncoordinated self would have mastered the precision skill was lower than the depth of the Mariana Trench. Especially in the three months Olita had given me. It wasn't like I was a young and suspiciously capable heroine in a fantasy story.

Sam rubbed his hands together and picked up the messy burger, and I directed my gaze away and down to my own. I was starving. The end of the bar was filled with not-so-subtle chewing noises when the bartender came back with our second beers. The man's face was an exact copy of Olita's. I smiled at him with a mouth overstuffed with food.

Picking through my fries, I started up our conversation again. "What other powers do you guys have?"

Sam took a few long swallows of beer to wash down his last bites and wiped his hands on a napkin. "We get more each time we rank up, but we're all faster and stronger than humans and heal quick. We can do basic charms like hiding our presence and erasing parts of memories if a human sees us doing shit we don't want 'em to."

"Like what you did at the camp?" Sam nodded. I peered at him with suspicion. "Have you ever done that to me?"

He shrugged and didn't meet my eyes. "Possibly."

I raised a skeptical eyebrow. His "possibly" sounded an awful lot like a "probably" which, in my experience, is nearly always a "definitely." I tilted my head and watched his face. "What does it feel like?" The idea of having someone erase your memories was creepy, but also opened up interesting opportunities for consenting parties.

Sam took a sip of beer and shrugged. "I dunno; divines can't do it to each other." He looked over at me. "Wanna find out?"

I grinned. "Yes!"

"Alright, move a bit and I'll make you forget doing it."

I tapped my lip and thought through weird things I could do so I'd be surprised when I came to. My gaze flicked over to Sam— bonus points if I messed with him in the process. I reached under his elbow where it rested on the bar and dug my fingers between his. His head pulled back in surprise, and an amused smile tugged at his cheeks.

"Okay, I was thinking more like standing up, but this works."

I watched his lips form a low noise—

For some reason, I was staring at Sam's mouth. My gaze drifted upwards; he had an expectant eyebrow raised. I looked down at my arm and hand entwined with his. "What the fuck?"

He winked. "You did it, not me." I continued staring at him. "You wanted me to erase a memory so you could see what it's like."

"Oh, yeah." My hand lingered on his for a moment before I slid it away.

"So, what did it feel like?"

I wrinkled my nose. "Like nothing, I guess?" My eyes widened. "Jesus Christ, are you guys going around doing things like raping people and making them forget?"

He recoiled. "Fuck no!"

I wanted to point out that the myth of incubi having sex with women in their sleep might be based on some truth, but just glared at him instead.

He sighed. "The chances of a divine being a rapist are the same as a human. Most of us only kill and do evil shit to each other. The majority leave humans alone." He took a sip of beer and watched me from the corner of his eye. "And I take care of the ones that don't."

I nodded and drug a lazy finger around in the ring of condensation my glass had left on the bar top. The silence stretched on until I cleared my throat. "Um, what else can you guys do?"

He leaned back and crossed his arms. "At my level, we can do basic substitution. Like how I swapped the bloody piece of blanket with a different one. It's hard to do as an incubus; you gotta replace things with something similar. It gets easier at demon rank. They can swap air for things."

I remembered the keys Olita had popped into existence. "Ah." I paused and tilted my head in confusion. "Why don't you just magic the blood straight out of each other?"

Sam shook his head. "Yeah, it doesn't work like that. I can't take anything outta another divine." He rubbed the stubble on his chin. "Although, in theory, it might be possible to exchange like for like..." He considered it for a moment before shaking his head again. "Eh, even if you could swap, you have to drink the blood, not just have it in your veins."

I nodded; I'd already assumed as much. There was no way Olita would've let me dirty up her condo if she could have just used magic.

Sam continued. "Angels can control humans and make 'em talk, for a few minutes anyway." He acknowledged my gaping jaw and horrified expression with a nod of agreement. "Then there's the ability to give powers to humans." He dipped his head at me. "Demons can have one assistant and each rank after that can add another."

"So Dram has two assistants?" Sam nodded, and I frowned. "Do we all have the same power?"

He shook his head. "Nah. With a few exceptions, divines can give whatever powers they want. I've only met a few other assistants, and their powers were…well, they definitely weren't the same." Sam's haunted gaze shifted away from mine as he took a sip of beer. "What power did Olita give you?"

"No pain, no fear."

He turned to me, squinting with confusion. "Two powers?"

"Is that not normal?"

His brow furrowed, and he shook his head, eyes unseeing as he pondered the line of liquor bottles on the wall. "Huh."

My fingers itched to trace the flames of his neck tattoo down and peek beneath his collar as I waited for him to elaborate. When he didn't, I got us back on track. "So we have no idea what Dram's people can do?" He nodded. "Well, that sucks." I stared down at my empty basket. This was going to be even harder than I'd thought, and I'd already considered it to be ninety-nine percent impossible. Seems we were approaching a solid one hundred.

He finished his beer as my meager hope dwindled further. The bartender came by again to gather our baskets and leave the tab on the bar top. Sam pushed over his empty glass. "Another one please, mate." The bartender gave us a flat smile before walking off to fulfill the request.

I fished around in my purse and pulled out the *Magia Deorum*. "What the hell is this? Olita said it was a children's book about divines, but it's written in a weird language I can't read."

He winced as it left a trail of water in its wake when I pushed it over to him.

"Hmm," he said while flipping through the pages. When the door of the bar swung open with a bang, his head snapped up. A large, muscular woman in a tight tank top strode in. He shoved the book back to me. "Put it away. We're leaving."

My gaze darted between the two of them before I shoved the book back in my purse and pulled my wallet out. I slapped a wad of twenties on the bar and stood. Sam nodded to her as we walked by, and she narrowed her eyes at me and didn't nod back.

Outside I asked, "Who was that? Someone you owe money to?"

He said nothing for several blocks and glanced behind us before answering. "Name's Mara; she's an incubus and a mean sonuvabitch."

"One of Olita's?"

He nodded. "She's been tryna shank me for years."

I jogged a step to keep up with his longer stride. "Why would she want to kill you?"

He looked down at me. "Competition, Jeanie. It's all a big fucking competition."

When he slowed his pace, I broke the tense silence. "Where are we going?"

"Back to my place. It's safer there."

I had made some unflattering assumptions about where Sam might live based on his career choice and thus was pleasantly surprised when we arrived at an elegant brick apartment building. A charming stone archway marked the entrance to a small courtyard garden full of roses and vibrant green mosses. I pulled a flower toward me and inhaled its fragrance while Sam dug his keys out and opened the front door.

"Not what you were expecting, aye, Jeans?" he said when we walked into the warm entryway that had the sweet smell of old paint.

Diamond glass windows looked out onto neatly trimmed hedges, and a carved wood balustrade led us upstairs. "No, it is not," I agreed.

After unlocking his apartment, he gestured me inside and I stepped into the short hallway. He followed, closing and locking the door behind him. Instead of a dark cave like Olita's library, Sam's place was full of sunlight, bright colors, and hanging plants. The fresh breeze from the open windows carried a hint of tree sap and lemon. He pointed me to an old wood and brocade chair at a small dining table as he shuffled out of his coat. The clean oak floors gleamed in the light, and colorful artwork lined the walls.

I admired the pieces as I sauntered by. Many of the prints were of similar styles to artworks I'd collected in my old life. I froze in front of *Figure with Meat* by Francis Bacon and had a vertiginous moment of nostalgia. As a joke, I'd hung a print of the same disturbing painting over the dining table in Tom's and my apartment. He hated it. To get back at me, he hid postcards featuring hackneyed, conventional works from an overrated artist in my things and cackled every time he heard me groan at the newest discovery. I took a deep breath against the sorrow that tightened my chest.

After circling through the open living and dining space, I settled down in the chair and directed my attention back to Sam. He was taking off a shoulder holster with a large dagger in it, and another hung from his belt. Snaky tattoos circled their way up his arms and disappeared under his sleeves. I stared at the gray t-shirt straining to cover his well-muscled arms, shoulders, and chest. His belly protruded at his waistline, but overall, I was impressed.

"Damn, Sam, you're pretty stacked. Shame about your face, though."

He waggled his eyebrows at me. "Wait til I'm a demon; you won't be able to keep your hands off me."

I scoffed. "Yeah, nah. I can't imagine it makes you less of an asshole, based on Cummings, anyway."

"You're a bit feisty when you're sober," Sam said.

"I'm a bit feisty when I'm not afraid of you."

His head jerked back. "You were afraid of me?" His surprise was genuine.

I frowned in thought. "No...just afraid of pissing you off, I guess. You could've cut off my supply; seemed prudent to keep my sassy mouth in check around you."

He shrugged. "Makes sense. Want some coffee?"

"Sure."

It was surreal to be sitting in the quaint apartment of a man I knew only as a no-nonsense street hustler while he made coffee. It was too domestic, and I couldn't quite wrap my head around it. "How do you afford this place, anyway? I didn't think shaking down addicts would pay these kinds of bills."

"I got my ways."

"You're a mysterious man, Sammy." I crossed my legs and scanned the room. There were no photographs or personal artifacts in sight, not even a silly fridge magnet.

"Yeah," he agreed.

The silence became increasingly awkward. It was obvious Sam didn't want me in his sanctuary. "Where are you from originally?"

"Ireland, you heard of it?"

I rolled my eyes. "Where in Ireland?"

"Dublin."

"When did you move here?"

His gaze shifted to mine, then back to the coffeemaker. "When I needed to."

"Fine." I threw up my hands. "Sorry to invade your privacy or whatever. I'm just trying to get to know my new partner-in-crime. Who, as I shouldn't need to remind you, pulled me into this mess."

He set the two steaming mugs on the table. "Cream?" He was struggling to keep his habitual scowl from making an appearance. I nodded, and he grabbed a carton from the fridge.

"Lemme see that book," he said as he sat down and scooted the chair forward. I took it out and plopped it in front of him. He flipped through it, his eager gaze darting across the pages while I sipped my coffee.

"You can read this?" I asked after a long period of silence. He grunted in affirmation. "Care to fill me in on the contents? Any idea why Olita would give it to me?"

He closed the book and looked up at me, face inscrutable. "There's nothing in here that'd help you, so I dunno why she gave it to you." He frowned and made a point of holding it up to his eye and scrutinizing it from every angle. He even held it to his ear for a moment. I watched him, amused. "I think she put a spell on it to keep track of you. It reeks of magic."

I snorted. "Yeah right, sounds like bullshit. If that's true, then why didn't she just put a spell on the children's book she promised me?"

He shrugged. "Who knows why Olita does what she does?" He tapped the cover. "I should hold on to this for you. The magic could attract other divines."

My eyes narrowed. Sam was living up to his nickname and giving off some seriously shady vibes. I took a moment to consider his offer and decided that if I couldn't read the book, and he wouldn't tell me what was in it, then I had no use for it; Olita's threats be damned. "Fine, whatever."

His shoulders sagged in relief before squaring back up when he caught my skeptical look. He leaned back in his chair and took a casual sip of coffee. There were so many questions I wanted to ask, but I sensed he'd rather be alone, so I got right to the point. "Why tell Olita to make me her assistant?"

His face was carefully neutral. "Cuz you're the most likely person to come up with a good plan. You're savvy and you're smart. You've got a master's degree, for Christ's sake."

I closed my eyes and let out a long, irritated breath. "Ok, A, I have a master's degree in art history, not murder; and B, just how much digging into my past have you done?" When I recalled Olita's blunt summary of my life, my jaw tightened. Evidently, one or both of them had done a fair amount of digging.

He waved the question away. "Look, Olita wanted another plan in place, so I told her about you. But, Jeanie, you don't need to do anything. I'm taking care of it; you'll barely be involved."

His face remained impassive while I waited for further details. After a long, expectant pause, I pushed my coffee cup away. "Well, fuck you, and thanks for your help." I stood up to leave and hesitated. "Got any good stuff? I can pay."

He shook his head. "Not here."

A disappointed sigh escaped my lips. "Guess I'll be going, then."

He inhaled as if he wanted to say something, but frowned and stood up instead. The fresh scent of soap mixed with a tantalizing earthiness trailed in his wake when he walked by me to open the door. I breathed it in and hummed a pleased note to myself before deliberately brushing against him on my way out. He gave me a tight smile as I left. "See you round, Jeanie."

Back on the streets, I debated my next move. It was pushing 2 p.m., and I was no closer to anything resembling a plan or to figuring out what part I was expected to play in Sam's. The only thing I could think of trying next was to meet Dram in person. I sat down in a narrow alley and looked up his law office phone number. A woman with a bright and friendly voice answered. I claimed to be a reporter interested in interviewing Mr. Nguyen for a piece I was writing on charitable giving in the Seattle area. She hummed while she checked his availability.

"Let's see...Oh! He had a cancellation for tomorrow. Can you come in at eleven?"

"That would be perfect!" I gave her my name and hung up.

My gaze crept down the alley wall to stare at the cigarette butts littering the ground around my feet. I was starting to feel a little twitchy. Too much time on my hands would not help with my still-tentative stab at sobriety. While I was considering whether I *really* needed to give up my emotional support drugs, a calendar notification popped up on my phone. It was a reminder for the salon visit Olita scheduled for me. I hadn't planned on going, but with nothing better to do (except track down a dealer), I set off to find the place.

After a mani-pedi, facial, haircut, and body scrub, I felt like a new person. As I walked to my hotel, I reflected on the last time I'd enjoyed a proper pampering. It was before Tom's cancer had surfaced: a bad flu that turned out to be acute leukemia. The memories of shared nights trading massages, making love, kissing, and talking about our dreams for the future drifted into my mind like sparkling dust in a sunbeam. Through the warmth of the recollection, the heartache and grief set in, and then the bitter anger at him being taken from me far too soon.

I stopped walking and pushed my palms against my eyes, trying to block out the pain, like if I couldn't see the outside, then I wouldn't have to see the inside, either. Instead, my brain filled the void with the memory of Tom lying in a hospital bed, his once stout body frail beneath the thin blanket, and his round face gaunt and tinged yellow-green. I took a deep breath and willed the tears to stop squeezing out through my eyelids. My thin hope that spending two years in a drug-fueled oblivion would count towards the time needed to move through grief was a false one. It was still too fresh, and still too much to bear.

Time to go back to the hotel and smoke like there was no tomorrow.

7

A STRIKING WOMAN with smooth brown skin and pink-tipped hair glanced up when I strode into the lobby. She was typing away on a computer while talking into the phone held between her shoulder and ear. "Kaytee Seeger" was etched onto the brass nameplate atop her desk. She held up a manicured finger and shot me the professional just-a-moment look. I nodded and perused the various awards and accolades for Dram's work as a vulnerable populations' advocate, troubled youth softball coach, and charitable organizations' leader. The gleaming plaques and award ceremony photos covered an entire wall.

After a cordial goodbye, the woman hung up the phone and smiled at me. "How may I help you?" Her voice was the perfect blend of friendly and professional.

I copied her tone. "Hi, I'm Jeanine Bennett. I have an appointment with Mr. Nguyen."

"Hi Jeanine, I'm Kaytee, Mr. Nguyen's assistant. Let me take a look." She clicked through her computer. "Ah, yes, here you are. May I ask what your meeting is about?"

My eyebrow rose. I was pretty sure she was the person I'd spoken to on the phone. "I'd like to interview him for an article I'm writing."

"Oh?" Her eyes narrowed a fraction, and some of the friendliness dropped from her tone. "And what publication are you writing for?"

"Um, it's an online news site that focuses on inspirational stories about people in our community. It's new, you probably haven't heard of it."

"Mm-hmm." Her expression was still professional, but definitely not friendly. She glanced at her computer again. "Oh, shoot, I double-booked him for this time slot. How about I give you his email so you can send him your questions and he can answer when he has time? He's just so busy. I can't fit you in."

"It will only take ten minutes."

She shook her head.

"I can make it five. Surely he's got five minutes?"

"Sorry," she said without a hint of apology in her tone.

"Seriously? I kind of figured he wouldn't mind discussing all the wonderful things he's done for the community so he can inspire others to do the same."

She leaned forward, elbows on the desk, fingers clasped in front of her. "Look, Jeanine, I know what you are and I know you're lying." She responded to my dumbfounded face with a sigh. "I'm Mr. Nguyen's *assistant*. I don't care which demon you work for, I'm not letting you in to see him."

"Oh," I said. "Um...hmmm."

She watched me go through my slow mental gymnastics and shot a meaningful glance toward the door. As I considered whether I could knock her out and charge into Dram's office, she frowned and crossed her arms.

"Don't try anything funny." She looked me up and down. "I'm pretty sure you can't take me, and I know you can't take Marcus." She leaned back and let out a tired sigh. "Please just leave."

I winced—I'd forgotten Dram had two assistants. "I'm not the first one, am I?"

"Nope. We get someone coming in here every six months or so."

The air blew out of my lips in defeat. "Look, I don't want to hurt him. I just wanted to see if he's as nice as his online profile suggests." Her eyebrow rose. "But, I get it—you're just doing your job." I took a step toward the door, then hesitated and turned around. "I know it's weird, but can *we* talk? I'm new to this, and it'd be nice to have someone to compare notes with." My hands came up in a placating gesture. "No funny business; I promise."

Her eyes searched mine for a long, appraising moment. "Fine. I've got my lunch break at noon today. We can meet somewhere and talk."

"Seriously?! Thank you. I really appreciate it."

We discussed lunch spots and decided on a place. I walked out the door feeling better than I had since waking up to the new life Sam had foisted on me.

Kaytee joined me at the outdoor bistro table where I'd been sitting, nursing iced teas and trying to ignore the stares from people waiting to be seated. As she pulled out the chair, I admired the way her tailored pink suit hugged her curves. A pang of jealousy crept up from my gut to say hello. I was stuck wearing the blouse and slacks Olita had given me. I'd donated everything else, and my new collection of ironic t-shirts and faded dresses didn't exactly scream earnest professional. We exchanged polite smiles and small talk while we waited for the server.

By the time we'd placed our orders, I was bursting with questions but wasn't sure where to begin. "How long have you worked for Dra...I mean Mr. Nguyen?"

She twisted her lips and gazed up in thought. "It's been about five years now. And you can call him Dram."

"That long?" I considered my assignment from Olita. "I thought we were all pretty short-term."

She shrugged. "That might be true for assistants working for... less civil divines. Especially the ones looking to ascend. Dram isn't into the whole violence thing, so we stay pretty safe. We run defense rather than offense." She sipped her ice water.

"Huh." It figured I would win the shit lottery when it came to working for a divine. "How'd you two meet?"

She shifted in her seat like she had an itch on her back that needed scratching. "He, um...we met at a charity fundraiser. We chatted for a while and he offered me a job. It wasn't what I was expecting, but it's been working out pretty well." She brushed invisible dust off the sleeve of her impeccable jacket.

"So is Dram actually as nice as he looks on paper?"

She nodded and smiled. "He actually is."

"Fuck," I whispered. She raised a questioning eyebrow while I contemplated the sunlight shining on the windows of the tall buildings around us. "I was hoping he was secretly a total asshole."

"Ah," she said. "I can see how that would make your job easier."

"Yeah." I took a deep breath and let it out in a defeated huff. Once I got my disappointment in check, I smiled at her. "What's your power?" She hesitated, so I offered her mine. "I don't feel pain or fear."

She nodded slowly. "That must be...weird." Her eyes narrowed, and she watched me with careful calculation while assessing whether I could be trusted. Apparently I could, because she answered. "I can tell when people are lying."

"Really? That's awesome!" My mind churned through all the ways I could mess with someone if I had her power.

"It's...okay." She looked down and fidgeted with her gold and pearl bracelet. "It sucks for relationships, though. Having space for little white lies is kind of crucial for getting close to someone."

"Oh. Yeah, I could see that." While I pondered the negative aspects of her power, the server brought our food, and we took a moment to settle in with napkins and utensils. "Can a divine take away their assistant's power, or is it like a permanent thing?"

"They can take it away."

"Will Dram ever let you retire?"

"Sure. He said he'll let me go whenever I want." She took a bite of her sandwich.

"Aren't you worried about dying if he dies?"

Her head jerked back, and she shot me an incredulous look while choking down the rest of her mouthful. "What? No, it doesn't work like that."

"Really? Did Dram tell you that?"

She rolled her eyes. "Yeah. I'm pretty sure I wouldn't have agreed to the job if that was one of the conditions."

"Can you tell if a divine is lying?"

"Of course," she said, then hesitated. "Well...I'm almost sure. I've only ever talked to Dram, and he has no reason to lie to me, so I've never confirmed it." She raised a curious eyebrow. "Did yours tell you that you'd die if they die?"

"Yeah, but I don't think I can trust anything she says. If she lied about it, then that's excellent news for me." I took a happy bite of pasta.

"Yours is a woman?"

Whoops, probably shouldn't have divulged that. Oh well. "Yeah, an extra bitchy one," I answered.

"Ah, Olita."

My head pulled back. "You know Olita?"

She nodded. "She's been trying to take Dram out since he took over the territory."

I pursed my lips. Olita really was expecting me to do the impossible.

"How did you meet her?" Kaytee's curiosity was genuine; this was probably the first time she'd had a friendly chat with another divine's assistant, too.

"Um, she kidnapped me and kind of forced me into servitude." Her mouth gaped while I took a bite.

"Oh my god, that's terrible," she said in a low voice.

I shrugged. "Eh, same shit, different day. But you're right; it is terrible. Especially considering I'm probably the worst person she could've picked. I guess she's going for the whole least-expected angle in this stupid murder game, but personally, I think she's got some screws loose."

Kaytee's eyebrows dipped in sympathy. "I'm really sorry, Jeanine."

"Call me Jeanie."

"I'm sorry, Jeanie."

"It's...whatever. I'm just glad that not all divines are horrible people." I then asked about the only other line of attack I'd come up with thus far. "Does Dram want to ascend?"

She squinted up at the colorful awning and wrinkled her nose. "I doubt it. He's pretty happy with what he's got going on."

My shoulders slumped as I frowned down at my bowl. It seemed the possibility that Olita taking Dram's place if he ascended was a nonstarter.

I dredged up a smile and changed the subject. "Do you just sit in the office and interrogate people when they come to see Dram?"

She laughed. "No, that would be boring as hell. I'm also the office and IT manager for the firm."

My eyes widened. "That's a lot of hats to wear. Dram sure scored when he found you."

She smiled. "I suppose he did."

We finished our lunch in thoughtful silence, and the server brought the check. I grabbed it and pulled out enough twenties to cover the tab, plus an extra for a tip. Then another one because I felt guilty about hogging the table for so long. It was nice to spread the wealth around.

I walked Kaytee back to the office and hesitated as we stopped in front of the door. "Maybe this is crazy, but...do you want to hang out sometime? Like get a drink? I don't have anyone else to talk to about, well...anything." She narrowed her eyes. "Again, no funny business. Ask me anything you want."

She watched me for a long moment. "Do you plan on trying to kill Dram?"

"Almost definitely no. And for sure not anytime soon."

She sighed. "Good enough for now, I guess." She rifled around in her purse and pulled out a business card, wrote her cell number on it, then handed it to me. "It was nice talking to you, Jeanie."

"You too, Kaytee. And I know you know I mean it."

She laughed and waved as she pushed open the door.

I might have just made a friend in the strangest way possible.

8

THE NEXT MORNING, I partook in the time-honored tradition of procrastination. I had my first appointment with a personal trainer and signed up for lessons at an MMA gym. Based on my lack of coordination, cardio capacity, and balance, I doubted I'd progress very far, but why not go for it? The muscle and moves might come in handy if I was going to be hanging around shady characters like Sam and his cronies. Visits to the army surplus store for holsters and a high-end boutique for a fancy power suit kept me busy until the afternoon.

Getting all the easy business out of the way left me with time to consider all the headway on my task I wasn't making. If I didn't want to kill Dram for his blood, and he didn't want to ascend, then…? If I helped him ascend, would he let Olita take his place? The whole situation was ridiculous. Olita did a terrible job preparing me. It was becoming apparent why she hadn't been able to pull it off yet. With my annoyance levels rising, I had to deliberately redirect myself away from areas with dealers as I walked to my hotel. Sobriety is fucking hard.

Back in my room, I cuddled up with the *Annals of the Divine Lineage and Hierarchy* book to check out the competition I'd be facing. The other demons in Dram's territory were spread out evenly across Washington State, with one across the Canadian border in Vancouver, B.C. They were all younger than Olita, which meant they might be less powerful. Their assistants, however, might be complete badasses. Especially when compared to me.

On a whim, I looked up angels in adjacent territories. Perhaps Olita would be okay with a change of location? The archangel of the western United States was a woman named Juanita Tarantello. Under her were eight angels, including Dram. My finger hovered above Jackson Greene of the Idaho and Montana region. Maybe he was evil enough to make me reconsider my no-murdering stance. Or dumb enough to let me steal his blood.

I bombarded Sam with a barrage of texts:

> *Do you have to stay in the territory of the higher rank you kill?*

> *If a divine dies and no one takes their blood, who replaces them and how?*

> *If Olita became the angel of a different territory, how pissed would she be?*

It took about an hour for him to reply:

> *Jesus Christ, don't text about this shit. What if someone hacks our phones?*

I rolled my eyes and responded:

> *OK. FBI if you're reading this, I'm talking about an RPG called Angels and Demons. It's going to be all the rage*

He typed back:

> *Fuck you. Meet me at Cal Anderson park in an hour*

I smiled and replied:

> *Now you're making it sound suspicious. See you there*

Cal Anderson Park is in the middle of Seattle's bustling Capitol Hill neighborhood and is a great place to meet someone for just about anything. An abundance of visitors fill the park with distracting flurries of activity, while the restrooms and mostly clueless public draw in the less savory characters who use the general hubbub to cover for their dodgy dealings. In quieter parks, druggies stand out like pimples on a smooth backside. In Cal Anderson Park, they blend in with the rest of the acne scars that are the hoi polloi.

I found Sam sitting by the reflecting pool, popping the last bite of a burger into his mouth and putting the wrapper into the crumpled bag on the bench beside him.

I pointed to it. "I was going to tell you to eat a bag of dicks, so I'm glad you took the initiative on your own."

It's a stupid joke almost everybody in Seattle has made at some point, referencing the popular local burger chain named Dick's. Sam made the only appropriate response, which is no response at all. I sat down beside him and watched the eclectic array of people going about their business. It was nice to sit back and stare at everyone. No fear. No feeling like I needed to hide. Even a pair of police officers on patrol elicited no internal reaction despite my drug addict's conditioning to run.

Sam sipped his milkshake, and I intercepted it when he moved to set it down and took a sip myself. He eyed me, amused.

I tilted my head and looked at him. "Vanilla? I would have pegged you more as a strawberry guy."

He shrugged. "Sometimes you gotta keep it simple. Besides, only children and psychopaths go for strawberry."

I gave him a pointed look, and he shook his head, the faint traces of a smile on his lips. We passed the milkshake back and forth in companionable silence.

When it was gone and he'd deposited the empty cup and greasy bag into a nearby garbage can, he sat back down, ankle crossed over his knee, arm along the back of the bench behind me—the picture of a man at ease. I knew better, though. His gaze was darting around, taking in every movement and potential source of trouble.

His deep baritone startled me out of my musings. "Got yourself a haircut. Looks nice."

I was surprised he noticed, though the change was pretty dramatic. My long, straight hair had been an absolute mess from the poor treatment I'd subjected it to over the last two years. The stylist hadn't even touched it before recommending cutting most of it off to get a fresh start. My new choppy style had echoes of my punk rock past without being a too-obvious midlife crisis call for help. Hopefully. I ran my hands through it, enjoying the feel of my new silky locks.

I caught a glimpse of the knife handle beneath Sam's trench coat. "Do all divines carry their knives with them? Why don't you just magic them to wherever you are rather than carting them around?"

He shook his head. "That power doesn't work on magical things like knives and blood."

"Well, that sucks for you." I waggled my eyebrows at him. "Check this out, Sam." I pulled the skirt of my dress up higher than necessary to reveal the knife holster strapped to my thigh. "Functional *and* fashionable." His gaze slid up my leg, and he nodded slowly, eyebrows lifted in tacit approval. A faint flush crept up his neck, and I gave him a wide grin in response before pulling my dress back down.

"So about my questions. If I took out an angel from somewhere else, would Olita have to move there? Would she be okay with that? Seems like her main concern is she won't live much longer, and beggars can't be choosers."

He scratched the stubble on his chin as he pondered the question. "She might be okay with it. As you said, it's not like she's got a lotta options left. But, Jeanie, you don't have to worry about it. I'm taking care of it. I only need you for a few pieces of my plan—nothing that'll put you in danger."

"Care to elaborate? It would be nice to prepare. Or at least know what's next in your plan for derailing my life."

He looked at me directly for the first time. "The less you know about it, the better. Seriously though, I'm not gonna let anything bad happen to you."

I rolled my eyes. "Well, that's reassuring, but I guess I've put my life in your hands plenty of times before—trusting you were selling me the real deal and not something that would land me in the morgue. What's one more roll of the dice?"

His eyebrows drew together. "Your life in my hands? What the fuck are you talking about?"

"Olita told me that I'll die if she dies."

His eyes narrowed. "She did, did she?" He hesitated for a moment and then shook his head. "She was just fucking with you. That's not how it works."

I let out a sigh of relief. "Oh good, that's what Kaytee said, too."

"Kaytee?" Sam lifted an eyebrow.

"Oh, uh, yeah." I turned away and focused on a college boy climbing to the top of the nearby fountain sculpture while his friends snapped photos.

"Jeanie, who's Kaytee? How many people have you been talking to about this?"

I crossed my arms and stared at him with my best none-of-your-business look.

His jaw clenched, and he scooted closer before leaning over until his lips were next to my ear. "Who. The fuck. Is Kaytee?" His voice was deep and dangerous. Goosebumps erupted on my arms.

I shooed him away. "No one."

His hand on the bench behind me reached up to wrap itself around my neck and hold me down when I tried to stand up in protest. Thanks to my somewhat recent acquisition of a proclivity for masochism, the grip sent a pleasurable shiver down my spine.

I laughed. "Sam, it's not like you can intimidate me or hurt me right now. Plus, we're in public. What are you going to do?"

There was a note of hopeful anticipation in my tone as I issued the challenge, and I wondered if he'd heard it. He just kept staring at me, eyes narrow and threatening.

I sighed. "Fine. She's one of Dram's assistants."

He let go. "Seriously, Jeanie? You went and chatted with one of his people? Are you nuts?"

I threw up my hands. "Obviously! You should know that by now." He continued to stare at me, but now with a bonus gleam of incredulity in his eyes. "Look, I just wanted to know if Dram is as nice as he seems, and if he's looking to move up. That's all."

"And?"

"*And* he is nice, and he's not looking to move up."

He raised a suspicious eyebrow. "Why do you care if he's nice? Did you actually meet him?"

"I thought I'd be asking all the questions today," I said in a huffy tone and crossed my arms like a petulant child. His stare pierced through my reluctance, and I sighed. "No, I didn't meet him, and I *care* because I'm not a psychopath looking to murder innocent people."

Sam's voice was a low growl in my ear, and the vibration raised the hairs on the back of my neck. Heat crept into my cheeks. "We're not people, Jeanie. Never forget that. All of us have done fucked-up things and Dram is no different. And, since he's an angel, guaranteed he's done a *ton* of fucked-up shit to get there. Killing and getting killed is part of the game."

"Yeah, *your* game." I poked his chest for emphasis. "You brought me into this, and I'm not going to play by your rules. Besides, even if Dram did fucked-up shit in the past, he's not doing it now. He's helping people, for Christ's sake. I'm not going to hurt him."

Sam leaned back and gazed up at the sky in frustration. "Look, *never* trust a divine or their people, and don't talk to anyone else about this, okay?"

"Fine." We sat in annoyed silence before I turned to him. "So, *in theory*, would it matter if Olita got blood from an angel besides Dram? Like, for example, Jackson Greene of Montana?"

The corners of Sam's mouth curled up. "That would actually be pretty hilarious."

"Does it make any difference?"

He shrugged. "Not really. She'd be an angel, which is what she wants." He stared off into the distance, and his smile turned into a toothy grin. His crooked eyetooth was, in a word, adorable. "I can't picture her in Montana. Wearing cowboy boots and roping cattle or whatever the fuck they do over there."

I snorted. "Don't forget camping and hiking. I can totally see her roughing it in a tent."

He chuckled. "As funny as it would be for us, she would definitely be pissed. It's hard to start over in a new territory, and I doubt Dram would cede this area to her. That would be a whole different fight."

I pointed at my chest. "And not my fight." My holster strap itched, and I scratched at it while considering my dwindling options. "If we do manage to make her an angel, will she release me?"

He glanced at me before looking away again. "I'll make sure she does."

My gaze ran over his profile. His face was kind of fascinating in how the different planes and textures met each other in strange and captivating ways. What was the phrase describing Ringo Starr? He's so ugly, he's cute? It almost applied to Sam—until he started growling, anyway. I tilted my head. No, that made it more applicable.

I nudged him with my elbow. "How do you know Olita will give you her place if she ascends?"

He shrugged. "I dunno, but I'm covering my ass in more ways than one."

"Does that mean taking out all your fellow incubi?"

"Some of 'em. The newer ones can't compete with me." His gray eyes twinkled when he smiled down at me. "And thanks to you, Johnny's out, so that's one less for me to deal with."

"Glad I could help. Does it take a while to build up power when you ascend to a new rank?"

"Yeah. The longer you stay in a rank and the more blood you drink, the stronger you get. Til you get too old and then..." His hand dove through the air like an airplane on a final, unplanned flight path.

"Oh yeah, that reminds me. What if a divine dies and there's no one around to take their place?"

"Either someone else claims their knife, or a higher rank promotes someone. Both are shite ways to ascend; you start with zero power."

I nodded and decided I might as well fact-check more of Olita's information while I had Sam in a state where he didn't mind me questioning him. "What if someone drinks your blood but doesn't kill you? What happens then?"

"You lose your powers and age fast. I've heard of a divine that lasted ten years, but most die within five." He glanced at his watch. "Anything else? I've gotta meeting I need to get to."

"Yeah, better not leave your addicts waiting. I hear they can get kind of twitchy."

He stood up. "Take care of yourself, Jeanie, and don't do anything stupid. Just lie low til you hear from me."

I saluted. "You got it, boss."

I had no intention of doing any of the things he just asked me to.

I contemplated Sam's hulking form as he strode away and thought back to what I'd said yesterday about being afraid of him. Interactions with other dealers were always sticky affairs, never knowing if the deal would devolve into violence or if they'd get creepy and demand sexual favors. As far as I could recall, Sam had never so much as touched me. It was true I'd been afraid of pissing him off, but I'd never been afraid of *him*. I always felt safe in his presence, like I knew if he was around, nothing bad would happen. Save for some growling threats and titillating intimidation tactics, that is. I squirmed against the bench when I imagined what he might do to me if I managed to royally piss him off and if it would involve him pressing me up against a wall and putting his tattooed hand around my throat.

I sat in the park for a while longer, admiring how the pigeons and seagulls deftly hopped about to pick up crumbs while staying just out of reach. How does one go about catching a bird? Bait in a trap? If I trapped an angel, I could leave Olita to deal with the rest. Then I wouldn't have to kill them myself—although technically I'd still be complicit in their death. But the less actual blood on my hands, the better. I dusted off my thinking cap and put it on. What kind of bait would an angel take?

9

THE CREAKING OF old floorboards echoed through the rental house like the footsteps of a ghost. I'd moved in two days prior and discovered the place was haunted by thoughts of what might've been. It was larger than the last apartment Tom and I shared, and the furnishings were, of course, different, but I still found myself waiting for him to come home. I pictured him sitting on the couch groaning, sighing, and sometimes laughing over the latest batch of essays from his English students. I could almost hear him in the kitchen singing made-up songs about the food he was cooking. I opened my eyes in the morning expecting to feel his soft weight pulling me to him like a lonely piece of space debris into a gravity well. Now, only pale apparitions and distant echoes remained of the life that died alongside my husband.

God, I missed him.

With a shaky sigh, I swept the ghosts under the rug and stuffed figurative cotton in my ears. I was sitting at my new desk with my new computer and staring at the relentless flashing of the cursor in my document titled "Fucked up Demon Shit." I'd listed all the angels in the western United States region along with where they lived and worked. Many of them had little to no online presence, which left large blocks of empty white on the screen. Until you scrolled to the section with questions and to-dos. That was packed full of the sickles, stalks, and dots of question marks and exclamation points. My focus constantly wavered. I got up to get more water, then to fix a snack, and then to use the bathroom. Wash, rinse, repeat until it was time to go to my MMA class.

Hungry and sweaty, I grabbed my own bag of Dick's after my lesson and headed to a bench in the dusk-lit park to eat. When I tossed the bag in the garbage and cut across a dark patch of lawn, a shadow darted behind a tree about twenty yards ahead. It was probably just a tweaker or a person looking for a place to crash, but on the off-chance it was someone worse, I walked over to investigate. A friend of mine had been assaulted in a park and struggled to fend off her attacker until a drag queen in six-inch spike heels hauled the man off her and beat the shit out of him. I could be that savior queen for someone. It's what RuPaul would want.

When I got to the tree, there was no one there. Frowning, I circled around the nearby shrubs. Nothing. I shrugged and started up the hill to my house.

Hands grabbed me from a dark alley, and I gasped in surprise as I was jerked off my feet. My attacker dragged me in and threw me to the ground behind a dumpster.

"Ow!" I cried out of habit and peered up. The light from the street served only to cast their face in shadow. "What do you want?"

A no-nonsense female voice answered. "To play a little. Where's Sam?"

My first and only idea was to play dumb. "I don't know who you're talking about." I shifted to stand up, and she pushed me down again.

"Who do you work for?" She pulled a knife out from behind her back. "You someone's little human pet?"

I squinted up at her darkened face and then down at the blade. In all likelihood, I was dealing with a divine. The realization sent an unexpected thrill of anticipation through my chest. I straightened my back against the wall while surreptitiously placing my right hand on the handle of the knife strapped to my belt.

"What are you talking about? I'm not a prostitute. *But* for the right drugs, maybe I could be." I waggled my eyebrows at her.

"Don't play games with me," she growled. "I know you're up to something with Sam. You're gonna tell me what it is, and maybe I won't kill you." Her knife flashed when it caught the light of a nearby streetlamp.

"I have no idea what he's up to. Want me to call him for you and ask?"

When my left hand reached for my phone, she kicked it away from my coat pocket and stepped on my wrist. In lieu of fear, excitement flooded my system at the chance to test out my new skills. I lifted my leg and slammed my heel against her knee while pulling my knife out and bracing against the wall. She cursed and pitched forward onto the blade before staggering back, clutching the wound and snarling in pain. With my limited repertoire of quasi-MMA moves spent, I switched to my patented rabid-squirrel jitsu. I jumped on her and stabbed while she bounced from alley wall to dumpster to alley wall, trying to dislodge me. The grunts and metallic clangs echoed their way up to the sky until I finally got her in the throat. She dropped to her knees, gasping for air, her hand squeezing the gash to keep the blood from spilling out.

She spat at me. "You fucking bitch."

Her face caught the light, and recognition hit. It was Mara, the incubus Sam and I had run into at the bar and whose presence had been enough to make him flee the premises.

My gaze darted back and forth between my bloodied knife and Mara's gasping form. A few steps outside the alley, I called out, "Hey! Any goblins around here looking to ascend?" No answer, so I shouted louder. This time someone leaned out of a window three stories up and yelled at me to shut the fuck up. I guess not, then.

Mara was still on her knees, wheezing, with blood trickling through the fingers at her throat. I turned the knife over and over in my hand, uncertain what to do next. "Any tips on how to stab a heart on the first try?"

"Fuck you." Her face was a tight grimace.

I bit my lip and wondered how long it would take for her to recover, and whether I should try to finish the job or just run. I was reluctant to go with option A. As I turned to dart away, she lunged for my leg and yanked me down. Olita's knife clattered and spun underneath the dumpster. After some ungainly ground tussling on the grimy pavement, I crawled out of her reach and fumbled around for it before she dragged me back again. This had to be the slowest and stupidest knife fight of all time.

Mara got in a few good swipes with her blade before I grabbed it from her by slamming my elbow into her nose and biting her wrist. She snarled when I took my turn swiping at her. Somewhere amid my clumsy slap fighting and her trying to grab the knife, I stabbed her in the eye. This time when she reeled back and cursed, my survival instinct kicked in like a punch to the face. I pushed her over, straddled her, and plunged the knife down a dozen times. I didn't stop until her ribcage sank and turned into dust. With trembling limbs and a hollow chest, I crawled over to sit against the alley wall and catch my breath.

With no corpse in front of me, it was easier to ignore the ramifications of what I'd just done. No sign of the heinous crime I'd committed. Nothing but a pile of dirt to ponder. As brains often do when confronted with horrific events, mine fixated on trivial details: the texture of the rust below the flaking paint on the dumpster, the taste of iron in my mouth, the odor of stale beer and rancid meat, the cool dampness seeping into my seat. My vacant stare drifted down to Mara's knife in my bloody hand. Maybe if I found a nice goblin, I'd give it to them. Or maybe I'd just throw it off a pier into the Puget Sound. I sat in shock until the tide of horror receded and only a tarry lump of self-loathing remained.

After fishing Olita's dagger out from under the dumpster, I stood up to get a better look at myself. I groaned at the dark splotches covering my jacket and tank top. Too bad divine blood didn't also turn into dust. I fingered a slash mark in the fabric and let out a long sigh. A lot of the blood was my own.

I shrugged out of my coat and used it to wipe up the spatters on my hands and face, mostly just smearing the blood into a thin film like a sicko tanning lotion. I balled up the jacket and wrapped it around the knives before sticking the bundle under my arm. In the evening light, the splatters didn't show up against my dark athletic pants and looked enough like a pattern on my white top to disguise the stains tolerably well. Otherwise, I'd have to hoof it up the hill in my bra and panties, which would draw more attention than walking around covered in blood. In my well-to-do neighborhood, anyway.

When I got home, I tossed the bundle on the floor and headed to the shower. I grimaced at my reflection in the mirror. Lines of dark red oozed down my face where Mara had caught me with her blade, and beneath the bloody veneer were plenty of bruises and stab wounds on my arms and torso, too. I wished upon my sub-par lucky star that the quick-healing from Olita's power wasn't a one-off. I didn't know what I'd do if I had to go to the hospital and answer questions from the authorities. "What's that, officer? Oh, I'm just really clumsy and happened to fall on my knife like two dozen times."

Thankfully, by the time I got out of the shower, most of the bleeding had stopped. I slapped bandages on the worst of the cuts and headed to bed. A black cavity lined with disgust gouged its way into my stomach as I stared up at the ceiling. I was officially a murderer now. Maybe I did have what it takes to be a demon's assistant.

10

"OH THANK GOD," I mumbled and let out a long, relieved breath. No visible cuts. When I pulled the bandages off, the deepest stab wounds showed up as thin pink lines, but otherwise it was as if I'd never been in a dark-alley knife fight. At least not based on my physical body—my soul was a different story. Fortunately, I'd gotten fairly adept at dissociating from painful emotions over my two years as a self-medicating widow. I added the new ones to the garbage pail, stamped them down, sat on the lid, and smoked a bowl.

After breakfast, I walked to the drugstore and bought wrapping paper and a small card with a picture of a cute kitten. I cleaned and wrapped Mara's knife as neatly as possible, complete with a sparkly bow.

In the card I wrote:

> *Dearest Sam,*
> *You're welcome.*
> *All my love,*
> *Jeanie*

I put everything in a box with his name and apartment number on top. On my way to the gym, I dropped it off on the doorstep of his building. Someone was bound to bring it inside. If not, then some thief was going to end up with a murder weapon.

When I was done with my personal training session, I pulled out my phone. Sam had texted me half-a-dozen times:

> *Where are you?*

What happened?

Are you okay?

You better text me back.

Don't make me come find you.

I'm coming to find you.

I smiled. He could try.

I assumed he'd been across half the city before his steps crunched on the dirt path behind me at the street end under the ship canal bridge. I was throwing the last bits of bread from my sandwich to the ducks gathered near the slimy logs of the shoreline.

"Glad to see you're alive and well," Sam said as he eased down beside me. "Care to tell me what went down?" he asked in a politer tone than I thought he was capable of.

"Care to tell me the plan for getting Olita up to angel rank?"

He put his elbows on his bent knees and propped his forehead on his hands like a sports-obsessed father whose son told him he wanted to take up the violin. "You're not making this easy for me, Jeanie."

"Oh, really? What's that like?"

He lifted his head and looked out over the water. The lines on his brow and dark circles under his eyes stood out in the reflected light.

I bumped my knee against his. "By my count, you now owe *me* a favor. Two favors, actually."

He sighed and watched me from the corner of his eye. "Probably," he agreed. He seemed drained. I wondered if he was due for a goblet of goblin blood or whatever. "Look, the thing with Olita is...complicated. There's a lotta loose ends to work out and too many moving parts to pin down."

I straightened a leg out and leaned back on my elbows. "I've got a check-in with her in less than a week, and I'm not sure what to tell her other than I've taken out two of her incubi."

He scratched at his stubble. "Yeah, probably shouldn't mention that."

"How much blood does she need from you guys?"

"She gets donations almost every day, depending on who she can track down and threaten enough."

I squinted in confusion. "Wait, *she* has an endless parade of sketchy people going in and out of *her* condo?" I couldn't picture her welcoming the underbelly of society into her home on a regular basis. Once had seemed like a stretch for her.

He chuckled. "Not all goblins and incubi are sketchy like me, but she doesn't meet with us. There's a secret chute to her place we use to send her our containers of blood. She had me come in when you were there to impress you or creep you out or something."

We sat in silence for a while, watching the ducks as they dove their heads in and out of the water. A warm breeze tickled my skin as it blew through the neckline of my dress. I studied Sam's hunched shoulders, and something stirred in my chest. "What about you? You look kinda tired or sick. How much blood do you need?"

He twisted his head around and looked down at me. "I'm behind a bit, but I'm fine."

His gaze shifted to my bent leg where the skirt of my dress had slid down my thigh, revealing my knife holster and probably my panties. My heart skipped with excitement when his focus lingered for a long moment. A faint blush crept up his neck before his gaze traveled back up to my arms and chest. His brow furrowed.

"Mara was a fucking nightmare, and you don't have a scratch on you. How'd you pull that off?"

My mouth curled into an innocent smile. "I'm just really good at knife fights, I guess."

He considered me for a long moment before standing up and offering me a hand. "Come on, let's go find a goblin to suck dry."

It didn't take long to find one sleeping under the bushes along the ship canal. According to Sam, divines can sense when another is nearby, so all we had to do was walk around until his proverbial hackles rose. He prodded the wad of blankets with his foot, and a long string of colorful curses erupted. An angry woman with a face like a bumpy potato emerged from the nest.

"Come on, Baby, up and at 'em." I raised an amused eyebrow at Sam. "It's her name," he explained.

Baby stood up and eyeballed me. "Who the hell is she?"

"Don't worry about her. I'm here for your dues." He beckoned her away from the nearby trail and toward the water where they'd be mostly out of sight.

She grumbled and stumbled after him. "I just gave you some, Shady. You're gonna bleed me dry," she whined. Her hand was clasping something under her dirty t-shirt. Before I could say anything, she whipped out a shiv and lunged for Sam. He caught her arm easily and twisted until she dropped the knife.

"Nothing funny today, okay, Baby?"

She spat before plopping down in defeat, whining more when Sam took his knife to the inside of her elbow. My face scrunched in disgust, and I stepped back up to the trail and looked around, expecting to find a crowd of onlookers watching in horror at the atrocity being committed right under their noses. Two cyclists rode by in matching kits. Then a woman followed by a man walked by, both staring intently at their phones. I was used to seeing people ignore others who were strung out or incoherent in public, but to think a woman could be brutalized twenty feet away and they wouldn't even notice? Or maybe just not care?

When Sam was done, he scrambled up the small rise to join me.

"Pretty messed up that you can get away with that shit in broad daylight," I said to him.

He wiped a drop of blood from the corner of his mouth and shrugged. "I used a charm to hide us from humans."

My brow furrowed. "But I could see you."

"It doesn't work on humans who already know we're there."

"Well, that's a relief," I said acidly before turning towards home.

He fell in beside me, his step jauntier and a gleam in his eyes. He clapped me on the back. "It's a wonderful world, ain't it, Jeans?"

Sam was more amiable than usual and didn't brush me off when he started on his incubus rounds. As we made our way around his part of town, I saw what he meant about not all goblins being the same. He shook down one at a high-end mechanic's shop and another working in the kitchen of a fancy restaurant. We caught one of his goblin women striding out of an architecture office. She was surprisingly pretty, with thick blond hair and soft blue eyes. Her smile was sweet and suggestive when he stopped her. An answering smile played at Sam's lips, and I looked away to hide my inexplicably tight jaw.

He didn't take any of their blood, he just asked how they were doing in a menacing manner and told them when he expected their next quote-unquote donation. Most nodded and agreed, but a few got grumbly. He had to push one up against a wall with his knife to their throat, and he broke the arm of another.

"He'll be fine," he said and waved a dismissive hand when I protested the harsh treatment. "It'll heal in a couple of hours."

"Speaking of healing, how did you get that scar on your face if you all heal so fast?"

Sam's stride checked, and his voice was quiet when he answered. "Our abilities don't start til puberty. Before that, we're basically human."

"Oh."

Sam definitely had some, well, demons in his past I knew he wouldn't want to talk about. I'd be treading on dangerous ground if I asked, and I was enjoying our time together and didn't want to ruin it. It was a comfortable kind of companionship I'd been missing for years.

When he was done with his rounds, we headed back to Capitol Hill.

"How come some goblins end up on the street and some don't?" I asked him after we'd crossed the bridge over the noisy freeway.

"How come some humans end up on the street and some don't?" He asked back.

"Well, that's a question with a multi-faceted answer; how much time you got?"

He sighed. "Most of the reasons are the same, but more divines get orphaned as children. Goblins die young or get killed, so their kids end up on the street or in foster care. A few get adopted into nice families. A lot don't." His tone softened. "Being an ugly kid really lowers your chances of getting into a good situation."

"That's...really sad." I hesitated before carefully asking, "Did your parents die when you were young?" I knew I was prying too much.

His face closed up into a hardened expression that was all too familiar. "Let's just say I got my street smarts from somewhere and leave it at that."

"I'm sorry, Sam."

"Want me to walk you home?" he asked, not looking at me.

"Nah, I don't want you to know where I live." It was a joke. He'd always been able to find me when he wanted to.

"I'll see you around, then." His hands were in his pockets, his gaze somewhere far away. I had a powerful urge to hug him, like he was my friend now that we'd hung out for more than an hour. He also looked like he needed one.

Instead, I took a deep breath. "Okay, see you around."

I turned and trudged up the hill to my place, lost in my thoughts. By the time I got home, my disappointment had made way for a bratty resolve. If Sam wouldn't let me in, then I saw no reason to tell him about the stupid plan I'd been brooding over and was ready to hatch.

11

THE ENGINES ROARED to life, and the sudden burst of speed scooped my fellow passengers and me into the air with barely a wobble. As the plane circled and headed east to Billings, Montana, I mulled over my decision to make the trip. It was obviously a bad one. Heading into angel Jackson Greene's territory with no backup was a terrible idea, but the desire to get out of Seattle trumped any common sense that might have weighed in on the decision. I hadn't left the area in three years, and the same streets and people had become monotonous. Besides, I was too restless to just sit around and wait for Sam to put his secret plan in motion.

I'd booked a hotel in the city center and stopped there first to check in and drop off my bag before heading out to explore the nightlife scene. There wasn't much going on; it was Wednesday, so no surprises there. I found the busiest tavern and took a spot at the bar to watch people and see if I could attract someone interested in a good time.

Trying to hook up at a bar was not an activity I especially enjoyed. I'd never been beautiful enough to garner much attention, and the older I got, the more invisible I became to charming men looking to get laid. Still, when it worked out, there was something thrilling about not knowing what kind of toy was at the bottom of a stranger's sexual cereal box. The potential for danger brought an excitement that would have shocked me before my life took its dark turn.

For a long time after Tom died, I didn't want to be touched by anyone, not even myself. Eventually, desire did find its way back into my life, but not in the form it had existed in before. I didn't want any loving touches or caresses, nothing that could be construed as intimate. Instead, I sought out meaningless hookups that scratched the itch without intruding into the barrier I'd built around my heart. I had brief flings here and there with fellow addicts and a surprising number of dalliances with clean-cut men who got off on fucking dirty street chicks. After an intense encounter with a man in a classy suit that resulted in a bout of almost-but-not-quite-serious choking (and two hundred guilty dollars afterwards), I discovered I enjoyed the pain. I don't know if it was because pain in my body meant less attention was available to acknowledge the pain in my head, or if it was because I thought I deserved it—a punishment for choosing to jump the conventional life ship after Tom died rather than powering through to a brighter future. I'm sure it would take years of sessions with a licensed therapist to untangle those knots.

After two drinks, I caught the eye of a balding late-forties man, and he ambled over to talk. Most of my predictions about him were true: adult kids, working his way up the corporate ladder at some unremarkable business, and an ex-wife so horrible that he couldn't stop bitching about her—even to a woman he was trying to pick up. Ultimately, I excused myself and walked back to my hotel alone. A bout of disappointing sex followed by an awkward morning was not appealing enough to break my latest stint of celibacy.

Back in my room, I took matters into my own hands and wasn't surprised when Sam popped up in the middle of my sexual reverie. He was a regular visitor in my fantasies already, and the memory of him squeezing my neck on the bench and whispering menacing words in my ear got me flushed and ready. Then, the mental image of him bending me over said bench and holding me down with his muscular arms sent me over the edge.

Now calmer, I reviewed the small amount of information I'd gathered on Jackson Greene. According to sources on the web, he owned a shitload of real estate in downtown Billings, along with lucrative properties stretching all the way into Idaho and Wyoming. His name was associated with a property management company called Angel's Real Estate, LLC. Way too on the nose with that one, Jackson. I wasn't sure what angle to play yet, but maybe something would come to me when I stopped by his office in the morning.

I peered through the large window of the plain one-story brick building. A petite blond receptionist was chewing gum and filing her nails behind a desk in the empty lobby. She slid the nail file into a drawer, and her bored mouth snapped into a plastic smile when I swung the door open. She looked me up and down, and some of the eagerness dropped from her expression.

"Is Mr. Greene in?" I asked, making sure my designer bag logo was visible in case she thought I wasn't worth enough to have dealings with the largest real estate owner in the area.

She turned to her computer. "Do you have an appointment?"

I gave her an embarrassed smile. "No. I happened to be traveling through the area and figured I'd take the opportunity to discuss a potential investment property with him. I hear he's the one to talk to." She straightened up at the word "investment."

"Let me see what's on his schedule for today. May I ask your name?"

"Jane Booker."

"Ok, hmmm. He's got an opening at ten o'clock. Does that work?" I glanced at my watch. It was 9:15.

"That's perfect, actually."

"Okay, we'll see you back here at ten, Ms. Booker." She shot me another artificial smile before I turned to leave.

I walked to a cafe to grab a coffee and come up with a plan. First, I looked up ski resorts in Big Sky, Montana. Maybe I could convince Jackson that one of them was up for sale, or a neighboring area was ripe for development. There was also a golf course nearby. Okay, my misinformation machine was starting to warm up.

Of course, the key component of the meeting would involve violence. If he was alone, should I rush him? If by some magical chance I immobilized him, then how would I collect his blood and get away afterwards? My eyebrows dipped as I scrutinized my paper coffee cup. How does one go about smuggling blood through airport security? I sighed. With too many unknowns, I'd just have to go in blind and fumble my way through, as per the usual. I opened my purse and made sure the knife was still easily accessible. I'd taped the sheath near the top so I wouldn't have to rifle around in the bottomless bag if stabbing was called for.

With the smallest inkling of a plan in place, I drained the rest of my coffee and headed back to the office. My hands smoothed the jacket of my new power suit before I walked in. I didn't compare to Kaytee, but I did feel more powerful.

Jackson rose from behind his desk to greet me with a handshake. He was tall and thin, with deep green eyes and a bland but pleasant face suitable for both real estate agents and serial killers.

"Please, have a seat, Ms. Booker." His voice carried a hint of a drawl.

I thanked him and sat prim and proper, with my purse balanced on my lap.

"My secretary tells me you have an investment opportunity you'd like to discuss?"

I beamed at him. "Yes, thank you so much for taking the time, Mr. Greene. An associate of mine informed me that a property is coming up for sale in Big Sky between the ski areas and golf course. I think it's an ideal location for a new five-star resort. I have a few investors on board already and have a meeting with the current owner in about…" I glanced at my watch. "Five hours. Your name has come up several times in my business dealings, so I swung by on a whim to see if you might be interested."

He propped his elbows on the arms of his chair and steepled his fingers, swiveling from side to side as he studied me. "Funny, I haven't heard of you before. My secretary wasn't able to find anything about you, either."

I waved a casual dismissal. "Oh, I prefer to operate in the background under various LLCs." I leaned forward and said in a conspiratorial whisper, "I prefer to spread my investments around under the radar; I'm sure you understand." I sat back up and gave him a broad smile. "I have some information here if you'd like to review it."

As I reached into my purse, he held up a hand. "Before you do, I'd like to bring in my business partner." He pressed a button on his desk phone. "Jim, come in here, please."

A moment later, the door to the office opened and a burly man in a too-tight suit entered. His military-style haircut was the perfect complement to his meaty, trapezoidal face. He walked over and stood next to Jackson, crossed his thick arms, and tightened his mouth into a menacing scowl.

I faltered before offering him a pleasant smile. "Okay, Mr. Greene...and, Jim." I nodded to him. When I reached into my purse again, Jackson sighed.

"Cut the crap, lady. Who do you work for?" I stared at him in astonishment as a peculiar buzzing started up in my head. It made it difficult to think clearly.

"I'm sorry, I...I'm not sure what you're talking about." I stuttered out.

The buzzing ticked up several notches and drowned out all sound save for his voice. "You're going to tell me who you work for and what you're doing here."

The words were a command, not a suggestion, and almost impossible to resist. A dim memory of a conversation with Sam brought the realization into stark focus: angels can control humans. Shit, this was bad. I struggled to breathe as I attempted to fixate on anything other than my mission for Olita. "Money... rich people...skiing!" I gasped out.

Jackson stared at me, his eyes narrow and calculating, and the buzzing stopped. He gestured with a finger, and Jim nodded. I watched with mild curiosity as the glowering man walked over and reached for my forehead.

12

WATER DRIPPED IN an irregular staccato, and the stale air carried hints of rust and mildew. I licked my dry lips and tried to scratch my nose, but my limbs wouldn't cooperate. After a series of groggy blinks, my eyes focused enough to take in my surroundings. Chains bound my hands to the ceiling of a chilly concrete room lit by a solitary swinging bulb. I stifled a giggle. I could be on the set of any number of action movie tie-up-and-torture scenes. Jackson, Jim, and the secretary lurked in the shadows just beyond the circle of light.

Jackson's gloating grin came into view when he took a step forward. "Okay, Ms. Booker," he said. "We can do this the easy way or the hard way."

I snorted. "Seriously? How cliche can you get?"

His mouth hardened into a frown, and his eyes flashed red. "Fine. Stacy, you're up."

The secretary strutted over, gum popping. Her smile was a little too broad, and her eyes a little too bright. "Hi, Jane. This is what's going to happen. I'm going to torture you until you beg me to stop and then you're going to answer Mr. Greene's questions." She stared at me, smug and expectant, like she assumed I'd just spill the beans out of fear. Too bad I didn't have any. "Okay, then. Allow me to demonstrate my power." She flexed her hand and admired her long pink nails for a moment before swiping them across my abdomen and down my thigh. The tips left bloody red stripes behind as they ripped through my blouse and skirt.

With a quiet huff of annoyance, I stared down at my torn clothes. Damn it, the outfit had cost like $800, but at least they'd been kind enough to remove my jacket before chaining me up. When my gaze drifted back up to their waiting faces, I realized they expected me to be writhing around in pain. I squeezed my eyes shut in pretend agony and copied the classic tortured hero by groaning and jerking against my manacles.

Stacy's sadistic smile widened. "Round two, Jane."

She reached up and skimmed her nails along my face and throat with slow and sensual caresses before jabbing them into my shoulder. Sparks crackled across her fingers, and my body seized up as though two large hands were grabbing every muscle and wringing them dry. A subtle odor of blood and ozone drifted into my nostrils—she was electrocuting me. Even though my power blocked pain, the experience was something I didn't relish having to go through for longer than necessary. She stopped then dug her nails into my side and started again. During the next break, I struggled in earnest. My flailing legs tried to kick her, but I couldn't get enough purchase on the floor to make any real impact. Instead, I swung in lazy loops like the light bulb.

After the third bout of electrocution, phantom jolts of static were shooting through my limbs, and ripples of cold tingled beneath the warm blood trickling down my skin. I amped up my wailing and thrashing. All three mouths broke into broad grins, and Jackson's eyes gleamed red.

"Ok, Stacy. Let's see if Ms. Booker is more amenable to having a conversation now."

Stacy stepped back, still grinning like a possessed Barbie doll as she wiped her hands on a rag. The buzzing in my head started up, and I whimpered. I'd lost a fair amount of blood and possibly suffered a heart attack during the electrocution torture. My mind was struggling to collate my brainwaves into something resembling intelligence, and it was nearly impossible to resist Jackson's commanding voice.

"Who do you work for?"

"O-o-ol," I began before biting down on the words. The buzzing grew louder. "O-o-o-Oh, say can you see, by the dawn's—" Stacy stepped forward and cut me off with a clawed slap to my face.

Jackson's jaw clenched. "Cut the crap, Jane. Let us know who you work for and I'll be happy to send your shredded carcass back to your master. Maybe with enough life left so you can give them my regards."

The buzzing grew so intense it was almost like pain. I shouted out nonsense to cover up the sound of his voice. "We all live in a yellow sub—" A sharp slash across my belly. "I am the very model of a mod—" This time it was Jackson who silenced me with a punch to the face. I was woozy enough that his words barely cut through the haze in my brain.

His annoyed voice said to Stacy and Jim, "We'll leave her for now; she's too out of it to answer anything. I'll see if I can find something out about the knife. You two stay here until she wakes up. If she won't talk, lock up and come to the office."

The door creaked open and then slammed shut, and my consciousness promptly vacated the building.

My eyelids crawled upward, and my blurry sight sharpened into focus after a series of blinks. The room was empty. I let out a sigh of relief—nothing like some alone time to fully appreciate the consequences of my stupid actions. Still dazed, I looked up and examined the manacles. They weren't tight around my wrists like proper handcuffs would have been. Jackson must have cheaped out and decided a one-size-fits-all model would be sufficient for his torture games. There had to be a way to dislocate a joint or break a bone in order to free myself.

I tugged—nothing. I pulled harder, resting all my weight on one hand. Also nothing. I pumped my legs in and out to gain enough momentum to hop up before bringing my full weight back down. After a dozen fruitless attempts, it worked. Blood lubricated my lacerated hands as I slid them out of the manacles before landing in a heavy pile on the cold ground. A wave of motion sickness passed over me now that my previously swinging body was hugging the motionless floor. I curled up on my side, and hot prickles of blood crept back into my arms.

I lay there, breathing deeply, until the vertigo had run its course and I could sit up. With my nose scrunched in anticipation of gory horror, I examined my mangled hands. The manacles had torn deep gashes into the sides and revealed an unsettling glimpse of bone. I suppressed a gag and tested the use of my fingers by gingerly tearing strips of fabric from my shredded shirt and clumsily wrapping each hand. Shuddering with nausea, I considered either throwing up or lying back down, maybe both, until a dull murmur came from behind the rusty metal door. I shuffled over on my knees and put an ear to it. A man and a woman were talking, but their voices were too muffled to make out words. I slid down in the door's blind spot to think.

What I knew so far was Jim could knock people unconscious with a touch, hopefully only with his hands, maybe only on bare skin. Stacy's power was having nails like knives mixed with jumper cables and an appetite for torture. Jackson had given his assistants some questionable powers. Not that mine were any use for getting me out of the current mess I was in. I didn't have my knife, obviously, or even my shoes to throw. I cast my gaze around the room. It was empty save for the manacles and light bulb. The dank cement soon had me shivering as I leaned against the wall and gave myself time to recover.

When my breath was steadier, and the thought of using my hands didn't send a sickening shudder down my spine, I stood up to inspect my surroundings. The manacles were worthless to me; if they hadn't budged during my thrashing marionette movements, then brute force wouldn't bring them down. So much for my chance to beat someone with a chain. My gaze drifted to the naked bulb next and then to the doorway. If my eyes were adjusted to the dark, I'd have an advantage when the dickhead crew returned. It took half a dozen tries before I got a good enough grip on the bulb to crush it. Darkness fell.

I felt my way over to the door and sat down next to it with my ear to the cool metal. Time stretched on until the scraping of chairs roused me and footsteps approached. I stood up, my body tense and ready.

When the door creaked open, Jim cursed. "Light went out," he called back to the other room before inching his way inside.

I waited in the shadows, heart pumping with adrenaline, with no idea what my next move would be. When Stacy stepped up behind him to peer in, and Jim turned around to head back out, I saw my chance. I leapt out and shoved him, grimacing as my palms slid against his sweaty shirt. He gasped in surprise and stumbled, hands out for balance, and ran into Stacy. She collapsed into an untidy heap of spindly limbs and platinum blond hair.

Jim's knee folded forward at the impact of my reasonably well-placed kick, and he tripped over Stacy and fell. A giggle escaped my lips. While Jim struggled to get up, I jumped over him and ran out of the cell, eyes blinking rapidly against the light. I raced to grab one of the two metal chairs flanking the rickety card table. Jim was on his feet and staggering in my direction by the time I turned around, his teeth bared and snarling in his purple face.

My veins pulsed with fiery anticipation as I rushed him and pushed him back with the chair until he tripped over Stacy again and landed in the doorway of the dark cell. His head smacked against the concrete floor, and his pelvis presented itself like the posterior of a cat in heat. With a barely suppressed smile, I stomped his crotch. There was a moment of expectant silence before his breath whooshed out and he grabbed his balls, wheezing in pain, and flopped to the side. I watched him writhe around in agony for a moment, and a tiny speck of guilt floated by. It was a low blow, but then again, chaining me to the ceiling and torturing me was also a dick move. I raised the chair and whacked it against his struggling arms until it finally struck gold. With a triumphant yell, I brought the chair down on his face one more time. He went limp.

My breath came fast and heavy from the adrenaline still pumping through my system. While my heart and lungs attempted to get ahold of themselves, I considered my options. I was not okay with murdering a human. That was the hard line I'd agreed on with myself during my long, sleepless vigil after killing Mara. My gaze traveled from Jim's slack and sweaty face up to the dark opening of the cell. Thankfully, I had the perfect alternative to murder at my immediate disposal. For good measure, I hit him with the chair one more time before setting it down and looking him over. I prodded his gut with my foot before crouching and poking his cheek. He was out. I snaked an unwilling hand into his clammy pockets and rifled around until my fingers met a ring of keys and a car fob. I let out a long sigh of relief. Escape Part Two was shaping up to be a success.

It took a lot of breathless pushing, pulling, and rolling of Jim's limp body before I got him into the cell. Stacy went next. After shutting and locking the door, I leaned against it and caught my breath.

My eyes had finally adjusted to the garish fluorescent lights, and I took stock of my surroundings. I was standing in what appeared to be an old break room, or possibly a nuclear fallout shelter, for what must have been the most depressing workplace on earth. My purse was sitting on the dingy counter next to a dusty coffee machine, and my phone was on the card table. I picked it up and snorted when I read the screen; it was disabled from too many incorrect password entries. Nine more minutes until the next attempt. Much to my non-surprise, Stacy and Jim weren't expert hackers. I tossed it into my purse.

With a preemptive wince, I looked down to check myself out properly for the first time. I groaned in annoyance. Bloody shreds were all that remained of my blouse and skirt; it was a miracle they were still hanging on. I swiped a saliva-moistened finger across one of the cuts on my side. There was a thin gash beneath the dried blood, but the bleeding had stopped.

My blazer was draped over a pile of boxes and clutter in the corner, and I grinned like I'd spotted a free bottle of laudanum. I pulled the rest of my torn and bloodied blouse off and put the jacket on. That was the top half covered, at least. I sorted through the mess and found nothing but old office and cleaning supplies. Stacy's pants popped up as a possibility when I glanced over to the prison door, but I discounted the idea immediately; they were probably four sizes too small. The thought of peeling Jim's pants off his unconscious body prompted my gut to reverse direction, so I scanned the room again. There were no signs of my shoes either. With a resigned sigh, I picked up an empty box and punched the bottom out, stepped through it, and pulled it up to my waist. Fortunately, I was accustomed to having very little dignity when it came to my appearance. I hiked my purse strap farther up my shoulder and headed out.

At the end of a short hallway with the same peeling yellow paint and fluorescent lighting, a heavy metal door opened to a stairway that led up through a cold concrete tunnel. Where the hell did Jackson find this place? Did he make it a point to have an assortment of creepy torture rooms in his real estate portfolio? A dark and echoey warehouse greeted me at the top of the stairs. My bare feet made quiet slapping sounds on the smooth cement as I crossed to the huge sliding door. I struggled to open it wide enough to peer out.

A loud creak announced my exit, and I paused to survey my surroundings. Muffled vehicle noises drifted over on the cool night air, and distant lights illuminated a scattering of stacked pallets in the otherwise dark and silent lot. My back bumped rhythmically across the corrugated metal as I sidled along the warehouse wall to the corner. I stopped and peeked around it. In front of the smoking stacks of a refinery, two forklifts were moving pallets of barrels, taking them off of neat rows and lifting them onto idling trucks. Across the yard, the overhead lights of another warehouse shone on three people in hardhats standing around and shooting the shit. Another swept the area with leisurely strokes of a push broom.

While I was considering walking over and explaining my situation (did you guys know there's an underground torture chamber here?), a low whistle sounded. The workers walked off, their shift over, and the forklifts finished their loading and drove away. I crossed my fingers and hoped there wasn't a night shift. Darting from shadow to shadow, I paused periodically to listen as

I made my way to the warehouse. A few stragglers dawdled inside, but most were heading out through the doors at the far end. Relief settled in as I waited for the last of them to leave. Halfway down the building was a pair of bathrooms. Another stroke of luck.

Only thin red lines remained after scrubbing my face and body with the rough paper towels. After pondering the clumsy bandages on my hands for a brief moment, I decided to leave their care up to my potentially dependable future self—AKA the Schrodinger's Jeanie who is simultaneously responsible and irresponsible until observed. I poked at the mottled purple and yellow bruises on my cheek and around my eye and wondered how long it would take for them to disappear and what the hotel staff would do if I walked in wearing nothing but a designer jacket, cardboard box, and signs of facial battery.

No one noticed me as I beat a hasty retreat out of the warehouse and circled around the gravel parking lot to a pair of shipping containers. I sat in the deep shadow between them and let out a relieved breath. The case of the bloody, bedraggled, and half-naked woman trespassing on private industrial property would remain unreported, for now, at least. A buzzing against my leg startled me, and I rooted around in my purse.

My phone had just connected to cell service and was alerting me to the fact that there were several voicemails and texts from Sam waiting. I read the texts first:

> *Where are you?*

> *Why aren't you answering your phone?*

> *Are you in trouble?*

> *Do you need help?*

I rolled my eyes. If I could answer my phone, then I wouldn't need help, would I, Sam? The voicemails went from angry to concerned:

"I need to talk to you. Call me back."

"Jeanie, what the fuck? Call me."

"I'm getting worried. Call me."

"I can't find you, Jeanie. You're scaring me."

I smiled at the last one. His voice had a certain quality of desperate and angry I found appealing.

My phone made an unhappy noise. The battery indicator showed three percent remaining.

I texted him:

I'm OK. Battery about to die. I'll call later.

He responded within seconds:

Where are you?

Billings

WTF...

He was still typing when the screen went black.

Rather than heading to my hotel, I decided to pay another visit to Jackson's office on the off-chance he was there. Maybe I could knock him out and steal his blood if he didn't have his two psycho cronies with him. It was a long shot, but I might as well take it. If nothing else, maybe I could get Olita's stupid knife back.

After several minutes spent stumbling through the dimly lit parking lot, a distant beeping answered my key fob. I threw my box skirt into the back seat and climbed into the sleek, black sedan. The engine hummed to life. I couldn't help but whip the car around in a tight circle, stirring up a ring of dust in my wake, before peeling out onto the road.

13

THE WINDOWS OF Jackson's office were dark when I did a slow drive-by, so I pulled into the alley behind the building, hoping to find another way in. It would be nice not to mess around with keys while pantless and in full view of a well-lit public street. I breathed out a sigh of relief when I spotted the back door. When I strode up with Jim's jingling key ring, my smile soon turned into a frown. The stiff handle wouldn't budge, even after trying every key. I growled in annoyance and grabbed the tire iron from the trunk.

It took about ten ill-aimed blows before the lever handle finally clattered to the ground and the door sagged open. I poked my head in and listened. Nothing. The soft light of street lamps glowing through the windows lit my way through the hallway and into the lobby. More bashing and prying got me into Jackson's office. I switched on the light. Everything was the same as when I'd visited in the morning. Just a neat and perfectly ordinary office: mahogany desk, leather chair, certificates on the walls—nothing to indicate that an evil, sadistic asshole worked there.

On his desk was a handwritten note:

> I'm following up on a lead. Meet me at the library and bring the knife. It's in the safe.

After a careful visual scan, I saw nothing resembling a safe. I checked the lobby next. The closet had only a printer and office supplies, and the large metal file cabinets held, surprise, surprise, files. I found lots of gum, nail polish, and, to my delight, gay porn mags in Stacy's desk. Another small office off the lobby, probably

Jim's, had only a chair and desk inside. Minus the computer on top, the desk contained nothing except an alarming amount of staples, paper clips, and a hand squeezer thing for working out forearms. Gotta keep those paralyzing-toucher muscles in shape, I guess.

I poked around in Jackson's desk next but found even less than I had in his assistants'. My hope dwindling, I tried the large bottom drawer last. It was locked. After letting out a long and frustrated groan, I tightened my grip on the tire iron and proceeded to bash the whole side of the desk in. Yay for particleboard! Inside was a metal cash box. I shook it, and something hard clattered inside. It better be my fucking knife.

The sound of distant sirens froze me in place as I stepped out of the office with the cash box under my arm. A string of expletives followed in my wake as I ran out the back door and slid into the car, punched the start button, threw it into gear, and took off with a satisfying squeal of tires. When I was halfway across town, I parked on a dark, dead-end street and debated whether I should go back to the hotel. Walking through the lobby while bruised, bloodied, shoeless, and pantless was not the way I would choose to wrap up my ill-advised trip to Billings. There was also the possibility that Jackson would find me. He might already be asking around about a middle-aged white woman with extremely poor judgment.

I tapped my lip. Maybe I could engage in some old-timey hijinks and steal clothes off a clothesline and head to the airport? My furrowed brow shot up in sudden realization, and I dove a hand into my purse. My wallet wasn't there—Jackson must have taken it. Loud curses filled the car as I banged my forehead on the steering wheel before remembering I'd pulled everything out of the purse in order to fasten the knife sheath to its side. It was possible I'd forgotten to put the wallet back in. Only one way to find out. I let out a resigned sigh and shifted the car into gear. Time to get ogled by the hotel staff.

In as dignified a way as possible, I walked through the bright lobby with the cash box under one arm and the cardboard box held up firmly in the other. I smiled and nodded to the front desk man as I passed by. His eyebrows rose higher and higher with every slap of my bare feet. Nothing to see here, sir! I took the stairs two at a time to my room and let out a quiet whoop of relief when I found my wallet tucked into a fold of the rumpled duvet. After tossing it into my purse, I set about cleaning myself up to a level more acceptable for public display. I stared at the bloodied bandages on my hands for a long moment before opting to slash into a pair of socks with my nail file to make fingerless gloves. I eased them over the shreds of my once-blouse. Sorry again, future self! I threw fresh clothes on, shoved the cash box in my suitcase, and was out the door in under ten minutes.

Next stop: the airport.

The keys made a satisfying thud against the side of the trash can when I tossed them in. I'd left the car in the short-term, high-rate airport parking lot as a final fuck-you to Jackson. Then I sidled into the small terminal, scanned the area for a tall and angry man, and let out a sigh of relief—only two desk agents and a glowering security guard in sight. The departure screens announced that the next flight to Seattle wasn't until five in the morning. A quick glance at the clock revealed it was nearing 1 a.m. I chewed my lip as I watched the doors. How long would it take for Jackson to track me down once he realized I'd escaped?

The bored woman at the car rental booth looked up from her phone when I approached. "Can I help you?" Her voice was the perfect pitch for appearing to make an effort while also not giving a fuck. Chef's kiss.

"Do you know how long it takes to drive from here to Seattle?"

"Let me check." She typed on her computer. "Looks like it's about twelve hours. Would you like to rent a vehicle?"

I shifted from foot to foot. "Nah, thanks anyway."

With my plane ticket purchased and bag checked, I got comfortable on the floor by the gate, head propped up on my purse, and sunglasses on. The way I figured it was that even if Jackson found me here, what was he going to do? Mutilate me in front of the half-dozen late-night occupants, TSA personnel, and security cameras? If he got the police involved, it might get tricky. I did technically burglarize his office, and there was probably footage of me doing so. All I could do was hope he didn't have enough cops in his pocket to get them swinging into action before five in the morning. My gaze darted in every direction like a stoned gonzo journalist at a police convention while I waited to see what the next few hours would bring.

My shoulders finally relaxed when the plane got airborne. The stretch between being seated and taxiing to takeoff felt like an eternity. I kept peering out the window, expecting to see blue and red lights careening onto the tarmac and police officers dropping into crouches with guns drawn. That probably only happens in the movies, but by that point my brain was having a hard time keeping fact and fiction in the appropriate lobes of my cerebral cortex. I was so tired I could barely keep my eyes open, and so hungry I could have eaten through an entire pasta buffet. I accepted the small cup of coffee from the flight attendant and leaned my seat back. Only two more hours to Seattle.

Sam was sitting on my front stoop when the car pulled up to the curb. He stood up slowly when our eyes met through the window, and my heart performed an unexpected flip.

The driver swiveled his head around to look at me. "You know this guy? Want me to drop you somewhere else?"

My reflection in the mirror of the airport bathroom had revealed the remnants of a bruise under my eye. I wondered if the driver had seen it and what conclusions he might have drawn. It was sweet of him to care.

"No, that's okay. It's just my secretary. Thanks for asking." I slid out and gave him a final wave before Sam closed the car door.

Without a word, he grabbed my suitcase and offered an arm to help me up the steps. It was obvious how tired I was as I swayed from side to side. My key kept missing the keyhole, so he guided my hand and unlocked it for me. Inside, I shuffled to the couch and collapsed onto it.

"Fuuuuuck," I moaned and flung an arm over my face when he turned on the overhead light.

"So, Jeanie, out doing a little sightseeing?"

I peeked out from under my elbow. Sam was leaned up against the door with his arms crossed. His tone was light, but there was an undercurrent of "you done fucked up now" in it.

I rubbed my face with both hands while my scrambled brain debated how much I should tell him. As I plopped my heavy arms down beside me, he stiffened and walked over to tilt my chin up to the light.

"The fuck? Is that a black eye?" I shrugged. "What happened over there?"

His voice was taking on the concerned tone I was liking more and more for some reason. Maybe it was because it sounded like he cared—a sentiment I didn't realize I was missing until his words dropped into the void Tom's used to fill.

My chest expanded with a deep breath as I gazed up at him towering over me, his face in shadow. "I *may* have got into a little bit of trouble with the Billings police." He tilted his head. "And definitely into trouble with Jackson Greene."

He stepped back. "Jeanie…"

He was trying to find the words, scanning the walls and rubbing his forehead in frustration. I didn't bother waiting to hear what he had to say. My eyelids refused to stay open. I hadn't had what I would call sleep in over twenty-four hours, lost a fair amount of blood, been electrocuted, and possibly suffered a heart attack. The couch drifted away when Sam picked me up and carried me to the bedroom.

He sat me on the bed and slid his hands under the back of my t-shirt and undid my bra before snaking the straps through my sleeves and over my arms. Waves of goosebumps and heat washed over my skin at his touch. Then he eased me down onto my back and slipped the bra out from underneath my shirt. His fingers tickled my stomach when he unbuttoned my pants, and I giggled as he pulled them off, taking my socks and shoes with them. He picked up my feet and tucked them under the sheets before covering the rest of my body, lifting my head briefly to rearrange the pillow. After a pause, a gentle finger traced across my forehead and brushed a lock of hair from my nose. The steady pressure of his touch on my bandaged hands faded into the background of my exhausted mind. I sighed in comfortable contentment before falling into the deepest sleep of my life.

14

THE ROOM WAS dark and disorienting. I thrashed around under the covers until I could free a hand and turn on the bedside lamp. I squinted at my watch: 8:45 p.m. With the loopy feeling of having slept through the day, I stumbled out of bed and turned the shower knob to cold to help shake off my sleep hangover. I shivered and shook just long enough to scrub the last remnants of Billings from my body before stepping out to towel off.

With a resigned sigh, I reluctantly turned my attention to my hands. My brow furrowed as I stared at the neatly wrapped gauze bandages. With hesitant fingers and a face already scrunching into wince mode, I unwrapped them. Instead of mangled blood and bone, it was only smooth, pink skin over the areas where the manacles had scraped the flesh off. I grinned—looks like my future self didn't have to deal with the carnage after all.

A surprised squeak left my mouth when I walked into the kitchen and found Sam poking around in my cupboards, and the hot water kettle burbling on the counter. The corner of his mouth lifted into a pleased smirk when he saw me.

"Hey, sleepyhead, how're you feeling?"

"Like I slept through the day and woke up to find a man in my kitchen." His gaze slid down my body and stopped midway between my head and feet. I looked down. "Oh." I was wearing only panties and a short, tight tank top with the shaky outline of my favorite rock album rendered in puffy fabric paint. I turned and headed back to the bedroom to pull on sweatpants. Sam was grinning when I walked back in.

"Looking pretty good there, Jeans. You been working out?"

I pressed my lips together to hide my pleased smile and shooed away the compliment. "Yeah, right, like you can tell. Wait till you see me in a few months; I'm going to get so ripped."

"I bet."

I padded over and reached past him to open the cupboard and grab mugs and tea before setting them down on the counter next to where he was leaning.

His jacket and shoulder holster were off, and I took a moment to admire the muscles bulging on his chest and crossed arms. My fantasies about him from the other night came swimming into focus, and I wondered idly what his preferred mode of sexual gratification was. His expression hovered somewhere between amusement and hunger when I finally tore my gaze away from the pattern of veins on his forearms to look up at him. Heat rose in my cheeks, and I scooted around him to sit down at the table.

When the water in the kettle reached a boil, he poured it into the waiting mugs and walked them over before heading back to the fridge and pulling out two takeout containers.

My eyebrows lifted, and he shrugged. "Figured you might be hungry, so I grabbed you something to eat." He put them in the microwave and hit start.

Oh no, this was too much. It'd been ages since someone had cared about my well-being. My chest twisted into an uncomfortable knot. "Um, thanks," I said and studied my mug of steaming tea. "And thanks for taking care of me last night—I mean this morning. You didn't have to do that."

He set a fork and the warm containers down in front of me. "It was nothing." The small laminate chair squeaked in protest when he sat down across from me. "You ready to talk about what went down?"

I took a deep breath. Where to begin and how much to tell him? "Well, I made an ill-advised trip to Billings to visit Jackson Greene." Obviously. His eyes never left mine while he sipped his tea and waited for me to continue. "I talked to him, one thing led to another, and he and his two assistants locked me up for a bit."

His eyes narrowed. "Okay. Then what happened?"

"I broke free and made a run for it."

"Did they hurt you?"

"Obviously, no. I mean, if they could have, then yeah, but overall it was just a melodramatic attempt to get me to talk. Which failed. I'm pretty sure they don't know my real name or where I'm from."

His jaw tightened. "They tortured you?"

"They tried to." I tilted my head. "You know, at first I wasn't sure why Olita gave me the powers she did, but I'm starting to get into them."

"What kinda torture?"

I raised an eyebrow. "Why? Do you get off on that kind of stuff?" He didn't respond or break his stare, and my intrigued shoulders shrank back down in disappointment. "One of his assistants knocked me out with a touch and the other one has these, like, magic fingernails she used to cut me up and electrocute me. Pretty lame power, if you ask me. Just buy some knives and a shitty extension cord, you know?"

He looked at my hands curled around my mug. "Your hands are healed, the bruise under your eye's gone, and you don't have any other marks on your body."

So that's what this was all about. He was just confused about my healing ability. My gaze lowered, and I shrugged half-heartedly at my tea. "Just a piece of the power Cummings gave me, I guess."

Sam's eyes were narrow and calculating when I lifted mine back up to meet them. "That's not a power she can give you."

"Okay then, you tell me how I'm healing so fast."

He leaned back in the chair and rubbed his face before letting out a long, defeated breath. "I dunno." He pondered the ceiling for a moment before his gaze snapped back to mine. "You said they tried to get you to talk. Was it Jackson?"

"Yeah, he made my brain go all buzzy-like." I wiggled my fingers by my ear.

"But you didn't answer him?"

"I came close to but then forced myself to think of other things so I could ignore him." I shrugged and sipped more tea.

His puzzled eyebrows lowered, and his narrowed eyes became dangerous. After a moment of tense silence, I opened up the takeout containers and offered him one. He shook his head and stood up. "I gotta get going."

My heart sank as I watched him put on his shoulder holster and shrug into his coat. When I got up to see him out, he turned to me and rested his hands on my shoulders, his eyes soft and pleading, his default menacing expression gone. "Jeanie, please, for the love of all that is holy, just lie low for a while, okay? I'll look into Jackson Greene and find out if he's on your tail. If you need anything, call me. Please."

I hesitated before letting my own protective mask drop. "Okay," I said softly.

His eyes lingered on mine for a moment longer before he turned and walked out the door. My heartbeat quickened as it closed behind him. We'd been real with each other, and it had been terrifying. My nipples perked up in response, and I gazed down at my braless chest. Instead of being embarrassed or creeped out, the memory of Sam undressing me and putting me to bed filled me with a pleasant warmth. My gaze drifted over to the takeout containers on the table, and my chest tightened again. Why was he being so nice to me? Sudden tears prickled along my lashes, and I closed my eyes. Because he still needed me for something. *Sam doesn't care about you, Jeanie. No one does anymore.*

15

EVEN AFTER WATCHING a marathon of boring documentaries, my night was restless and peppered with vivid dreams of blood and violence. Still, having slept for roughly eighteen hours over the past twenty-four left me invigorated the next morning despite the tossing and turning. Full of energy, I decided that going to the gym and my MMA lesson counted as lying low. There was guilt attached to the decision, but not enough to keep me in my house when I was ready to bounce off the walls.

Some physical energy spent, I felt better. Now, if I could only get a good dicking down, the day would be perfect. I considered calling Sam, but my hand shook when I reached for my phone, so I gave it up. Stupid idea—getting involved with a murder associate, pusher, and incubus. Just keep it light. Despite all that, or maybe because of it, I fantasized about him again when I took it upon myself to bleed off excess sexual tension.

Afterwards, I was still too antsy to stay home. It was Saturday night; I could sit in a bar until another paunchy, divorced dad worked up the courage to try his luck. I closed my eyes and sighed. A widowed addict isn't exactly a catch, either. Jesus, middle age can be depressing.

What I really needed was companionship. The junkie friends from my recent history weren't a good choice since I was finally making progress toward sobriety. Besides, the last time I went on an epic bender, I landed myself in an alternate reality full of blood-sucking assholes. Instead, I wanted to get high in a "healthy" way for once. With legal substances, for example. I considered calling old friends from my pre-widow era, but quickly discounted the idea. I'd been off the radar for too long. It would only open up a massive emotional clusterfuck that I didn't have the bandwidth to deal with. Then I remembered Kaytee.

I dug her business card out of my wallet and texted her:

> *Hi Kaytee, it's Jeanie. What are you up to tonight? Want to go out?*

Twenty minutes later, she responded:

> *Yes! Marcus and I are heading over to a club in Belltown. Want to come?*

> *OMG, yes!*

At 10 p.m. I was standing in line outside the club with her and Marcus, Dram's other assistant. He had flawless light-brown skin and adorable hazel eyes fringed with long, dark lashes. He couldn't have been over twenty-five, way too young for this old hag.

When I took a survey of the other women in line, I gave my dress a self-conscious tug. I'd found it at the thrift store two hours earlier. It fit decently and had enough sparkle to be appropriate for a dance club, but was definitely lacking when compared to the youthful, glammed-up babes around me.

Kaytee was stunning. She was wearing a slinky silver number that plunged way down in the front. I kept stealing glances at her impressive bosom when she wasn't looking. Marcus blushed when I winked at him after I caught him doing the same. She'd done her nails to match, and her large hoop earrings sparkled in the light when she moved. On me they would have been overwhelming, but on her they somehow guided your eyes to her lips and the dusting of glitter that shimmered on her eyelids.

She asked me her obligatory question when I first stepped beside them in line. "Are you going to try to hurt me and or Marcus tonight?"

"Nope."

"Are you here to party?"

"Hell yeah!"

She laughed then looked me up and down before pointing to my dress. "Did you just grab this off the rack at a thrift store?"

My shoulders raised into a sheepish shrug. "Maybe."

"Damn girl, if you're looking to get some, you need to try harder." She reached into her purse. "I have some makeup so we can at least try to perk up your pasty-ass face."

I grinned. "Yes, please."

By the time we made it to the door, Kaytee had dabbed her reddish-brown lipstick on my lips, darkened my eyelids with kohl, and plastered thick mascara onto my lashes. She showed me my reflection in her small mirror. I giggled—I hadn't seen myself in club makeup for ages.

"How do I look, Marcus?" I asked him.

He examined me. "Better," he announced. Kaytee and I laughed. He couldn't say more in front of Kaytee without her calling him out.

"You look good, Jeanie. Those white boys will come running for you."

"Yeah right, only after you turn them down." She rolled her eyes before we headed into the thick of it to dance our asses off and forget the dark world of divines for a while.

Around 1 a.m., Kaytee tapped my shoulder, and I abandoned the sweaty, manic man I'd been dancing with for too long. "Thank you," I mouthed to her as we walked out of the crowd. When we were far enough away from the speakers to hear each other, she asked if I wanted to go somewhere chill before ending our night. I nodded enthusiastically.

Twenty minutes later, we were ordering drinks at a table in the corner of a cozy bar. I was pretty tanked at that point. Tunnel vision was creeping in, and my words were threatening to slur. My gaze roamed over the eclectic decor on the walls to give Kaytee and Marcus privacy while they had a quiet conversation. It suddenly occurred to me that I was a third wheel. Whoops. With that in mind, I pulled out my phone.

"Hey, Kaytee, wanna find out if you can tell when a divine is lying?"

She raised an eyebrow at me. "The fuck are you talking about?"

"I wanna text Sam. He's an incubus. I'm working with him on my, uh, project."

They both stiffened, and I put out a reassuring hand. "No, it's not like that. He won't even know who you are. I'll tell him you're old friends from way back."

Kaytee bit her lip and met Marcus's eyes. He shrugged. "Do you think he's lying about something?" she asked.

"Definitely. I just wanna confirm my suspicions."

She took a deep breath. "Okay, this is probably a bad idea, but since Marcus is here..." she trailed off. I eyeballed Marcus. I didn't know what his power was, but if it was for defending Dram, it must be pretty badass.

It took a string of curses and a lot of squinting to type out a text and send it:

> Hey Sam come to the speakeasy in Pioneer
> Square. I want you to meet some of my old
> friends.

I worked out a plan with Kaytee and Marcus in case he showed. As I was ordering my last-call drink of the night, a tingling heat prickled along my spine, and Sam was there. He wasn't wearing his usual trench coat, and I crimped my lips together to hide my hungry smile. Instead, he was looking very fuckable in a black bomber jacket over a white t-shirt and clean pair of jeans

He slid onto the chair next to me and looked up at the server. "Whatever she's having." He pointed at me, and the woman nodded.

My hand curled around his arm. "Sam! I want you to meet Sasha and Manny, my friends from before my, uh...drug thing." I gestured to them. "Guys, this is my friend Sam."

Kaytee and Marcus said polite hellos, and I made up a story about how we'd met. Kaytee leaned in towards Sam. "I gave Jeanie a little makeover. What do you think?"

He pulled his head back, and his gaze glided up and down my body. "I think she's looking pretty good." I blushed and changed the subject.

We discussed our favorite drinks and music until eventually Kaytee and Marcus started talking to each other, as planned, and Sam leaned over to whisper, "Clubbing? Getting low isn't the same as laying low, Jeanie." His breath against my ear sent sparks of desire across my skin.

"I needed to get out and have some fun. Live a little, huh?" I bumped him with my elbow. "Besides, it's not like I've got anything to worry about. Jackson doesn't know where I am, and you've got a plan for getting Olita to ascend, right?" Kaytee was watching him out of the corner of her eye while she pretended to chat with Marcus.

"Yeah," Sam said.

"See!" I threw my arm out and nearly knocked over my drink. "Nothing to worry about."

He leaned back and cocked an eyebrow in mild amusement. "How many drinks have you had?"

"Pfft, just the right amount."

"Okay." He sipped his whiskey.

My eyes had trouble focusing on the amber liquid in my glass, and I decided that any more would take me from just the right amount to too much.

I stood up and announced, "I'm going to the bathroom."

Kaytee glanced at her watch. "I'll come with you and close out the tab. It's time to get my ass home."

I turned to her as soon as the door closed behind us. "So?"

"So, he thinks you look good." I smiled despite myself. "And... he doesn't have a plan for Olita."

My face fell. "Shit." I slumped against the wall with a lopsided shrug. "Well, on the bright side, now you know for sure you can tell if a divine is lying."

Her eyes were soft with a sprinkling of pity when she patted my arm. "Yeah, that's good to know. Come on, let's get you home."

After I tidied up my renegade eye makeup, I staggered out to the table. Sam had finished his drink, and when he saw me swaying, he grabbed mine and downed it, too. Kaytee was at the bar settling up. I reached into my bra and pulled out a wad of sweaty cash and tried to give it to her when we all ended up outside. She grimaced and pushed it back. "My treat. You can get the next one."

"I'll get us a car, then." I struggled to open the rideshare app on my phone.

"Already done," Sam said and kept a steadying hand on my low back. I leaned into him. They'd agreed to share a car to the Central District to drop Kaytee and Marcus off before Sam and I headed up to Capitol Hill.

The car arrived, and I slid into the middle seat. Sam tucked his bulky frame in next to mine while Marcus squeezed in on the other side. Kaytee sat up front and chatted with the driver while we all got settled. Sam threw his arm over the seatback to give me more room, and I shifted closer to him—only because I didn't want Marcus to feel too squished.

Sam's voice was a low rumble in my ear as they talked about the bars and restaurants we passed, discussing where the best Thai or Ethiopian food was. I sat back with my eyes closed and enjoyed the warm comfort of his body beside mine. My mind drifted into pleasant thoughts about being wrapped in his arms before heading into steamier territories with visions of kneeling before him with my hair twisted up in his tight grip. Heat crept up from between my legs and flooded my stomach. I turned my head a little and inhaled. He had a fresh, bright scent with an undercurrent of intoxicating musk.

Somehow, we were already pulling up in front of Kaytee's apartment. I flashed her a wicked grin and flicked my gaze over to where Marcus was standing and then back to her. She snorted and shook her head. "Okay, crazy woman, see you around," she said before closing the door.

The driver pulled back out into the street, and I stayed put. Sam didn't say anything, but he shifted his arm so my head rested more comfortably against his shoulder. My eyes closed, and I sank into him with a quiet sigh of contentment. A breath of sweet whiskey stirred the hairs on my forehead when he asked if I was okay. I nodded against his jacket while my heart pounded—his lips were so close. If I just tilted my head up...wait, what had I been telling myself earlier? That getting involved with Sam was a bad idea? Ridiculous. I just needed to get laid and get it out of my system. Then he'd do whatever the hell he was planning, and we'd be done with each other. Maybe I'd end up in the Caribbean surrounded by beautiful men catering to my every desire; maybe I'd end up dead. I giggled. His head turned toward me again, but I didn't look up.

The ride was too short, and I wasn't ready for the chill that shot up my side when Sam got out. He reached in and helped me, grabbing me by the waist when I almost fell over. He thanked the driver and kept an arm around me as he guided me up the steps. On the landing, I fished my key out of a flowerpot and promptly dropped it. His waiting hand caught it, and he unlocked the door and hung back as I walked in and kicked off my shoes, sending them flying across the room.

I turned to him. Without a solid agreement from my brain first, my hands reached up to land on his chest. I took some time to appreciate the firmness of his pecs before gazing up at him in what my sloshy mind hoped was a passable come-hither stare. His eyebrows drew together, and after a long, breathless moment, his hands slid along my lower back. My heart thudded. His eyes searched mine before he sighed and brought his hands around to rest on my own before gently pulling them away from his chest.

"You're drunk, Jeanie." His voice was soft.

"Pfft, so?"

"So, I'm not gonna take advantage of you."

His face was serious, and I laughed. "You've taken advantage of me plenty of times before."

He dropped my hands. "Yeah, for money." He pulled his coat collar forward in a dignified manner. "I'm a hustler, not a rapist."

"Okay, fine." I stepped away and crossed my arms. The rejection, however valid, still stung. "I'd just regret it in the morning, anyway." As soon as the words left my lips, I wanted them back. Sam's face turned into the stony mask of his street persona.

"Yeah, probably," he agreed, his voice wary. He opened the door. "Lock this behind me." And then he was gone.

I hovered my hand over the doorknob. Part of me wanted to open it and run after him, and the other part wanted to sit down and cry. I stood there and debated my options until it'd been long enough that I wouldn't be able to catch him if I tried. My lips trembled as I reached up and threw the deadbolt. Jesus Christ, I couldn't even get a pity fuck from the ugliest man I knew.

16

I SUCKED AIR in through my teeth and grimaced at my reflection in the mirror. Black eye makeup streaked down my face, and smears of dark lipstick lined my cheek like war paint. I could pass as Gene Simmons after a sweaty Kiss show. Once I got coffee in me, a shower would be next on my list of priorities. My hair was a bedraggled mess, and I combed a hand through it, hoping I hadn't looked as much like a train wreck when Sam had seen me last night. My heart dropped to the floor. Last night. The sinking feeling in my stomach had nothing to do with a hangover. Not only did I feel horrible about what I'd said, which I was ninety-nine percent sure wasn't true, I felt horrible for putting him in the position I had.

From his perspective, he'd just been doing his thing when a disaster of a woman hit on him while sloppy drunk. The whole situation probably grossed him out, but he'd been too polite to say anything. Sam, being polite. it didn't quite jibe with the picture I had of him in my head, but he did still need me for his mysterious plan. Then I remembered what Kaytee said—he didn't have a plan. Not for helping Olita, anyway. What the hell was he up to?

My queasiness finally ebbed after getting food and water into my stomach. I shouldn't have had so many cigarettes and mixed drinks; my tolerance for that kind of behavior was fading fast. Thank god I didn't have to experience what would have been a raging headache. While I sipped at my second cup of coffee, my gaze drifted over to the suitcase on the floor. Time to see if my final visit to Jackson's office paid off. I zipped it open and pulled out the lockbox.

My elderly neighbor's eyes widened when he opened the door to me standing on his stoop looking like Beetlejuice's deranged sister. He retreated into his house with a quick hobble to retrieve the screwdriver and hammer I requested, and the lock clicked immediately after he shut the door behind him.

It took about an hour of cursing and banging before I finally got the stupid thing open. Inside was a black leather sheath with a carved ivory handle sticking out. I groaned. It had to be Jackson's knife. Or one of them, anyway. He was definitely not going to let this slide. Olita's sneering face popped up in my mind. She was definitely not going to let this slide either. I had no idea how to fix the problem, which brought me back to thinking about Sam.

I curled up on the couch with my phone in hand, and my heart sank lower and lower as I stared at his name in the messaging app. When the phone buzzed, I almost dropped it, hoping and also dreading that it was a text from Sam. Instead, it was a calendar reminder telling me I had a video call with Olita in ten minutes. I gave my face a rough rub. What was I going to tell her? That I'd killed two of her incubi, made no progress on taking down Dram, lost her knife, and had royally pissed off another angel in the process?

Her eyes were sharp and her voice crisp when I joined the call. "Hello, Jeanie, I hear you've been busy." She squinted at her screen. "Jesus Christ, you look like a whore after shore leave."

I plastered on my best fake smile. "Hello, Ms. Cummings, I hope you're well."

She narrowed her eyes. "I am not, thanks to you taking out two of my incubi. And two of my most powerful, to boot. Now I've got a newbie and a bloodless in their place. Do you know how much power you've cost me?"

I had no idea what a bloodless divine was, but assumed it meant Sam had given Mara's knife to someone. I rubbed the back of my neck. "Yeah, sorry about that. They did kind of attack me first, though."

Her gaze lifted to the heavens, begging the gods to give her patience, before resuming her stare. "Please tell me you have a plan for getting to Dram?"

I let out a long mental breath. Time to fabricate some untruths. "I've got a rough plan in place, but there are a lot of moving parts I haven't pinned down yet. I have several good leads, though, and I've been gathering lots of important information." Jesus, I sounded like Sam.

"Uh-huh." Her stare didn't waver. "Care to share any details?"

"Well, I know what one of his assistant's power is, so I'm coming up with workarounds for that. And, um, I've got more info on his routines. He's getting some kind of humanitarian award in a few weeks, and I think I can get to him at the event." I wondered how good her bullshit detector was because this was turning into an entire rodeo's worth.

"What event?"

"Um, it's in my notes. Let me see." I made a point of shuffling around papers on my desk. "Uh...I guess I left it at the coffee shop. I can look it up again."

Her eyes closed, and she took a deep breath. "It sounds like you're not making any progress."

"More than you, anyway," I muttered.

"What was that?" Her eyes snapped open, and her nostrils flared like a bull's before a rampage.

"Sorry, Ms. Cummings, it's going to take more time. This guy's had a lot of practice evading divines and their assistants." I fought to keep my eyes from rolling—it wasn't like she'd done any better with all the years she'd had to pull it off. "Plus, Sam has his plan he's working on, too." No point in mentioning it was a plan that didn't include helping her ascend.

"When I check in on you in another two weeks, you *will* have a feasible plan together and you *will* be ready to act on it. Otherwise..." she paused, and her mouth twisted up into a sinister smile. "I'll need to give you a little more motivation. Perhaps a few more bouts of excruciating pain would do the trick?"

My brain helpfully conjured up the memory of the utter agony demonstration she'd put me through. I swallowed. "Yes, of course...but I kind of thought I had another two and a half months."

"So did I, but there are rumors that another demon is in town. The deadline has moved up."

"Oh."

"Tell Sam he owes me more blood now that you've taken away my sweet Mara and Johnny."

"Can do."

"Two weeks, Jeanie." Her inky eyes bored holes through the screen.

"Two weeks, Ms. Cummings."

The screen went black.

I breathed a sigh of relief. Thank god that was over with and she didn't know about Jackson or her knife. Two more weeks to figure this shit out. Or to see how far I could run before she found me.

Despite my best efforts to ignore it, my misstep with Sam was gnawing at me and making it impossible to focus on anything else. Even Tom, to my surprise. It figured that the one time I was open to thinking about him would be the one time I wasn't able. Instead, the grief of losing the love of my life was getting folded into the icky feeling of hurting someone and morphing into a giant ball of suck. I couldn't even distract myself with my usual justified heartache routine. It's hard to play the Victim of Widowhood card when you're also holding the Certified Asshole card, and it certainly doesn't help when the Cave into Your Addictions card keeps popping up in the deck.

My brain decided to indulge itself in one of my favorite brooding pastimes: sifting through all the evidence that proved I was an irredeemable person and deserved all the bad things that came my way. As I lay down on the couch and rubbed my temples, flashbacks of my worst blunders played in my head. Like when I told my dad I wouldn't speak to him anymore because I was sick of him defending my mother when she was out of line. A month later, he died of a heart attack. Then there was the time I stormed out after Tom tactfully suggested I seek therapy rather than rely on drugs to deal with my issues. Apparently, my need for substances trumped the respect I had for my husband and his valid concerns. Even worse, it happened more than once. The missteps with my mother were too numerous to count. Not surprising—mixing a narcissistic mother with a rebellious daughter is like combining baking soda and vinegar. That she shared plenty of the blame for our rocky relationship didn't erase the fact that I was a total piece of shit for refusing to visit her after she was in a car accident. I'd been convinced she was lying to manipulate me into having a conversation with her. Turns out it was the one time she was actually telling the truth.

When I'd exhausted my supply of self-castigating thoughts, I groaned and sat up on the couch. Strangely enough, I felt better and vowed to make a custom rosary with a bead for every one of my major fuckups. Then I could flick through them daily like a penitent nun to comfort myself with the reminder that some things, at least, will never leave you. I stared out the window as I contemplated what a normal, well-adjusted person might do in my situation. The first step toward redeeming myself for my most recent blunder would be an apology, and I wasn't sure how to go about it.

After a lot of pacing in my living room and a long walk around the neighborhood, I texted Sam:

> Hey, I'm really sorry about last night. I didn't
> mean it.

My heart raced as I clutched my phone and waited to see if he'd respond. After twenty minutes, I couldn't take it anymore and smoked a ludicrous amount of weed to deaden the yucky feelings. Then I listened to the entire catalog of songs that had seen me through the crushes and heartbreaks of my younger days. I channeled my early pre-Tom self and sway danced around the living room, taking breaks to wipe the tears from my eyes. So, this was what my midlife crisis was going to be like. Jesus fucking Christ.

When I sobered up, I checked my phone. Sam had texted back:

Water under the bridge Jeans. Can you come over? I need to check something.

I sighed. It sounded very businesslike and not what I was secretly hoping for. I replied:

Ok. See you soon.

I stood in awkward silence on the front stoop when Sam opened the door and followed him up the stairs and into his apartment without a word. Olita's book sat on the table, along with an array of archaic implements that looked to be pieces from a medieval alchemy set.

He gestured to the chair and scratched the back of his neck. "Sooo, I need some of your blood."

I raised my eyebrow and made brief and uncomfortable eye contact with him. "Okay, why?"

"I think I know what's going on with your healing and the other stuff." His flat expression was all business.

My shoulders slumped as I held out my arm. When he picked up a syringe from the table and stuck it in, I bit my lip and looked away. I hated needles. To distract myself, I examined the artwork along his wall. His tastes trended toward the abstract with delightful forays into futurism and surrealism, but there were a few dark offshoots into post-war expressionism as well. If I'd co-majored in psychology, I could've come up with quite a few interesting theories about the inner workings of Sam's mind.

When my blood reached the halfway point, he slid the needle out and squirted it onto a silver plate, then lifted the book and read a passage out loud. The words were deep and guttural and made every hair on my body stand up and quiver. He waved his hand over the plate and touched the rim with his finger. A glowing drop of blood separated from the rest and formed a small iridescent bead. When he read another brief passage, the bead flashed a brilliant red. He stared at it, nodding to himself and breathing heavily through his nostrils. After a long pause, he touched a finger to the drop and then put it to his tongue. He waited for several seconds, brow furrowed, before his jaw hardened, and he uttered some especially demonic-sounding words. The remains of the drop burned to nothing. Abruptly, he walked into the bedroom and closed the door behind himself. The sound of something shattering and then a muffled "Fuck!" came from the room.

I sat through the outburst and then for a minute into the ensuing silence while I debated if I should leave. As my legs flexed to stand, he walked back out, his hand rubbing the angry blotches on his face. I waited a few long moments to see if he would say anything before asking in a tentative tone, "Everything okay?"

He took a deep breath. "No, Jeanie. No, it is not."

"Care to share? Otherwise, I'm happy to show myself out." I stood and took a step toward the door, anticipating his customary refusal to let me in on his thoughts.

He put his hand out. "Stay, I need to talk to you."

He gestured me back to the chair, and I perched on the edge. The veins in his neck stood out like wet spaghetti on a wall when he clenched his jaw. He was angrier than I'd ever seen him. His hands tightened into fists as he paced the room before turning to me. "I know why you can heal fast, resist an angel's charm, and have an extra power." His eyes scrutinized the ceiling and then shifted to inspect the floor. "Olita put a blood curse on you. She put a spell on her blood and injected you with it."

"Okay, so?" I asked when the pause stretched to an uncomfortable length.

"It means she was telling the truth when she said you'll die if she dies."

"Oh."

"That fucking bitch!" He drew his fist back to punch the wall and hovered it, tense and ready, until his shoulders sagged and his hand dropped to his side.

"Well, that won't matter if I can help her ascend, right?" He remained silent, and I sighed. "I already assumed I was going to die. It doesn't really change anything."

His chest rose and fell with deep, shaky breaths. Eyes on the floor, he said, "It changes everything for me, though."

I crossed my arms. "Sam, just tell me what the fuck is going on. I know you don't have a plan to help Olita, and I'm tired of trying to figure out what the fuck you want from me."

His head whipped around. "What? How did you know?"

"At the bar. That was Dram's assistant, Kaytee, and she can tell when people are lying."

He tilted his head back. "Fuuuuck."

"I'm going to ask you again. What are you up to, and why did you involve me?"

He covered his eyes with a hand and let out a long breath. "My plan's always been to kill Olita. I've been tryna take her down my whole life and now I can't without killing you, too."

Probably there was a tragic story behind his confession, but at that moment I didn't care. I was done with being pulled into his tangled web of secrecy and scheming against my will. I just wanted the fucking truth. I studied Olita's book on the table, and some pieces fell into place.

"That book. You swapped it after you gave her your blood, didn't you?" He nodded. "Do you need it to kill her?" He nodded again, head still in his hand. My eyes narrowed. "How the hell did you convince her to let you into her library, and why get me involved?"

His eyes met mine, and I saw the regret in them before his gaze darted away to stare blankly at the floor. He took a deep breath. "I convinced Olita her strategy was flawed, and she should try something new. Her other assistants were all bloodthirsty psychopaths, so I told her she should find someone different, someone smart and resourceful, and only give 'em the basic rundown so they'd have fresh eyes on the whole thing." He glanced up at me again, eyes soft and pleading. "I told her you'd be perfect." He rubbed his face before studying the floor again. "Then I said I should come over in case you needed extra convincing or reassurance from someone you knew."

I nodded slowly. "So this whole time you were just using me to get the book."

He looked at me, eyes full of remorse. "I had no idea about the blood curse, Jeanie. I swear. I never woulda told her to pick you if I'd known she could do that."

I let out a humorless chuckle. "That's sweet of you. I suppose you were going to use me again to get close to her once you figured out how to kill her?" His nonresponse told me everything. I shook my head. "Well, as an expendable junkie I guess I do make an excellent tool. I can see why you and Olita wanted to use me." I stood up. "Nice to know you think of me as the most gullible of your little addicts."

My heart was pounding in my ears, and my mind was hovering somewhere between anger, humiliation, and...something else. Disappointment, maybe. I bit my lip to stop it from trembling and didn't look at him as I strode to the door. When I reached it, I paused and pushed my face into my shaking hand. "Jesus Christ, I can't believe I fell for it when you said you picked me for a reason. Like you actually thought I was smart, or special somehow." My eyes squeezed shut. "You told me yourself not to trust divines, and there I was, thinking that maybe you actually cared about—" My breath hitched.

His hand touched my shoulder. "Jeanie, I'm so sorry. I shoulda told you sooner. I—" I shrugged him off.

Tears stung my eyelids, and I clenched my jaw. My voice was quiet when I turned the doorknob. "Sorry I fucked everything up for you, Sam. Just do what you want. Kill her, kill me; I don't give a shit and you shouldn't either."

I slammed the door behind me and raced down the stairs before walking with swift strides out of the building, fingers dashing away tears like a hormonal teenager dumped at prom. My mind was busy bouncing between anger at Sam for using me, and myself for not seeing it sooner. Before I knew it, I was home. I threw myself onto my bed and moaned into my pillow. I was such a fucking idiot.

17

IT TOOK A lot of palm greasing, pavement pounding, and runarounds before I finally scored some acid. With a bouquet and the beginnings of a solid trip, I trudged up the grassy hill to my husband's grave.

I blinked down at his simple granite headstone.

Thomas James Bennett
1/16/1984 to 4/21/2017
Beloved Husband
i carry your heart with me (i carry it in my heart.)

I pictured my own next to it:

Jeanine River Bennett
7/15/1981 to Sometime really freaking soon/2019
Heartbroken Wife
i fear no fate (for you are my fate, my sweet.)

I took a moment to appreciate the coincidence that the poet who penned the lines I used for Tom's epitaph shared the same last name as the blood-cursing demon who entrapped me. I put the flowers in the vase and sat cross-legged on his grave.

"Sorry it's been a while, Tom. I've been off doing all the shit you asked me not to do when you were gone." My fingers plucked at the grass by my knee. "I've really fucked things up." I tilted my head back and willed my tears not to fall.

The leaves on the trees were starting to glow with dancing fractals, and I stretched out to enjoy an open view of sky. It was comforting, in a way, to know I was hovering above Tom's last mortal remains with only a few feet of dirt between us. My body relaxed and sank deeper into the grass, and my heartbeat thumped in my ears like the rhythm of the earth itself. I closed my eyes and pictured him there at my side, arms crossed behind his head, wire-rimmed glasses glinting in the sun. It wasn't a perfect hallucination, none of my trips ever were, but I could work with it.

In life, we could talk about anything: hopes, fears, embarrassments, triumphs. Every significant confession (and some ridiculous ones) ended with Tom writing it down on a piece of paper. Then, he'd either burn it on the stove if it was a bad one, or put it in a scrapbook titled "The Compendium of Awesome" if it was a good one. "This way the best memories live forever and the worst die in a fire," he told me. Whenever one of us was in an especially dark place, we'd pull the book off the shelf and read out loud from a random page. Things like, "I located an obscure painting that my client's grandfather painted before being taken to an interment camp. It was the only surviving heirloom from her family." Or, "I want to see the northern lights before I die." Or, "Today I honest-to-god slipped on a banana peel while walking to class, but it made my non-verbal student laugh, so it was totally worth it."

I wanted that life again so much it hurt. I whispered to the sky, "I'm not doing great, Tommy."

"You're doing what you can, Jeanie," his ghost replied.

I shook my head. "I don't know how to do this without you. We were supposed to die together so we never had to be apart." My tears left hot tracks as they curved their way down my cheeks.

"I know. Sorry I fucked that up." His ghost turned to me with an apologetic smile. I ached to reach out and run my fingers through his unruly mop of graying hair.

I let out a shaky breath. "Well, it doesn't matter anymore. I'm probably going to be joining you soon. Wherever you are."

"I'm in your head, for one."

"True. Thank god for LSD."

He laughed. "A-fucking-men."

We lay in silence while halos of green light swam in and out through the alder leaves, and puffy white clouds floated in an endless parade across the sky.

I sighed. "I'm such an idiot, Tommy. I thought a guy was into me because he was nice to me a few times, but it turns out he was just using me." My eyes squeezed shut in embarrassment.

"Is he hot?"

A laugh erupted from my mouth. "Nope. Not in the conventional sense, anyway, but he's got an intense presence and muscular build that's appealing." I shook my head. "I don't know why I bothered to get my hopes up."

"You can't give up, Jeanie. There's someone out there for you."

My eyes started brimming with tears again, and I rubbed at them in frustration. "No, there's not. He left when cancer took him. Jesus, look at me; I'm never going to be young again, and I'm never going to find what we had again. Everything good is gone forever."

"You're everything that's good, Jeanie, and you're still here."

Rainbow tracers swirled the sky around when I rolled my eyes. "Whatever, Tom." I turned to him. "But one thing that's cool about the predicament I'm in is that I'm not afraid of dying anymore."

"If you're not afraid of dying, then you shouldn't be afraid of living either." He winked at me.

I blew out a deep, defeated breath. "I'm not afraid of living, I'm just sick of it. I'm sick of not being able to talk to you every day. I'm sick of not being touched by you, of not feeling loved, of not having someone to love. I just...don't want to do this anymore."

"Jeanie, I'm always going to be here for you. Look at me; you're seeing my ghost, for Christ's sake."

My chest heaved with a painful sob. "But what if you fade away? You know my memory is garbage; what if you disappear one day? I'm not ready to let you go. I'll never be ready."

"You don't know what's going to happen, and no one's ever ready for the unknown." I could almost feel him stroke my cheek. "Hey, Jeanie." Through my tears, I saw him smiling at me like he used to when we shared secrets with each other. "Just remember in the winter far beneath the bitter snow, lies the seed that with the sun's love in the spring becomes the rose. You're in winter right now, Jeanie, but your spring will come again."

I snorted and shook my head at him. "Did you just quote Bette Midler to me?"

"Technically, you did; I'm only the echo."

I sighed. "Well, I don't buy it. I'm more like a gnarly, thorny old bush than a fresh seed."

"Gnarly old bushes grow the best flowers."

"Not without water," I mumbled before the breeze flowed over me like a wave on the beach and swept up my fragile vision of Tom with it. My eyes squeezed shut against the tears as he drifted away. "I miss you so much," I whispered. "I love you forever."

His voice was faint. "I love *you* forever." Then he was gone.

I lay there for a long time. The gentle breeze carried notes of cut grass and sunshine, and my tears created a kaleidoscope of rainbows along my eyelashes. I could almost see particles of energy floating through the air, and my thoughts swirled around the mystery of what awaits us beyond death. Would pieces of my soul free themselves and return to the world again? If they did, would the pieces of me be able to find the pieces of Tom? Maybe we would drift through the universe together on an endless journey of being and becoming. My body was floating as my acid trip peaked, and the answers drifted in the ether, just out of reach. I skated along the edge of nirvana, steps away from losing myself in the whole, the annihilation of self nearly in my grasp...but, as always, enlightenment eluded me and I sank back down to Earth again, the same tragically flawed person as before.

When dusk fell, I stood up, cold and shaky. I rifled around in my purse until I found the joint I'd packed and lit it up before gazing down at his headstone one more time. "I'll find you again, Tommy."

18

MY FOOT BUMPED against a small box when I went out to get my mail the next morning. It had my name on it and nothing else. After a long and suspicious scrutiny of my surroundings, I brought it inside. The contents thudded dully when I shook it, and the innocuous brown cardboard coaxed me into opening it. I froze. It was a framed picture of Tom. The photo was one I'd taken of him standing with a goofy grin and pointing to a sign where a shrub had blocked the crucial first letter for Canal Excavators, Inc. My heart raced—I hadn't seen a picture of him since his funeral.

Goosebumps erupted on my arms. It seemed like a meaningful coincidence that after my time at his grave yesterday, he would show up here, on my literal doorstep. As I traced my fingers over his face, I smiled despite myself. Behind the frame was a handwritten note:

> *Hey Jeanie,*
> *I found this on the internet and thought maybe you hadn't seen a*
> *picture of your husband in a while. Sorry if it upsets you. I'm*
> *not great at this kind of stuff. I want to apologize for everything.*
> *I care about you and don't want you to get hurt.*
> *Sam*

For someone who claimed to "not be good at this stuff," Sam managed to hit this one right on the nose. Either he was more sensitive than I gave him credit for, or he or his spies saw me rolling around babbling and crying on my husband's grave. My face screwed up into a wince before slackening into a sigh of resignation. He'd probably seen me do weirder things in the two years we'd known each other. I read back over the note and considered the possibility that he was trying to win me back so he could use me again, but a large part of me didn't really care.

Over the last two restless nights, my thoughts kept returning to his confession. Once my anger and embarrassment had subsided, I was able to look at the whole affair from a different and calmer perspective. Sam probably had a good reason for wanting to kill Olita, beyond just taking her place. If she'd done something terrible to him or someone he loved, then I'd rather be a patsy for a righteous cause than for a selfish bitch who wanted me to murder a kind man. I wasn't going to play their games anymore, but I wasn't going to stay mad at Sam, either. I *was* upset that I hadn't thought to take advantage of his contrition, though. Maybe I could've convinced him to take his shirt off so I could ogle his naked torso and use him, just a little, as payback. I may be nothing but a tool to you, Sam, but you're nothing but a hot bod to me!

My eyes lingered on his neat handwriting for a moment before I tossed the note in the trash and put the picture of Tom on the fireplace mantel. My other pictures of him were stored on the cloud somewhere, waiting for me to get over myself. I should print a couple to have around. Maybe I was finally ready for that, at least.

It took longer than anything online should take before I was able to log into my old email and cloud accounts. 10,354 unread emails. My fingers curled into my hair and threatened to pull it out as I contemplated whether I had the energy to tackle the formidable mess of my digital life. After a series of deep breaths, I sorted by the oldest first and read through the sender and subject lines. Most were from people expressing condolences or from the bank, hospital, and insurance company trying to track me down after I became overwhelmed by the absolute shitshow that is the American healthcare system. I didn't bother scrolling very far. About three months after Tom's death, they all turned into collection agency notices and legal bullshit.

But one name stood out from the rest: Jenny Bennett, Tom's sister. A deep heartache settled in as I read through her emails. They started off as delicate inquiries into how I'd been doing and if I'd like to go to grief counseling with her, before shifting to general concern and finally into angry missives about how terrible a sister-in-law I was.

The last one was brief:

> *Subject: Bye*
>
> *Jeanie, I'm done trying to help you. You're not the only one suffering because of Tom's death, you know. The rest of us are doing our best to heal, and I don't need my worry about you holding me back. I hope you get clean and find your way to the other side.*
>
> *Jenny*

Fuuuuck. I was a horrible sister-in-law and an even worse aunt. Isaac, Jenny's son, was close to seven now, which meant I'd missed out on nearly a third of his life. Tom and I hadn't wanted children of our own, so when Jenny got pregnant, we vowed to be the best aunt and uncle ever. I broke that promise, too. I banged my head on the desk. The hole I'd dug for myself was so deep I didn't think I'd ever be able to climb back out.

"Baby steps, Jeanie," I whispered to the keyboard. I owed it to Tom to at least try.

It took forever to craft an email and even longer before I was ready to hit send.

> *Subject: Sorry*
>
> *Jenny, I don't know how I can apologize enough for everything. It was selfish of me to just ditch you and Isaac and Ash. I want to set things right between us, but I understand if you don't want me back in your life. I'll be here if you do. I miss you.*
>
> *Love, Jeanie*

Even though I didn't care about the results anymore, I resumed my gym and MMA training. Mostly because I was bored and needed something to take my mind off my growing desperation for brain and body-numbing substances.

My rationale for staying sober was getting dangerously thin, so I kept junkie logic out of it by routinely sacrificing a ganja lamb to the smoke gods for the cause. "It's a plant! It's all natural!" I would say to myself when loading the bong. It was the lesser of my favorite evils, anyway.

Though marijuana helped to maintain my relative sobriety, it did nothing to lessen my aching loneliness. Every time I opened my email, my faint hope dwindled further. Still no word from Jenny. I considered reaching out to old friends I'd left behind when I hitched a ride on my downward spiral, but I didn't. Why bother? My life was heading back down in that direction again, and I wasn't sure how long I had left before Olita realized how worthless I was and sent me to the final oblivion.

The worst was realizing how much I missed Sam. I tried to deny it, but for every hour he didn't reach out, my heart fell a little lower. Soon it would be buried six feet under, just like Tom. I assumed he'd already forgotten me and was busy coming up with another way to kill Olita since I'd messed up his original plan. My real superpower: fucking up everything for everyone.

After two days in a pity haze, I opened my email, and a tentative ray of hope pierced through the darkness. Jenny had written back.

Re: Sorry
Jeanie, I'm glad you reached out. I don't know how I feel about letting you back in my life, but I'm open to talking. Do you want to grab coffee soon?
Jenny

The cafe was bright and cheery, with the delectable aroma of roasted coffee drifting through the air. There were several open tables, and I sank down into a chair with my brimming cup. I glanced at my watch: 11 a.m., our agreed-upon meeting time. I was sure Jenny wouldn't show and spilled coffee on my lap when she walked through the door ten minutes later. She looked older but even more beautiful than I remembered, with echoes of Tom in the arch of her eyebrows and wide, expressive mouth. When our eyes met, mine teared up of their own accord, and hers glistened in response.

She made her way to the table, and I stood up, awkward and uncertain. Her smile was flat, and eyes wary as she pulled out a chair.

"Can I get you anything?" I asked.

She shook her head—she didn't intend to stay long. I sank back down. Unsure where to begin, I opted for the low-hanging fruit. "How are Ash and Isaac?"

"They're fine. Isaac is about to start second grade, and Ash is still working at the hospital," she answered. "You're looking well."

My fingers fondled the smooth curves of my mug as I fought through my discomfort. "Um, listen, Jenny, I don't know what to say. I'm sorry for ditching you and your family after Tom died. Honestly, I don't really know why. I just couldn't...do anything anymore."

She was watching me closely, and my breath caught when a tear slid down her cheek. She let out a heavy sigh. "Jeanie, I was so pissed at you when you disappeared. I kind of thought we were closer than that, but you wouldn't even talk to me. It felt like both of you died that day."

When I closed my eyes, the tears slipped out.

"I'm sorry," I whispered.

"But...well," she paused and looked down at the table, trying to find the words. "Ash was in a car accident about a year ago and almost died."

"Oh my god! Are they okay?"

Jenny nodded, gaze distant. "Ash is fine now, but there were a few days when we didn't know if they'd make it, and um...it forced me to think about what would happen if they died." She examined the purse clutched in her lap. "It was the first time I seriously thought about it, and...I get it, Jeanie. If I didn't have Isaac, I don't know what I would've done. It scared the shit out of me." She chewed her lip. "So I can't exactly blame you for what you did. You and Tom had something special, and it must've been like losing a big piece of yourself, too."

It was hard to breathe. I picked up a napkin to wipe my eyes and nose, wishing I'd grabbed the entire stack. When I lifted my head, she was watching me, tears shining and eyebrows drawn together in sympathy. We held each other's gaze, expressions open and vulnerable, and she reached across the table to put her hand on top of mine. "I am so, so sorry, Jeanie."

I took a deep, shaky breath and blew it out. "I'm sorry too, Jenny. I should've been there for you...we could've been there for each other." My gaze darted away, ashamed. "I did have a moment of clarity before I left, where I saw the two roads ahead of me. I *knew* I shouldn't run, that I should pick up the pieces and live like Tom wanted me to. But I did it anyway."

We sat there, each lost in thought, before she broke the silence. "Isaac overheard me talking to Ash about coming to see you and he wanted to come, too. He misses you."

I put my head in my hands and sobbed. She stood up to get more napkins and pushed them toward me. When I could speak again, I said, "I miss him too. A lot." Isaac had looked so much like Tom when I last saw him.

"If you want to see him, I can probably talk Ash into it."

I stacked another crumpled and soaking napkin on my pile. "Ash fucking hates me, don't they?"

She let out a long breath. "Let's just say Ash is not excited about you potentially coming back into our lives."

I nodded slowly. "I get it. I'm not even sure about letting me back into my own life, considering all the dumb shit I've done to myself." She smiled, and there was a glint of hope in her eyes. I winced. "Speaking of dumb shit, I'm kind of involved in some... stuff right now." Her eyes hardened. "Not drugs!" I held up my hands. "It's something I can't talk about, though. In a few weeks, I should be free and clear of it." (Or dead.) "Can we talk more after that?"

Jenny held my gaze for a long moment before shrugging. "What's another few weeks?"

I gave her a tight smile. Another few weeks was going to be everything.

19

THE NEXT DAY started off like any other: gym, MMA training, watching a weird independent film at the local theater. In the middle of a late dinner, I got a call from Kaytee.

Her voice was shaky and on the verge of tears. "Jeanie? I need your help. Some serious shit is going down."

My heart skipped a beat. "Okay, can you tell me what's happening?"

Her words spilled out like water from a burst dam. "It's a demon. He kidnapped Dram's family and is holding them hostage until Dram gives himself up." Hysteria laced her rising tone, and I had to strain my ears to understand her. "But Dram's in San Francisco! He can't get up here fast enough. Flights are full and he's having trouble finding a private charter." Her breath hitched with a sob. "The demon says he's going to kill one of his boys at midnight if he doesn't give up his blood!"

I paused for a moment in shock. "Dram has a family?"

"A wife and two little boys." Another sob.

"Kaytee, breathe. Where are you?"

My phone vibrated with her shuddering breath. "I'm at the office."

I knew my course of action before I'd finished reviewing my two options: continue my apathetic existence in the liminal space between life and death, or do something worthwhile with my life before it ended. The latter definitely sounded better for my CV if heaven turned out to be a thing.

"Stay put. I'm coming."

Kaytee was pacing, phone in hand, when I peeked my head into the lobby. She ran over and threw her arms around my neck and sobbed into my shoulder.

I gave her an awkward pat on the back. "It's going to be okay."

She stepped back and took a long sniff in an attempt to hit the emotional reset button. "I'm sorry, Jeanie. I didn't know who else to call. Can you think of any way to get Dram here? Anything would be better than the zero options I've come up with."

I flashed her a wide grin. "I can do you one better. I'm going to take the demon down and get Dram's family back." She scrutinized me for a long moment, trying to figure out why I was willing to step in and risk life and limb. Then her eyes widened. I threw my hands up. "I have no interest in taking over the hostage situation to get Dram's blood for Olita. She can suck a royal fuck for all I care. I'm doing this because I won't let a piece-of-shit demon hurt kids." Her eyes started welling up again, and I put a hand on her shoulder. "Kaytee, we're going to get them back. Do you know where the family is? Where is Dram supposed to meet them?"

"They're on Bainbridge Island, somewhere near Dram's house."

My brow furrowed. "I thought he lived in Magnolia?"

"That's his cover. He has a secret way out to a dock from there and a speedboat to get to Bainbridge." My eyebrows shot up. Dram was a total badass.

"Has the demon told you their exact location?"

"He gave Dram an address." She walked me over to her computer and showed me the map pulled up on the screen. When I switched to satellite view, it revealed only trees and the corner of a structure.

She perched on the edge of her desk while I paced around the office and threw out ideas. "Okay, we need to stall him somehow. Maybe we can find someone that looks like Dram? No, too difficult; there's not enough time. Maybe I can sneak up on him? Probably not; we don't know what kind of place it is. There could be security cameras or something." I froze. "He must have an assistant which means there's at least two of them there." I squeezed my eyes shut. "Damn it, Jeanie, think! What would an asshole demon do?" I hesitated and glanced over at Kaytee. "Uh… does Dram know if they're still alive? Did he talk to his family on the phone?"

"He did like thirty minutes ago…oh my god, do you think they're already—" She covered her mouth with her hand, eyes brimming with tears.

"Nah, if they were alive thirty minutes ago, then he'll wait until his deadline." (Whether the demon was planning to let them live *after* the deal was done was another matter.) "Alright, so he's got them stashed somewhere, locked up, tied up, possibly both, and maybe at the address he gave Dram. Wherever they are, he'll probably lie about it. Based on every other divine I've met, anyway." I sighed. "I'll have to go meet the guy in order to find out more."

Kaytee sucked in a deep, decisive breath and squared her shoulders. "I'm going with you."

Her lips trembled, but her eyes were fierce and resolute. My nod was slow at first then sped up as a plan took shape. I grinned. "Fuck yeah! That'll make this a lot easier." I resumed pacing and stroking my chin like I was Sherlock Holmes. "Okay, you're going to need dark clothes that are easy to move around in. We'll have you hide somewhere so he thinks I'm alone. That way, you can listen in when I talk to him and see if he's lying about anything." I tapped my lip. "Hmm…I'll need something that looks like angel blood so I can pretend I'm there in earnest." My memory rewound to the glimpse of Olita's blood Sam had pulled from my own. The drop had sparkled and glowed with a dim light. Then my mind shifted to craft nights with my nephew when he was going through his mad scientist potions phase. I listed the items on my fingers. "We'll need a small jar, kid's glue, red food coloring, and glitter. Oh! And glow sticks."

She furrowed her brow in thought. "I'm pretty sure I have all that except the glow sticks."

"Awesome. Next we're going to need weapons. Do you have Dram's knife, or a gun, or anything?" My hand reached down and patted the sheath of Jackson's knife to confirm it was still securely fastened to my belt.

She shook her head. "Marcus is with Dram and has his knife, but I can maybe borrow a gun from my neighbor."

"Okay, if nothing else, grab some kitchen knives and wrap them in a towel." I glanced at my watch: 9:33 p.m. "Do you have access to a car and a boat?"

Kaytee nodded. "Dram's car is here and we can use the boat at his Magnolia place." The tension in my shoulders softened in relief—taking the state-run ferry would not be the most efficient way to go about this.

"Drop me off on the Pike and Pine strip then run to your place to get the stuff."

Kaytee's knuckles were white on the wheel as we waited through what felt like every red light in the city. She dropped me off on the nightclub strip, and I set out to find glow sticks. Thank god it was still Pride Month; I only had to ask four groups of scantily clad people before I scored some. They shot each other knowing looks when I took a deep, relieved breath and thanked them with wild and earnest exclamations. "This could save a kid's life!"

By the time Kaytee pulled up to the curb, I had the glow sticks and a bag of supplies from the pharmacy in hand. If this mission was at all like my other dealings with divines, then I'd need something appropriate for cleaning up blood. I slid in next to her and grinned. Every article of her clothing was black, complete with a black satin hair wrap to hide her bright pink tips.

I rubbed my hands together. "This guy is going to wish he never fucked with us. Now let's go get that boat!"

20

THE SLEEK SPEEDBOAT bobbed in the water next to the dark dock, and I saw a flaw in my plan. "Uh, Kaytee, do you know how to drive a boat?"

Her lips folded into a smug smile. "I'm a goddamn genius at piloting this one."

I let out a whoop, and the boat dipped and pitched in protest when I climbed in. Kaytee prepped the engine, and it came to life, its pleasant hum echoing against the dock. She untied us and we set off, moving at an infuriatingly slow speed past the houses lining the waterfront.

I stared at her, and she shook her head. "We're close to the locks and there's lots of buoys and pilings out here. Plus, these fucking rich people will one hundred percent call the authorities if we exceed the noise and speed ordinances. I doubt they'd catch us, but I'm not taking any chances. We'll be able to open it up in a couple minutes."

I took advantage of the momentary calm and dumped my shopping bags out on the bench seat in the stern. Kaytee handed me her backpack, and I found the craft supplies in the front pocket. The small jar still had the remnants of a sticker displaying THC percentage. I waved it in the air. "We should hang out more!" She rolled her eyes and went back to steering.

The fake blood came together by mixing the glue, glitter, food coloring, and water. When I shook the jar, the liquid swirled around and sparkled in the faint light of the boat's interior. I activated two glow sticks next before cracking them open and adding their solution to the mix, hoping the subtle glow would convince a demon it was angel blood.

I held up my most exciting scores from the pharmacy and showed them to Kaytee. "Check these out, tactical fanny packs!" She flashed me an are-you-fucking-kidding-me look, and I laughed. She threw the throttle open, and I meted out the first-aid supplies between the two packs before sitting back to enjoy the ride. The boat flew through the water, leaping from wave to wave, the tail of spray behind us glowing white against the black of the Puget Sound. This was some serious secret agent shit. The wind snatched my laughs away as I bounced from side to side. The whole situation was so absurd it was hilarious.

Kaytee eased up on the throttle, and the sudden cessation of deafening wind made my ears echo against the relative silence. A smattering of twinkling lights betrayed the homes tucked within the trees, and soft splashes of water lapped against the shore as we neared the black mass of Bainbridge Island. She killed the engine, and we drifted to the dark and silent dock. With her expert guidance, the boat slid up next to the waiting cleat, and I threw a rope around it. I checked my watch: 11:10 p.m.

We collected our supplies and jogged inland to the first line of trees before stopping for a whispered conference. Kaytee pointed up at the bluff. "Dram's house is up these steps. It looked dark from the water, but someone could be there watching for a boat."

"How far is the meeting place from here?" She opened her phone, and the sudden light made us blink and squint. We huddled over the glowing map, zooming in and out between the two points. The place was about five miles away. "Does Dram have a car here?" She nodded.

I held out a fanny pack to her, and she took it with a sigh of resignation. After wrapping it around her waist, she opened her backpack and pulled out four shurikens. An incredulous grin spread across my face. She shrugged. "My ex was really into ninja stuff, and they're the only weapons I had." I took the two she handed me and tucked them into my pack. Next, she pulled out a sword-like object straight from the Ninja Turtles. A sai maybe? She stuck it through her fanny pack's belt and tightened the strap.

"More stuff from your ex?" She nodded. "Do you know how to use that thing?"

"I guess we'll find out. Last thing." She pulled a pistol from her backpack.

"Holy shit." I said. "Do you know how to use *that* thing?"

"Not really? My neighbor gave me a quick rundown. You pull this thingy back and push this button down over here." She mimed cocking the gun and pointed to the safety switch. "He said it was loaded."

"Can I borrow it?"

"Yep; I'm not trying to get caught with a gun if the cops show up."

I tucked it into my pocket. "Alright, let's do this."

We channeled amateur ninja vibes as we climbed the stairs and slunk along the side of the two-story house at the top of the bluff. A dim light shone from the windows, but there was no movement inside, and all was quiet. Kaytee paused when we reached the front, and we peeked around the corner of the house together. Across the well-lit entry was a detached garage.

We looked at each other, and I shrugged. "Go for it?" I whispered.

She shrugged back. "Okay."

Like kids in a water pistol fight, we ran with bent knees from shrub to shrub, pausing each time to look and listen. We let out a joint sigh of relief when we made it to the garage unchallenged. She unlocked the side door with a key from under the mat. Inside, two cars gleamed in the faint light: a station wagon and a sleek sports car.

She shut and locked the door, and we waited a tense breath before I said, "Okay, let's call Dram and get an update."

She nodded and pulled out her phone. After hitting the speed dial, she flipped the call to speaker mode, and Dram picked up in an instant. "Kaytee? Are you okay? What's happening?"

"Hi, Dram, I'm fine. I've got Jeanie here. We're at your house on Bainbridge."

A moment of silence passed before he spoke again in a tentative tone. "Hello, Jeanie, I don't think I've had the pleasure of meeting you."

"Hello, um, that's because I'm Olita's assistant. But I'm here to help you and your family," I added quickly.

"She's telling the truth," Kaytee reassured him. "Where are you? Have you heard anything else from the demon?"

"Marcus and I were able to get a charter from San Francisco to Portland. We're waiting to board a private helicopter to Bainbridge, but we won't get there for another hour, at least." His voice was strained. "I spoke with Lupita at eleven. She and the boys are okay so far." I glanced at my watch: 11:22.

I chimed in. "Was she able to tell you anything about where they are or if there's more than one kidnapper?"

"No, the demon only let her say they were okay." His breath hitched.

"Tell me everything you said to each other."

"He put Lupita on the phone and she confirmed they were still alive, then he asked me where I was. I told him and said I couldn't make it there before twelve thirty at the earliest, and he said I'd only have one son by then." He sucked in a shaky breath. "Then he hung up."

"Okay, it's going to be okay. Did you sound scared when you talked to him?"

In the ensuing silence, I assumed Dram's face matched the confused expression on Kaytee's. "What? Um, I don't know."

Marcus's voice piped up. "No, he sounded like he always does on the phone. Very professional."

"That's great news," I said. "If you talk to him again, pretend like you don't care."

Kaytee's incredulous eyes met mine. She shook her head and chimed in. "Jeanie and I have a plan to get them back." She shot me a look that said she wasn't convinced but didn't want Dram to know it. "We're going to silence our phones. I'll call you as soon as I can."

Dram's voice was now firm and commanding. "Kaytee, please don't do this. I can't have you in danger along with Lupita and the boys. It will be too much if I lose all of you."

Kaytee's eyes were brimming with tears. "I have to try. I love your babies, too." She hung up.

Sympathetic tears welled up in my eyes. "Wow, you guys are all, like, really close."

She wiped her wet cheeks with her sleeve and pressed her mouth into a weak smile. "They're my family."

After switching my phone to silent and fumbling it into my fanny pack, I said, "Okay, I'm not exactly great at coming up with plans, and we have no idea what we're walking into, so we'll have to do a lot of improv on the fly." She gulped and nodded. "Here's what I'm thinking so far: the demon will probably meet me when I drive up and make sure I have something to offer before he shows me someone from Dram's family. You're going to hop out before we get to the house and hide so you can listen in while I question him. If all goes well, you'll be able to figure out where the family is being kept based on what he says." I paused in thought. "Do you need to see the guy to tell if he's lying?"

She nodded. "I need to see his face."

I frowned. Hopefully, there'd be decent lighting for this venture. "Okay, once you know where they are, you'll sneak off to rescue them while I use every stalling tactic in the book." I glanced around the immaculate garage. "Fuck, do you think Dram has any bolt cutters here?"

She shook her head, eyebrows raised in concern. "I don't think so?"

"Okay, that's fine. Let's hope they're not chained up." She bit her trembling lip.

"Hmm, how are we going to hide you so you can get out and sneak away?" I was back to the Sherlock Holmes chin rub again. "Aha!" I went to the rear of the station wagon and lifted the trunk door. It opened easily and without a sound. "Okay, we'll put you in the back." I frowned at the trunk light and walked up to open the driver-side door. Kaytee held her phone's flashlight steady while I crouched and peered around the side of the dashboard until I spotted the crack running through the vinyl and popped it off to reveal the fuse panel.

As I started pulling fuses out, she mumbled behind me, "What kind of shady shit..."

I glanced up at her and grinned. "I've just dealt with a lot of crappy old cars in my day." When I found the right fuse, the trunk light went out. "Well, that's one thing I'm glad I thought of in advance."

After replacing the cover, I stood up and gave her shoulders a firm squeeze. "Real talk time, Kaytee. Dram was right when he said you shouldn't put yourself in danger. If you find the family, grab them and run. If shit gets dangerous, you run. If the demon takes me down, you run." She was about to protest, but I put up a hand. "I'm dead fucking serious right now."

Her eyebrows drew together. "You don't even know these people, though. Why put yourself in danger?"

I took a deep breath and listed the reasons on my fingers. "Well, for one thing, fuck divines and their games. Two, I heal fast and don't feel pain. And three, Olita put a blood curse on me." Her chin drew back, and she squinted at me in confusion. "She meant it when she said I'd die if she dies." Her jaw fell open. I put a reassuring hand on her shoulder and smiled. I was more sure of myself than I'd ever been. "I'm saving that family, or I'm going down. This might be my only chance to redeem myself for all the pain I've caused people and to make up for breaking my promise to my late husband. Regardless of what happens, I'm going to die soon anyway."

Tears glistened in her eyes. "But what if you can lift the curse? What if Olita releases you?"

I snorted. Either of those scenarios were as likely to happen as a billionaire getting visited by three spirits in the night and waking up with a conscience. "You want those kids to live, right?"

She nodded, her wet cheeks glistening. "More than anything," she whispered.

"Well, it is a far, far greater thing I do than I have ever done, and a far, far greater rest I go to than I have ever known." Her brow furrowed, and I clapped her heavily on the back. "Poorly quoted Charles Dickens, baby! Now get in the trunk."

21

FOLLOWING THE DIRECTIONS Kaytee called to me from her hiding place in the back, I turned onto the dark, wooded drive and stopped. The faint light of our destination was just visible through the trees. I swiveled my head around. "All good?" Her hand popped up from behind the back seat and gave me a thumbs up. I released the latch, and the car dipped before the trunk closed with a soft click. Show time.

The headlights swept across the tall firs to rest on the white facade of an enormous garage. I stopped about fifty feet away, shifted the car to park, and turned it off, leaving the keys in the ignition and the lights on. The gun had a reassuring weight to it when I lifted it from the cup holder and stepped out.

"Helloooo!" I called. "I'm here on behalf of Dram Nguyen!"

The door of the garage swung open and a man in black pants and turtleneck peeked out, shielding his eyes from the glare of the headlights. A shadow shifted against the trees at the edge of my sight and stopped behind the dense line of shrubs. Kaytee was in position.

"Turn your fucking lights off!" the man yelled. I reached in and switched them off. An old fluorescent light above the garage door flickered, but the sudden darkness was disorienting. I blinked the afterglow from my eyes, and the man's steps crunched on the gravel toward me.

"Stay back," I warned him. "I've got a gun." His footsteps stopped when I waved it in the air.

"Where's Dram?" His voice was deep and menacing. In the dim light, I could just make out his compact, wiry build and head of close-cropped black hair. Shadows hid his features, and I doubted Kaytee had a clear view from where she was hiding.

"Are you the demon?" He nodded. "Well, something more important came up and Dram can't make it. He sent me to make a deal with you."

He was silent for a long moment. "Something more important? What the fuck are you talking about? I've got his family, for Christ's sake!"

I held up a hand. "Sir, you're getting hysterical. Please calm down." His hands curled into fists at his sides. "Listen, you have Dram's *secondary* family. They're kind of a decoy for his primary one. That's why he isn't coming, and that's why he sent his second-best assistant to talk to you."

"Bullshit," he growled.

"I know; he's a wily guy. It must sting to be outsmarted by him, but here's the deal. I have intel on another angel coming to town. He's the one you should go after because he's a way easier mark than Dram. Hell, I'll even help you. Where's your assistant?" He didn't answer. "Come on, someone else has to be here for you to pull this off. Are they in the garage with the family?" He pulled a knife out of his leg holster. "I'm not making a deal with you until you tell me where the family is. Are they in the house back there?" I gestured with the gun toward the partially concealed single-story tucked into the woods fifty yards behind the garage. "You have to at least show me one of them so I know this isn't just a ruse."

He spat off to the side and pointed his knife at me. "Dram talked to them. He knows this is the real deal."

"Dram talked to *someone*, but he said it didn't sound like Lupita. He thinks you're bluffing. What if you don't even have them? What if they're somewhere else? How do we know you haven't already killed them?" The man took a step toward me, and I raised the gun, making a point of sliding the top back into a satisfying click before taking aim. He stopped. "Where are they, asshole? I'm going to start firing if I don't see them soon, and my power is I never miss. I'll shoot your eyes out first and then stab you. Dram will be so stoked if I kill you; I'll be able to retire off the coast of France."

He raised his hands and pointed with his knife toward the garage. "In there."

"Yeah, right. Go get them. I want to see 'em."

With his hands still raised, he walked backwards and stepped out of sight when he was through the door. When he stepped back, he was pushing a bound and gagged woman in front of him. He stopped outside the doorway and put the knife to her throat. "Here, see? I've got them."

The light from above finally lit up his swarthy, shrewd face. I shook my head. "You have *one* of them. You have the other two in the house, don't you?"

"No," he growled through tight teeth, "they're in the garage."

"I bet your assistant is in there and ready to kill them as soon as we finish our deal here."

He clenched his jaw. "No, he's not. Now cut the bullshit and give me what I want; Dram, or she dies." There was the barest hint of rustling bushes off to my side, and I let out a quiet breath of relief—Kaytee was on the move. Step one accomplished, now for step two: performing some Olympics-level stalling to give her time to free the kids.

The demon pushed the knife into Lupita's throat, and the trickle of blood was black in the sickly glow of the overhead light.

"Okay, okay!" I held my hands up in surrender. "I was bluffing. Stop it and let's talk."

"No more lies. Where's Dram?"

"I think we both know if he'd shown up, you would've killed him and then his family. This way, we have a little more bargaining power." His eyes narrowed, and Lupita struggled against his iron grip. "I've got Dram's blood and his knife," I said quickly, hoping he would ease up on the poor woman.

He lowered his knife a fraction. "Show me."

Since he didn't tell me to drop the gun, I tucked it into the back of my pants before reaching into the car to grab the jar of fake blood. I shook it and smiled at the soft phosphorescence that glowed within. I stepped out from behind the door and held it up then slid Jackson's knife out of my holster and held it up, too.

"See, it's right here. I took the blood from Dram myself with his own knife. If you drink it, you ascend."

He paused for a long moment. Tears glistened on Lupita's cheeks, and I held my breath. "How do I know it's his?" he finally asked.

"Drink it, dumbass." I shook the jar, and it lit up a bit more. I wondered if he was buying it. "Let her go so I can see you mean to play nice, then we'll make the exchange."

His dimples darkened in the half-light when he smiled. "Carlos, get the knife and gun away from her." A hand closed around the back of my neck and squeezed the sides of my throat. "Dram's assistant, meet my assistant Carlos."

⌒ ⌣ ⌒

I kept my hands up and didn't turn. "Hey, Carlos," I said in a friendly tone. "You're really good at sneaking up on people. Any chance we can talk this through? You don't want to hurt kids, do you?" He said nothing as he reached up and twisted my hand until the knife fell out and clattered to the ground. Then he slid the gun from my waistband.

The demon was grinning. "Carlos, bring her to me."

I was shoved forward. "Okay, take it easy," I said amicably. He shoved me harder, and I stumbled.

When we were ten feet away, the demon said, "Carlos, stop and hold her still." Carlos tightened his hands around my upper arms in a vice-like grip. The demon grinned at me, his white teeth flashing. "Hello there, my name is Antonio Rossi. It's a pleasure to meet you, Miss…"

"Miss My Ass, first name Kiss."

He closed his eyes and shook his head. "Very cute, though I suppose introductions aren't strictly necessary considering our time together will be very short. If this blood is fake, then you will die, this one will die," he shook Lupita, "and both of the children will die."

"Listen, Mr. Rossi, you probably don't want to kill the family. They're your only real bargaining chip here. Me, sure, I get it, but Dram's never going to give you his blood if you kill them."

"As long as I have one of them, I think he will." He pushed Lupita to her knees and kicked her over before taking a step toward me. "Now, let's see this alleged angel blood."

I let the jar go and did the best dropkick I could manage with my arms held and zero hand-to-foot coordination. It smacked the side of my toe and flew about ten feet in the opposite direction of Lupita's struggling form.

Rossi stopped in front of me and let out a dramatic sigh. His eyebrows came together like he was very sorry for what he had to do, but it wasn't his fault I'd stepped out of line. Then he hit me in the jaw. Hard. My equilibrium was thrown off, and I stumbled against Carlos, vision blurring. I blinked through the eddies of red and black and imagined little cartoon birds looping through the air around me.

When Rossi's steps crunched off toward the jar, I threw my head back into Carlos' face. A sickening snap came from his nose, and I winced. He grunted, but didn't let go. Okay...I slid a foot back and threw my weight forward and to the side, tripping him and throwing off his balance so he could do nothing but fall with me. His hands were still clenched around my upper arms after we landed. What was this guy's power? Super grip?

Rossi laughed as I struggled on the ground, trying to roll away and tear out of Carlos' grasp. Lupita's eyes were wide and glistening when they met mine. I mouthed the word "run" to her. I might be able to keep these two occupied long enough for her to escape.

With my favorite inane smile plastered on my face, I stared up at Rossi as he stood over me with the glowing jar in his hand. His eyes narrowed.

"Carlos, turn her over and pin her down."

In one smooth movement, Carlos flipped me over and landed on top of me. It happened so fast I had no time to react before I was on my stomach with my left arm twisted up behind my back and my right arm pinned to the ground with his knee. Gravel dug into my cheek, and I coughed and spat dirt out of my mouth. Rossi's shadow loomed as he stepped closer and crouched down in front of me. Through his feet, I saw the gun on the ground behind him. Carlos must have dropped it during our tussle.

Rossi chuckled. "You really are Dram's second-string assistant, aren't you?" I smiled through my squished cheeks. He reached out to tousle my hair, pushing my face farther into the sharp rocks while doing so. He set the jar down in front of me. "What, exactly, is this?" He shook his head and laughed. "Maybe you *were* telling the truth about Dram. He obviously doesn't give a shit about his family, since he sent me an idiot with a jar of glitter. Or maybe you're just trying to stall for time?" His eyes narrowed. "Well, time's up." He stood. "Carlos, get her up. We're going to teach Dram a lesson."

Carlos lifted his knee and pulled my arms up behind my back to raise me off the ground. When I was halfway up, I twisted, dislocating my left arm as I threw my weight toward the gun. Carlos' grip finally slipped, and I got my right arm free just as I planted face-first next to the weapon. When he let go of my now useless left arm to get a better grip, I snatched the gun and rolled onto my back, feet kicking to keep him away. He grabbed my leg and started dragging me. I pulled the trigger. Nothing. My thumb fumbled along the side of the cool metal barrel until it located the safety switch and flipped it off. I raised the gun and shot straight up. Bingo. I aimed directly at Carlos' head, but he ignored it.

Rossi cried out, "Carlos, get the gun!"

As Carlos spun and lunged for the gun, I brought it up wide, smacked it broadside against his head, and pulled the trigger. It wasn't the loudest gun, only a .22, but I imagined the sound of it right next to an ear was pretty intense. He staggered back with a hand over his ear.

Rossi yelled again, "Carlos, get the gun!" I fired at him, and he darted to the side, out of range.

Gravel slid under my hand as I pushed myself up with my one good arm and made the awkward transition from sitting to standing. Rossi was nearly on top of me, but jumped back as the gun swung toward him and fired. I'd only shot a gun three times in my life, and always with two hands and lots of time to aim. I missed. Another round went wide as he scrambled to duck behind the car. Gravel crunched behind me, and I turned to see Carlos straightening up. My gaze darted to the garage—Lupita was gone. A slow grin spread across my face. One hostage freed, only two more to go.

Before Carlos could shift into a solid stance, I rushed him, throwing my leg out and doing my best approximation of a flying kick to his balls. It wasn't perfect (I should probably pay more attention in my MMA class), but it was enough to get him to double over so I could bring the gun down onto his head. He grunted. Despite what movies had taught me, pistol-whipping was not a surefire way to knock someone out, at least not for my clumsy self. I bashed it against his temple and ear a few more times until he lost his balance. I shoved him over.

Movement in my periphery made me turn; Rossi was coming in for an attack. He slid to a stop and made another mad dash for the car when I raised the gun to take aim. I fired two bullets, and he jerked to the side, stumbling and cursing. He wrapped a hand around his thigh, and I laughed in triumph as he limped the last few steps before diving behind the hood. Carlos was pushing himself up with shaking arms when I spun back around. I kicked him in the face.

"I'm sorry, Carlos!" I yelled as I ran after Rossi. He stayed just out of reach as I chased him around and around the car; cue the Benny Hill music. I fired at him whenever he popped up opposite me until the gun clicked—empty.

Rossi rose from his crouching scramble and smiled at me. "What now, sweetheart?" I threw the gun, and he ducked. With a victorious grin, he straightened all the way up and limped around the car toward me.

I flashed him a sweet smile. "You know, Rossi, you're pretty hot. Maybe you should take *me* into some kind of *hostage* situation, if you know what I mean." I waggled my eyebrows at him.

He laughed. "You wish. I only fuck supermodels."

I pouted at him. "Oh, honey, one drunk pity fuck doesn't justify using a plural there."

He snarled and lunged at me.

Now it was my turn to run away. I reached my hand down to scoop up Jackson's knife from the ground as I ran by, but stumbled and gave up. My breaths were coming fast and heavy as I sprinted for the garage. Jesus, I needed to work on my cardio. I crashed against the door and shook the handle up and down like an angry maraca player. It was locked. Rossi was a couple of staggering steps behind me, and I dodged him to dash down the path toward the house.

"You can run, but you can't hide!" he called after me cheerfully.

I dug in my fanny pack and pulled the shurikens out as I ran. He was about fifteen feet behind me when I turned and threw the first one. I missed, naturally, so I paused to say a brief prayer and take aim. I threw the second when he was eight feet away and let out a gasp of surprised victory when it buried itself in his shoulder. He cursed, and I took off again. The limping footsteps stopped.

His incredulous voice called after me, "What the fuck? Is this a ninja star?"

The shuriken made a faint metallic ring when it hit the stone pathway, and I turned. He was heading back to the garage with uneven, stumbling steps. I followed on tiptoe and hid behind a dense shrub to watch. Carlos was kneeling, still dazed, as Rossi leaned over and said something in his ear. He shot up instantly. Blood was streaming down his forehead and nose, and he was listing to the side like a sleepy zombie.

"Carlos, get that woman." Rossi pointed in my direction and Carlos stumbled forward into a shambling run. I took off again.

"Please, Kaytee, don't be in the house," I said over and over in a breathless whisper as I ran to the door and tried the handle. Locked. A quick glance under the welcome mat revealed the key. I rammed it into the keyhole and shoved the door open, scrambled inside, slammed it shut, and twisted the deadbolt just as Carlos' body crashed against it. He continued to ram it as I stumbled through the dark house, pulling a lamp and side table down behind me as I made my way to the back. A soft light above the kitchen stove guided me to what I was looking for. The front door gave in to Carlos' frenzied pounding right as I swung the back door open, ready to dart through. I froze. A shadowy figure was standing outside.

Rossi was smiling as he stepped into the light. "Leaving so soon?"

I slammed the door in his face and locked it.

He jiggled the handle while the thuds and scrapes of furniture being kicked and pushed aside announced Carlos closing in. I twirled and made a survey of my surroundings. Either Kaytee and the kids were somewhere in the house, in the garage, or hiding outside. I really hoped it wasn't the first. If I could keep Carlos and Rossi busy inside, then the family had a solid chance of making it to the car and getting the hell out of there.

I darted out of the kitchen and into the dining room. French doors led out to a moonlit deck. My gaze fixed on the tall candlestick gleaming against the dark wood table. I snatched it and turned to face Carlos as he barreled in. The heavy brass was unwieldy in my one good hand, and I waved it from side to side, trying to hold him back. I kicked a chair over in front of him, and he yanked it aside, expression blank and emotionless.

"Carlos, leave the woman alone," I said in my deepest voice.

He jumped forward into a flying tackle, and the candlestick made a sickening thud when it smacked against his temple. We smashed through the doors and hit the decking hard, snapping my head back against the glass-strewn deck and knocking the wind out of me.

Rossi chuckled as I lay there, dazed, trying to suck in a breath while Carlos kneeled on my chest. "I'm starting to think you aren't even Dram's assistant. Why would he imbue an idiot with the power to almost get away? Now, should I have Carlos kill you here, or should I have him bring you back to the garage and kill you alongside the rest of the family?" He hummed and tapped his lip as he considered his options. His other arm dangled at an awkward angle from his shoulder; I must have hit a nerve or ligament with the shuriken. I grinned—at least I would die as a cut-rate ninja. Pretty fucking badass.

I rasped out, "Do it now, pussy."

Rossi jerked his head around in surprise a split second before an enormous body came hurtling through the broken door and slammed into him, knocking him through the railing and off the deck. Carlos paid no notice and continued to kneel on me, his dark eyes empty and lifeless.

I gasped for air, pushing uselessly against his chest. He didn't budge. My good hand touched the candlestick next to me and, with a pathetically feeble effort, brought it up to hit him. He slumped forward before it found his temple. With no breath left and only one working arm, I couldn't move his limp body. The moonlight faded to black.

22

I BLINKED UP at the vaguely familiar figure looming over me before hacking out a few wheezy coughs. The trip through the patio door and subsequent suffocation had done a number on me —my vision was still swimming.

"Hey there, Jeans, take it easy." His voice quavered as he brushed a strand of hair away from my forehead.

I squinted up at him. "Sam?"

He took a shaky breath and blew it out in relief. "Jesus Christ, Jeanie, you scared me there for a minute." I tried to get up but fell back when my useless left arm didn't bother to assist. "Easy, I've got you." He helped me sit up. After a few deep breaths, the thick fog in my head began to clear.

I couldn't quite make out his features in the faint moonlight. With a hesitant hand, I reached up and traced a finger across his smooth cheek until it hit the indent of his scar, now thinner and less pronounced. "The fuck?"

He grinned, "I told you when I became a demon, you wouldn't be able to keep your hands off me."

Still dazed, I let my finger slide down to his chin while my gaze roamed all over his new face. His pockmarks were gone, and the proportions of his jaw and forehead more balanced. I blinked down at his hand on my knee before looking back up at him in confusion. "What are you doing here?"

"You butt-dialed me when you and Kaytee were going over your plan. I got here as quick as I could."

I jolted and sat up straight, my head clearing fast. "Where's Kaytee? Are the kids okay? What happened?"

"I dunno. A car pulled out as I pulled in, but the demon is dead and his assistant is out cold and no longer has his power."

I dropped my head back and let out a relieved breath. "Thank god. Those guys fucking sucked."

"Can you stand up? I can carry you." Sam's voice had a delightfully worried edge to it.

"I can stand." He helped me as I rose, unsteady and weak, to my feet.

When I was more or less upright, he pulled me to him and wrapped his arms around me. "Please don't do something like that again, Jeanie."

Surprised by the embrace and the concern in his voice, I lifted my good arm and gave his back a tentative pat. "I'm okay, Sam."

He stepped back, hands on my shoulders. "That was too close; I almost lost you."

My gaze darted to his face and then away again. He was clearly Sam, but I didn't want to stare—it was too much like ogling a stranger. It was going to take time to acclimate to the fact that he was still the same man, but now a step closer to being out of my league.

His eyebrows drew together when his gaze traveled from my face to my neck. He squinted and leaned forward. "The fuck is this?" The skin of my throat shifted when he reached up and touched something. "Is that glass?"

I glanced at the broken door behind him. Jagged pieces of glass and slivers of wood were sticking out like snaggly teeth from the remaining lattice. "Probably?"

"Fuck. Let's get a bandage." He grabbed my hand when I reached up to pull the shard out. "It might be in an artery; you could bleed out."

I pointed to my fanny pack and grinned. "Guess what's in there?" He raised an eyebrow and zipped it open.

"Look at you being prepared for your own bullshit." He pulled out a roll of gauze and tore a strip off to fold into a pad. "Lemme do it." I dropped my hand and stood quietly while he slid the shard out and pressed the pad down with one quick motion. He held it in place by gently squeezing my throat while the fingers of his other hand traced along the rest of my neck, feeling for more glass. My nipples hardened—this was kind of hot. I gave my inner horny self a mental slap. He shook his head. "Let's get you inside so I can get a better look and check out your arm. Hold this."

He opened the door, scraping it across the shattered glass and pushing Carlos out of the way of its swing. The ex-assistant was still out cold, his blood drying into dark streaks on the side of his face and under his nose. I sucked in a guilty breath.

Sam put a hand on my back and guided me into the house. Without a word, he pulled a chair aside and lifted me up to lay me out on the dining table. "Eyes closed," he said as he switched on the light. After a long pause, I blinked my eyes open and looked up at him. He was staring at my chin. "The demon do this?" He slid a gentle finger along my jawline where Rossi had punched me. I nodded, and he closed his eyes and took a steadying breath before opening them again and unclenching his jaw. He dumped out the rest of the first aid supplies from my fanny pack and set them on the table beside me. "Alright, hold still."

For the next several minutes, I held the gauze pad in place while Sam pulled my bloodied hair out of the way and picked shards of glass and slivers of wood from my neck and scalp before dabbing the cuts with an alcohol wipe. His hand grazed over my shirt as he felt along my shoulder and arm. "Jesus, you have some here, too." He grabbed my collar and ripped it open to expose my skin. The heat rose in my cheeks—this was definitely hot. I closed my eyes and pictured him ripping the rest of my clothes off and pinning me down. Lust shoved my sensible self aside, and I squirmed against the table.

He paused his ministrations. "Are you okay?"

My eyes snapped open. "What? Yep. Totally fine." I doused my inner horny self with cold water and steered my brain to more neutral ground. "Sorry I butt-dialed you." He looked up from skimming his fingers along the back of my shoulder and drew his eyebrows together in confusion. "I mean, thank you, you saved my life, but you didn't have to come out here." I glanced up at him and did a double take when I noticed his eyes were now light blue.

"What the hell is wrong with you, Jeanie? Of course I had to come." Before I could protest, he pressed his hand against my mouth and gently pushed my head back down. "I told you I care about you, and I meant it." His fingers brushed against my lips before returning to work on my arm. I closed my eyes and took deep, calming breaths.

After a few more minutes of glass tinkling against the tile floor, he said, "I think I got all the pieces. If there's more, we'll cut 'em out later." He peeked under the pad on my neck and nodded. "Looks good." He dropped it on the pile of bloody wipes and helped me sit up before sliding my legs over and off the edge of the table. "Lemme see that arm." He lifted it from where it dangled and bent it up and down and circled it around. "Just dislocated. Good thing—I suck at setting bones." With one quick movement, he yanked down on my arm and pushed against my shoulder. It made a popping noise. Gross. I blushed and tried to look anywhere but at him as he stood between my legs to wrap a strip of torn curtain around me to make a sling for my arm. With his steadying hands on my waist, I slid to the floor. "Alright, should be good as new in a couple hours."

My phone vibrated, and I scrambled to get it out of my pack and answer it. "Kaytee, are you okay? Are the kids safe?"

"We're safe! We got out of the garage and ran to the car while you distracted them in the house. What happened? Is the demon still around?"

"I'm fine; Sam rescued me." I looked up at him with a soft smile. "He killed the demon, and his assistant is currently passed out on the deck. Are you somewhere safe? Is Dram there yet?"

"We just pulled into the grocery store parking lot. Dram and Marcus are going to call as soon as they touch down." She blew out a breath. "I can't believe we pulled this off."

"I told you we would."

"I know! I only went along because you weren't lying. Oh, Dram is calling. Let me call you back," she said and hung up.

I surveyed the furniture and glass strewn about and the bloodied body outside the door before meeting Sam's eyes. "Do you think we should leave a note?"

23

SAM OPENED THE rear door and flipped Carlos' limp body off his shoulder and pushed him in before opening the passenger door for me. When he slid into the driver's seat of the small plug-in hybrid, I raised an eyebrow. "Is this your car?"

"Yeah." He shifted into drive and circled around to head back to the road.

"Huh," I responded. I studied his tattooed knuckles resting on the perfectly ordinary vinyl steering wheel. It wasn't the type of car I'd pictured for him. I would have guessed an old 1970s beater sedan, rusty truck, or anything to which the term "hoopty" could apply. I was tickled to discover yet another facet of Sam's character.

He tipped his head toward Carlos in the backseat. "What was his power?"

I shrugged. "I don't know; he was like a brainless zombie and did everything Rossi told him to."

The veins in Sam's neck stood out as he nodded. His voice was quiet. "It's called 'the automaton', and it's a fucked-up power to give a human. It takes away their free will." He met my appalled gaze with a sorrowful shake of his head.

We watched the road in silence and followed the map's directions back to Dram's house. Kaytee opened the door and wrapped me up in a bear hug, tears glistening in her eyes. "You are one crazy woman, and I'm so grateful I met you!" She froze when she saw Sam standing behind me with Carlos' body slung over his shoulder.

He held up his hand. "I swear I won't hurt anybody." He pointed at Carlos. "I'm just the delivery guy."

Kaytee's shoulders relaxed, and she smiled and waved us in. Sam eased Carlos down against the wall of the entry hall, where he promptly slumped over. When Sam stood back up, Kaytee squinted at his face before nodding in understanding and approval.

Dram and his family were huddled together on a couch in the adjacent room. A small boy was sitting on his lap, and a larger one was between him and Lupita, his tiny arms clutching her waist. Marcus perched on the couch's arm with a hand on the angel's shoulder. Dram's eyes widened when he saw Sam, and Kaytee put her hands out to reassure him. "Don't worry, this is Sam, not the one that did it. He won't hurt anyone." She turned and gestured to me. "This is Jeanie."

Dram rose, carefully depositing the boy into Marcus's arms, and walked over with shining eyes. He embraced me, and I gave him a few hesitant pats with my good arm. When he pulled away and held my shoulders, there were streaks of tears running down his creamy beige skin. "Jeanie," he began before he choked up and had to pause. "You saved my family. I owe you everything."

I waved him off. "It's no big deal. I'm glad everyone's okay."

Lupita's eyes glistened when they met mine, and she smiled. She was beautiful. Dark black eyelashes framed her large almond eyes, and her plump, motherly body looked perfect for hugging. I had a powerful urge to go over and lay my head on her lap. I smiled back at her. The children were all spindly limbs and enormous eyeballs as they held onto Lupita and Marcus for dear life. The boy on the couch shrank away when he caught my gaze, and Lupita pulled him closer and stroked his hair.

Dram turned to Sam and held out a hand. "I understand you helped as well. I owe you my gratitude."

Sam took Dram's hand and shook it while his other hand scratched the back of his neck. "Nah, Jeanie did all of it. I was just the clean-up crew."

I tilted my head toward the foyer and whispered, "Speaking of clean-up crew, Sam said you might be able to get some answers out of the demon's assistant. He's currently knocked out cold in your entryway."

Dram nodded and told his family he needed to take care of something and would be back in a few minutes. The boy in Marcus's arms whimpered, and Marcus hugged him closer, rubbing his back and making comforting shushing noises.

In the foyer, Dram crouched down next to Carlos. "Do you know his name?"

I nodded. "It's Carlos. The demon's name was Antonio Rossi."

Dram frowned. "Hmm. I don't know him; he's not one of mine. Kaytee, could you look him up?" She nodded and walked down the hall, presumably to get the *Annals of the Divine Lineage and Hierarchy*.

Dram pondered Carlos' face for a moment before touching a finger to his forehead. "Carlos, can you hear me?"

He groaned, and his head flopped over toward Dram. "Yes." His voice was the barest wheeze.

I winced. "Is he going to survive?"

A concerned wrinkle creased Dram's brow when he pulled his hand away. "I think so, but I don't like the idea of questioning him in his current condition. It might put too much strain on his mind." I recalled the agonizing experience of being questioned by Jackson and nodded.

When Dram stood up, Sam leaned toward him and said in a low voice, "Your family might not be safe here." He lifted his chin toward Carlos. "He might know if other divines have the same intel on you."

Dram's shoulders sagged, and he nodded. "Let's take him to the guest room and make him more comfortable, at least."

Sam picked up Carlos and followed Dram down the hall and into a small bedroom. He laid him down on the bed and straightened him out so his head rested on the pillow. Dram switched on the bedside lamp to cast a pleasant glow over Carlos' bloodied face.

A flood of guilt washed over me. "I'll find a washcloth and clean him up."

I walked down the hall until I found a bathroom and closed the door behind me. The entire ordeal had left my face pinched and haunted, and a dark purple bruise lined my jaw where Rossi had punched me. Sam had cleaned up some of the blood, but streaks of crusty red still ran down my cheek and along my clavicle. My ripped shirt draped off my shoulder and revealed more bloody marks. No wonder the kid had been scared shitless when he saw me. I sighed and grabbed a washcloth to clean myself up before wringing it out and refreshing it with more water for Carlos. I didn't bother getting a fresh one. What's a little blood between enemies? Former enemies, I reminded myself. He wasn't under Rossi's control anymore and didn't have any powers. Now he was just a regular human with multiple head injuries and a broken nose.

Back in the guest room, I dabbed at the dried blood on Carlos' face and then the trickle from his ear. His black hair was matted down where I'd bashed him with the gun and then the candlestick, and faint bruises darkened his temple. Shame tightened my chest.

"I'm sorry, Carlos," I whispered.

Kaytee walked in, the book open in her hands. "It says Antonio Rossi is from Missoula, Montana."

Sam's eyes met mine, and we shared a moment of realization. Rossi was from Jackson's territory.

Dram thanked her and took a deep breath. "Okay, I'll see what I can do." He perched on the edge of the bed and touched his fingers to Carlos' forehead again. "Carlos, who did you work for?"

His eyelids twitched and his pupils moved around beneath them before he opened his mouth to push out a hoarse answer. "Antonio Rossi."

"How did Antonio find out about my family?"

It took Carlos several breaths before he answered in a halting voice. "He...got a call. Then...made a plan...to kidnap them."

Sam and Dram looked at each other. "Who was the call from?"

"Don't know."

"Did Antonio ever work with other divines?"

"Don't know."

Dram rested a soft hand on Carlos' shoulder. "Thank you, Carlos. Please rest."

Carlos went limp, and we all shared meaningful glances. Sam spoke up first. "Your family isn't safe here, Dram. You'll probably be fine for the rest of the night, but you should get somewhere off the radar soon."

Dram nodded in defeat, his eyes downcast. "You're right. I'd really hoped to not have to do this to them; it's so hard on the boys." He looked down at Carlos and shook his head. "Poor man, it's tragic what some divines will do to humans. I wish I could do more to help him."

Sam said, "I'll make sure he gets to the hospital."

Dram sighed and stood. His hand came to my shoulder, and his bright smile beamed me in the face. "Can I get you two anything? Anything you want, it's yours."

I scratched my neck in discomfort, not wanting to intrude on him and his family. Jesus, I was acting like Sam now. I dropped my hand. "I'll take a glass of water if that's alright."

"Of course!" He led us down the hall and into the kitchen, while Kaytee split off to head back to the family. He raised a questioning eyebrow at Sam as he pulled a glass out, and Sam nodded. "Two glasses of water coming right up!" He handed them to us and opened the fridge. "Are you sure you don't want anything else? There's some of Lupita's delicious enchiladas in here, lots of soda and juices. Beer?"

Sam and I shook our heads in unison. Dram's hospitality was making both of us equally uncomfortable. I smiled and said, "I think we'll just head out. Thanks, though." I chugged the water and set my glass on the counter next to the sink, and Sam did the same.

"Before you go..." Dram walked over to a nook in the corner and scribbled something on a notepad before tearing the page off and handing it to me. "Here's my private cell number; please call if you need anything. I owe both of you everything." His wide smile was all sincerity.

I tucked it into my pocket. "Thanks."

Sam didn't move when I turned to go. "I do have a favor to ask." Dram nodded at him with a bright and hopeful smile. "Can you lift a demon's curse?"

Dram's eyebrows dipped, and he frowned in thought. "In theory, I should; I suppose it depends on the nature of the curse."

Sam gestured to me. "Olita put a blood curse on Jeanie."

Drams's curiosity turned to horror as Sam explained what a blood curse was. The wrinkles on his forehead deepened. "I think I should be able to...I'm pretty low on power right now, but I'll see what I can do."

Sam held out his arm. "I don't have much yet, but take what you need."

Dram grimaced and glanced toward the living room. He lowered his voice. "I always hate this part, especially with my family around." He gestured Sam to a laundry room off the kitchen and closed the door behind them.

When they came back out, Sam was holding a paper towel to his arm, and Dram's eyes were brighter, and his skin shone with a faint inner light.

"Okay, Jeanie, go ahead and take a seat." He pointed to a chair in the breakfast nook. I sat down and jiggled my leg while he pulled his chair closer until our knees touched. He squinted as he scanned my eyes, as though he could see the curse if he looked deep enough. "Okay." He leaned in and placed a hand over my heart while the other rested on my shoulder, like a gentle doctor checking over his patient or, more aptly, a quiet priest exorcising a demon at a tent revival.

He closed his eyes, his face smooth and serene. After a long minute, his brow furrowed, and he angled his head toward me. A faint red light emanated from between his fingers over my heart. I glanced up at Sam. He was watching the glow with a naked expression of hope. The light flashed bright white for a brief moment before fading. Dram shook his head.

"Something's wrong." He lifted his hands away and leaned back, stroking his chin. "It's like I can almost get it, but there's something holding the last bit back." He looked up at Sam. "Is it possible that any of the cursed blood is outside of Jeanie's body?"

"I destroyed the drop I took outta her." He frowned in thought, then his face fell. "The vessel." He exchanged a look with Dram.

"The vessel?" I asked.

Dram turned to me. "It's the special container that's used when a divine takes on an assistant. A drop of blood from the divine and the human is placed inside, linking the power of the divine to their assistant. As long as the drop of Olita's cursed blood remains in the vessel with yours, I can't lift the curse." His expression was bleak. "I'm so sorry, Jeanie."

I shrugged. "Eh, it was worth a shot."

He took my hand, his eyes earnest and resolute. "Olita made you her assistant and ordered you to kill me so she could ascend, correct?" I nodded. The corner of his mouth lifted into a half smile, and his eyes shone. "You saved my family; my life is yours. Take my blood and release yourself from the curse."

My eyebrows shot up. "What? No. I'm not taking your blood." I looked up at Sam; his face was carefully blank. "I'm not going to take you away from your family so that b—" I glanced toward the living room and lowered my voice. "B-word can ascend in your place."

Dram nodded and examined my eyes. "Kaytee's right; you're an incredible person. I'm forever in your debt. If there's another way to lift the curse, I promise I'll help."

"Okay, thanks," I mumbled and stood up. Dram led us back to the front door after making a stop at the guest room to retrieve Carlos.

I popped my head into the living room to wave goodbye to Kaytee and Marcus and the rest of Dram's family. Kaytee beamed up at me and mouthed the words, "Thank you." Lupita's head was flopped back on the couch, her mouth open and eyes closed. The older boy was fast asleep across their laps, and Marcus was still holding the younger boy in his arms, his drowsing head resting on Marcus's shoulder. My tears threatened to spill out. The intimate love between Dram's family and his assistants was a lot to take in for a lonely woman. It made me think of Isaac and all the missed opportunities for creating the same sweet moments with him and Jenny.

Dram's hand squeezed my shoulder, and he pulled me into a gentle side hug when he saw the glistening of my tears. I glanced toward Sam when I turned to leave. His eyebrows were curled up and his eyes shining. My breath hitched when I realized Sam might be just as lonely as I was. He quickly turned away when he caught me watching him and hoisted Carlos farther onto his shoulder before opening the door. After a quick wave to Dram, we headed out into the cool night air.

24

THE QUIET CAR hummed down the road, and the silence inside was heavy. After a hesitant breath, Sam turned to me. "Jeanie, I'm really sorry about...everything."

I glanced over at his earnest face and shrugged. "Water under the bridge, Sammy." An awkward minute crept by. "Um...thanks for the picture of Tom. That was really thoughtful."

He mumbled, "It was nothing."

The window of the car was cool against my forehead as I watched the trees stream by on our way to the ferry terminal. I breathed a deep sigh of relief when we caught the first boat of the morning. It was 4:35 a.m., and I was struggling to keep my eyes open and my head upright. I was too old for this staying up all night and fighting demons shit.

Once we were loaded onto the ferry, Sam gestured up to the passenger deck. "Wanna check out the view?"

I nodded, and we made our way up to the observation platform that provided an open-air view of the crossing. The brisk wind livened me up a bit, and I filled my lungs with a deep, grateful breath. I shrugged out of my now unnecessary sling, and we leaned on the railing next to each other, watching Seattle's sparkling city skyline glowing against the faint outline of mountains in the distance.

Over the thrumming of the engines, Sam asked, "Do you remember when we first met?"

I wrinkled my nose and squinted up at the dim stars. "Vaguely?"

He gazed out over the water. "Brandy brought you to that old house off Dexter. You wanted to try ecstasy."

"Oh, yeah." Snippets of the encounter started coming back.

"I sold you some and you two went inside to party. After about an hour, you came to the back porch where I was sitting on the couch. You sat next to me and asked me how I was doing. I told you I was fine and asked how you were." He paused. "You put your head on my shoulder and said your life was fucked. You told me your husband died and you couldn't deal, so you gave up and were chasing the high and waiting to die."

I winced. I'd completely forgotten about the despair that came over me and how I'd unloaded all my troubles onto Sam. At the time, I assumed the stuff he sold me was a dud, but later found out that if you have a condition like clinical depression or bipolar disorder, then MDMA won't necessarily work the same. You need enough serotonin available in order to get the high from the drug dumping it all into your system at once. Instead, my sprinkling of serotonin molecules had partied for a minute before fucking right off like a deadbeat dad, leaving me in misery. While the others at the party were feeling up on each other, I'd left, dragging myself away under the weight of unbearable sorrow.

"Sorry about that, Sam. That was probably...weird for you."

He looked down at me. "Nah, Jeanie, don't be sorry." He paused. "It'd been a long time since someone felt comfortable enough with me to trust me like that. You reminded me of my sister."

I met his eyes. "You have a sister?"

"Had."

"Oh." I watched the dark water swirling below us. "Do you... want to talk about it?"

He studied the horizon. A lighter blue was glowing behind the mountains as dawn crept closer. "I was adopted by a demon named Maeve when I was a baby. My birth mother didn't think she could keep me safe, so Maeve raised me as her own." A fond smile softened his face. "She was an amazing woman who'd given up the divine lifestyle and devoted herself to helping others. She protected humans and didn't ask for blood from her incubi. In return, they did their best to protect her and donated to her freely when she got too weak. She fostered a lotta goblin children and adopted a human one." His eyes met mine. "My sister, Bridget." I held his gaze for a long moment before he broke eye contact and looked up at the dwindling stars. "Olita killed 'em both."

"Oh my god." My heart plummeted. No wonder Sam's entire goal in life had been to kill her.

"Yeah." His voice was quiet. "I was eleven when she killed Maeve for the *Magia Deorum* and then killed Bridget just for fun. Her assistant locked me in the bedroom and gave me this when I tried to get out and stop her." He pointed to the scar on his cheek. "Olita was already a demon when she killed 'em. She did it for the book, which Maeve woulda given her if she'd asked."

My gut roiled with anger, and I looked up at him. "We're going to get her, Sam. I promise."

He had a faint smile on his lips when his gaze shifted to mine. "No, we're not. I'm not putting your life in danger for an old grudge. It's not what Maeve woulda wanted." There was a glimmer in Sam's eye that may have just been a trick of the ferry lights dancing up from the water.

I hesitated before sliding my arms around his waist and giving him a gentle squeeze. He put his arms around my shoulders and squeezed back.

"I'm really sorry, Sam."

"It's okay, Jeanie." He let me go and lifted a hand to rub his eyes in shame. "I haven't been the man Maeve wanted me to be. I let my rage take me to some pretty dark places: killing divines I thought deserved it, and selling drugs to humans even though I promised to never hurt 'em. It's why I've been looking out for you, tryna protect you and make up for some of the bad things I've done over the years." He shook his head as he stared, unseeing, at the churning water below us. "When you told me about your husband and how much you loved him, it opened my shriveled black heart up enough to remember what Maeve tried to teach me." He met my eyes. "I asked Olita to choose you cuz I wanted you to get sober and have a second chance. You didn't belong on the streets."

"No one belongs on the streets."

He shrugged. "I know, but I'm a cruel man. I've got used to ignoring the usual victims. You stood out too much—a woman who couldn't handle the death of her true love? It was like some kinda Shakespeare story." His eyes lingered on me for a long moment. "Plus, you kinda look like Bridget."

The ferry slowed the rumble of its engines as it approached the landing, and the lights of the dock glimmered on the water. We traipsed back down to the car. The nature of the silence between us had changed. It wasn't uncomfortable per se, but charged with a new and vulnerable layer of understanding. I didn't want to say anything that would make Sam regret confiding in me, and I assumed he was processing his discomfort at sharing a secret part of himself. While I buckled myself in, the realization hit. We were the same—Sam and I. We'd both lost people we loved and spiraled down into darkness because of it.

The tires thumped over the ramp, and we followed the line of cars as they disembarked from the ferry and began their slow dispersal into the streets of downtown. Brake lights flashed on and off while I considered his confession that he'd been looking out for me. I'd been called Sam's girl more than once but assumed it was just a weird dealer-buyer ownership thing. The revelation that it was because he'd been protecting me sparked a warm glow in my chest.

As we drove up the hill, I broke the silence. "How'd you know where I was when you came to rescue me?"

He winced. "You're not gonna like it." His gaze shifted to my expectant face and then back to the road. "I turned location sharing on from your phone when you were asleep after your Billings ordeal." My eyebrows jumped up my forehead before furrowing in confusion. "Your code's written on a post-it on your desk," he added in explanation. "I'm real sorry, Jeanie; I was being overprotective."

I considered my response while we sat at a red light. A laughing couple staggered by, holding onto each other and doing their best to make it up the hill after a full night of drunken debauchery. I ached with longing as I watched them. Part of me wanted to be angry at Sam's invasion of my privacy, but the empty void in me felt a special delight.

I shrugged. "I guess it paid off, didn't it?"

Sam walked me to my door, and I stepped into his hesitant hug. I almost let myself get lost in the embrace, but let out a quiet sigh and pulled away with a shy smile instead. I wanted more than anything to ask him inside, but now that I knew I reminded him of his sister, I'd begun the process of moving him from my Potential Fuck Boi mental folder into my Platonic Friend category.

After I locked the door behind me, I began scheming. I now had a new and singular goal: destroy Olita Cummings.

25

NIGHTMARES OF SUFFOCATION caused my parched throat to wake me at 2 p.m. with a sudden spate of coughing. Still groggy and exhausted after a shower, I made myself coffee and sat down to stare at the new word document on my computer titled "Taking the Bitch Down." Despite my swirling rage of righteous indignation and strong sense of purpose, the page contained only a scant paragraph with an excessive amount of expletives. Get close and stab her was the main gist of what I'd come up with.

By 5 p.m., I was thoroughly annoyed by my lack of progress and because I hadn't heard from Sam. I went back and forth about texting him, but didn't have anything to say other than I missed him. Which I wasn't ready to admit openly to him or myself.

My gloomy self-doubt faded when I got a message from Kaytee:

> *Hi Jeanie, I wanted to check in on you and catch up.*

I texted back:

> *Hi Kaytee, I would love to catch up with you!*
> *Are you at the office? Can I bring you dinner?*

Kaytee responded:

> *I am at the office and that would be amazing!*

> *Ok, see you soon.*

Kaytee's eyes lit up when I stepped through the door with all the fixings for pho from my favorite Vietnamese restaurant, plus two iced milk coffees. "Oh my god, I just realized how hungry I am!" She was wearing tight jeans, snake print slingbacks, and a silky gold top. Even her casual attire was classier than my entire wardrobe. We prepared our soups and sat down in the small break room next to Dram's office.

After several bites of beef and noodles, I asked her about the rescue.

She put down her chopsticks and wiped her mouth. "Well, it turns out the whole family *was* in the garage, so I circled around back to see if there was another way in. I found a window and popped it out of its slide with the sai." She shook her head like she couldn't believe the ninja weapon had actually come in handy. "When I got inside, I found David and Joseph tied up and stashed in a fishing boat. Lupita was already outside by that time, so I untied the boys and started getting them out through the window. Then there were gunshots and Lupita ran in. I cut the ropes off her and we all got out and hid behind the garage while you were fighting with the demon and his assistant. I was going to sneak them through the woods to a neighbor, but then you got those two bastards to follow you to the house. We got in the car and the rest is history." She shook her head again and stared at her soup with raised eyebrows.

"Are Dram and his family somewhere safe now?"

She nodded. "He has another house under an LLC. He'd been renting it out as a vacation spot, but it's going to be their short-term residence until they can figure out something better. Marcus is with them, and I'm holding down the fort here."

"Marcus's power must be pretty badass to protect the family." Kaytee's eyebrows drew together, and I raised my hands in apology. "Sorry, I wasn't trying to get you to tell me what it is."

She smiled. "I forgot you didn't know. I think you've proven yourself to be trustworthy with our secrets. He can create a shield that keeps anyone inside from being hurt."

I nodded my head, impressed. "That's a pretty awesome power."

"It is." She picked up her chopsticks. "What happened at your end last night?"

"Well, there's not much to it." I sat back and gave her a summary of my escapades with Rossi and Carlos. When I was done, we looked at each other for a long moment, eyebrows raised in shared disbelief at how well things had turned out.

She shook her head. "Were you able to get the assistant to the hospital?"

I nodded. "Yeah, we dropped him off at the emergency room before going back to clean up the scene. Oh yeah! That reminds me." I pulled open my purse and took out the gun I'd wrapped in a pillowcase. "For your neighbor." I pushed it across the table to her and then the shurikens. "I managed to throw one of these into the demon's shoulder and mess up the use of his arm which helped Sam take him down."

She laughed. "I'm glad at least one of them did some good." Her brow furrowed. "How did Sam get there? Did you call him?"

"I accidentally called him when we silenced our phones, and he figured out we were up to something dangerous. He found me because, um, my location was shared with him."

It was still being shared with him. I'd decided that turning it off was not the best move with all the crazy divines roaming around. The only thing that had changed was he'd begun sharing his location with me, too.

"Oh. Are you guys like an item?"

I choked on a noodle and spent a moment coughing before I responded. "No. We're just friends."

"But you want it to be something more?"

I bit my lip and focused on my chopsticks. "Um, maybe, but he's not into me in that way."

"Are you sure?" She raised a skeptical eyebrow.

"Yeah, he kind of told me last night that he thinks of me as a sister or something." I stared down at the remaining swirls of noodles and bean sprouts in my bowl.

"Mmm, I don't know. I've seen the way he looks at you."

I shrugged. "Well, I don't think it's going anywhere, and I'm not going to humiliate myself by hitting on him again." Heat flushed my cheeks when I recalled the drunken debacle. "What about you and Marcus? Are you guys a thing?"

She threw her head back and laughed. "No, we're just really close. He's cute, but he's also six years younger than me. We're all more like a big family."

"I saw that. It must be...nice."

Her smile was soft. "It is. I don't have a lot of family out here; my folks are on the east coast, and I rarely see them. My cousin's nearby, but we're not on great terms right now. When I met Dram, I wasn't expecting to find a job *and* a family, but he's so open and loving. He introduced me to Lupita and the boys after about three months. Marcus was already working for him and fit into the family like an older brother. In a very short time, I became like an older sister. Those boys are just too damn cute."

My smile turned wistful. "I don't have much family, either. I burned a lot of bridges and lost the few people I had."

"If you don't mind my asking, what happened?"

"My husband died of cancer and I couldn't deal, so I fucked right off and disappeared, did a lot of drugs, and hid from everything and everyone that reminded me of him."

"I'm so sorry, Jeanie." The sincerity in her voice made me tear up.

I stared up at the ceiling and started some preemptive blinking to prepare for potential waterworks. "Turns out I don't have any healthy coping mechanisms. Even before Tom died, I smoked too much weed to deal with my depression and leaned on him too much when things got tough. In hindsight, I realize it wasn't fair to him or me. I should've diversified that portfolio sooner." I groaned and put my head in my hands. "The worst thing is I broke my last promise to him. He made me swear I'd move on and be happy after he was gone. I kind of did the opposite."

Kaytee was nodding to herself when I looked up at her. She took a deep breath. "I didn't meet Dram at a fundraiser. I met him at the women's shelter where I was staying after getting out of an abusive relationship." She squeezed her eyes closed. "I stayed with that bastard for way longer than I should have. I let him convince me that my self worth was tied to his approval, and I deserved whatever he did to me." She shook her head. "The worst part was I knew he was a piece of shit, but I stayed anyway. If it'd been any of my friends, I would have pulled them out of that situation in a heartbeat. It felt so good when I finally forgave myself."

I met her eyes with a soft smile. "I'm glad you found your way out of there and into something healthy."

She returned the smile. "You can do the same." She leaned back and contemplated my face. "You know, you haven't broken your promise to your husband." I raised an eyebrow. "I doubt he had a deadline in mind. You just haven't fulfilled your promise *yet*."

I looked away and frowned, unconvinced. "Maybe. I'm not sure I'll have time now. I don't know if I'll have time to make anything right."

"You saved a mother and her children. That has to count for something."

I shrugged. "You did most of the saving; I just made up shit, hit men with things, and ran around."

She laughed. "Well, it worked!" We shared another smile before she stood up and took our bowls to the sink. "What's next for you now?"

My gaze drifted up to the window where the distant buildings of downtown Bellevue were just visible through the summer evening haze. "Well, first I'm going to figure out how to kill Olita. Then I'm going to put that plan in motion and end her."

She whipped her head around to stare at me. "But won't that kill you, too?"

I shrugged. "That bitch has done truly horrific things. I'm thinking that taking her out is a decent step toward redemption." I rubbed my face and chuckled. "The universe will need eons to sort out my fucked-up karma."

She looked at me like I was wearing a pink lamé speed suit at a black-tie gala and shook her head. "You do you, I guess. I don't want you to die, though. You're an incredible person."

I shifted in my chair. I hated compliments—I never deserved them.

"I see you squirming over there." She pursed her lips and put a hand on her hip. "You know what makes me feel better when I'm going through some shit?" I shook my head, and a mischievous smile spread across her cheeks. "How do you feel about karaoke?"

26

IT TOOK A bit of convincing on Kaytee's part, and I was annoyed about having to change out of my sweats, but after a drink, I was starting to enjoy myself. Watching the human spectrum of confidence and musical ability parade onto the stage and take the mic did a remarkable job of lifting my spirits. Kaytee was amazing. She delivered the best cover of *I Wanna Dance With Somebody* by Whitney Houston I'd ever heard. Everyone on the path back to our table high-fived her as she went by.

I clinked my glass against hers. "To Kaytee, who can do anything with a level of grace and panache unachievable by most."

She winked. "Soon it'll be your turn to show the universe what you got. I put your name on the list." She laughed as I stared at her in disbelief. "Come on, I thought you had no fear?"

"I'm not afraid for myself; I'm afraid for everyone within earshot."

The poor suckers that had to follow her were a drunk duo attempting to sing *I've Had the Time of My Life*, which quickly devolved into senseless mumbling and laughing. "You can't be any worse than that," Kaytee leaned over and whispered as the couple stumbled off the stage to high-five a group of their equally inebriated friends.

I laughed. "Challenge accepted!"

When the emcee called my name, I had another drink under my belt and was feeling pretty good. I snorted when I stepped onto the stage and saw what song Kaytee had selected for me. En

Vogue's *Don't Let Go*. I strode up to the microphone and apologized in advance. Kaytee let out a loud whoop.

Things started out shaky, but then I found my groove. Kaytee was right when she said singing helped. It was helping me anyway. I was pretty sure I was actively hurting everyone else in the vicinity. After an especially impassioned delivery of the line: "Don't you want to be more than friends?" I opened my eyes and saw Sam standing next to our table and Kaytee sitting there with the biggest shit-eating grin on her face. I froze and squinted at him, trying to determine if he was actually there or if my sex-starved brain was projecting my desires rather than reality.

Others turned to look as he walked to the front, mouth serious and eyes unreadable. When he got to the stage, he beckoned me forward, and I abandoned the mic and took the hand he offered to help me down. He kept holding it as he guided me back through the bar. Several people clapped as I left, probably relieved they didn't have to listen to any more of my off-key yowling. I shot a helpless look at Kaytee when we walked by, but she just smiled and gave me two thumbs up.

Outside, Sam led me around the side of the building, through the small group of smokers, and into a nearby alley. He pushed me up against the brick wall, and his light blue eyes pierced into my own.

My breath caught, and I squirmed—being this close to him was making it hard to remember he was just a friend. "Um, am I in trouble?"

He put a hand on either side of me and leaned forward to whisper, "Jeanie, I want you."

The back of my head bonked against the wall as I looked up at him in surprise. "Like...in the carnal sense?"

"Like in most of the senses, but yeah, definitely the carnal one."

"Oh."

He pushed his hands into my hair, thumbs stroking my cheeks, eyes blazing. "Can I kiss you?" I trembled as the furnace in my low belly blazed to life.

My gaze went from his eyes to his lips, and I whispered, "As long as it leads to something more...full body."

He lowered his mouth to mine. The kiss was soft and sweet at first then deepened as his hands traced down my curves. The heat in my core turned into an inferno of desire, and I raked my fingernails through his hair. He pulled me closer. As my hands roamed over his muscled chest, his slid down my hips and back up from my hemline until he had a good grip on my ass. As I was debating whether it would be prudent to have him fuck me right there up against the wall in a dirty alley, a group from the bar walked by and saw us.

One woman yelled, "Hey, I guess he did want to be more than friends!" Another whooped out a catcall.

Sam laughed and looked down at me. "Yeah, since the day I met you."

I bit my lip and trailed a finger down his stomach to his belt buckle. "Prove it."

In the periphery of my mind, I felt bad for the driver of our ride. The level of dirty talk, fondling, and kissing in the backseat was totally inappropriate for a non-consenting audience. He didn't say a word as we stepped out and took off once we were clear of the car. Definitely not getting a five-star passenger rating from that guy.

Sam opened the front door and tossed me over his shoulder, and I laughed with every jostling step up to his place. As soon as we were inside his apartment, he set me down and pressed me up against the wall, his lips on my neck and my fingers in his hair. I pulled with panting desperation at his coat, then shoulder holsters, then t-shirt. He helped me take them off to reveal his muscled and tattooed torso before reaching around to the seam at the back of my dress and ripping it apart. I freed my arms from the straps, and his hands grazed along my bare sides and over my breasts. My breath ragged with anticipation, I undid his belt and tugged at his button and zipper with trembling fingers.

Before I could seriously grope the sizable bulge underneath, he picked me up and carried me to the bedroom with my legs wrapped around him and my frantic fingernails digging into his back. I bounced and giggled when he threw me down on the bed before pulling his pants and underwear off. My heart raced, and I squirmed with excitement as I stared up at his massive body looming over me. He grabbed the hem of my dress and ripped it off before doing the same with my panties. Starting from the bottom, he licked and kissed and caressed his way up until his mouth reached mine. My breath quickened with anticipation, and I gasped when my fantasies finally became reality.

My panting breaths soon turned into moaning cries. When my gasping and cursing ticked up another notch, Sam's neighbor banged on the wall, the international apartment dweller's signal to quiet the fuck down. In response, Sam lifted his hand from my throat and pressed it down on my mouth before doubling his efforts until I bucked up with a mind-blowing orgasm. He kissed my neck and held me down as my limbs threatened to shake themselves right off my body.

When my breaths evened out, he pulled my leg over his shoulder and trailed kisses along it, building up until I was panting with pleasure again. His breath ragged, he threw his head back and let loose a victorious string of curses. I ran my fingers up his stomach and over his chest while he gathered the fragments of himself back together. His muscles bunched and flexed when he lowered his lips to mine before collapsing beside me on the bed.

"Fuuuck," he said.

"Fuck." I agreed.

Sam turned to me, eyes twinkling in the soft light from the window. "Why haven't we been doing that this whole time?"

I shook my head and gave him a playful shove. "Screw you. It's not like I haven't been trying. I didn't think you weren't into me in that way."

He raised up onto an elbow with a bemused smile. "Why would you think that?" I shrugged. "Is it cuz of that night you were drunk?"

I shrugged again. "Partially."

He flopped back on the bed with a heavy sigh and rubbed his face. "Jesus Christ, Jeanie, I wanted to do unspeakable things to you that night. You standing there like some kinda deity of depravity and looking at me like that? Walking away from you was one of the hardest things I've ever done."

"Ooh, I like that, deity of depravity. I didn't realize you were such a poet."

He grinned. "I can be for such a beautiful siren of sin."

I laughed, and he pulled me into the nook of his shoulder. The soft down of his chest hair tickled my cheek when I settled my head down. I inhaled him in. Jesus, he smelled good. The calming rhythm of his heartbeat filled my ears, and the tension I'd been carrying for god knows how long melted away. My skin prickled with pleasure as he ran his hand in gentle strokes up and down my arm.

His voice vibrated deep within his chest. "I'm sorry I'm not great at, you know, making my feelings known. I don't like to make women uncomfortable, so I keep my cards close and wait for 'em to make the first move." He paused. "Then make sure they aren't coming on to me just cuz they want something, or are too drunk or high to care that I'm a mean, ugly sonuvabitch."

I sucked in a breath and lifted my head to meet his eyes. "I'm really sorry, Sam. I didn't mean what I said that night about how I'd regret being with you. I guess I said it because I knew I wouldn't, and it hurt when I thought you didn't feel the same way." I laid my head back down and stroked my fingers along his stomach and chest.

He squeezed my waist and kissed the top of my head. "So no regrets?"

I laughed. "Nope. Well…maybe that I didn't get a chance to fuck you with your old looks."

He lifted his head, confusion in his voice. "Seriously?"

I wiggled up closer to him, throwing my leg over his. "Yeah, I was way hotter than you then. I could've lorded it over you and got off on making you crawl on your knees and beg—like a duchess of debauchery."

He laughed and grazed his hand down my side, causing a delicious trail of goosebumps to erupt in the wake of his touch. "Like a paragon of perversion."

"Like all the things!" I sighed. "What is it about you, Sam? I've never orgasmed the first time with someone. Although I guess I have been priming the pump with all my fantasies about you."

His voice was incredulous. "You fantasized about me?"

I tilted my head to look up at him. "Yeah, ever since you held me down on the bench...and for quite a while before that if I'm being honest."

His eyebrows drew up in surprise. "Well...fuck. I've been wanting to hold you down and fuck you all over town for a long time now. I wish I'd known you were into me sooner, we'd be a lot further down on my *Depraved Things I Wanna Do to Jeanie* list by now."

My leg slid along his as I squirmed in excitement, and his fingers buried themselves into my hip. Heat spread through my body as my hand traced lower and lower down his stomach. I looked up at him. "You've got a whole list?"

His heart thudded to life, and he grinned. "It's a long one."

"I'm looking forward to finding out all about what goes on in that mind of yours." I stroked him playfully. "Want to explore some things I've fantasized about doing to you?"

His eyes watched my lips. "Jeanie, I'll take whatever you wanna give me."

With a seductive smile, I slid down the bed. His breath quickened as I rolled up my metaphorical sleeves and got to work. When his breaths turned ragged, his grip tightened in my hair and pulled my eager mouth away. I grinned up at him. With an answering grin, he sat up and pushed me over before sliding down to the floor and yanking my thighs to the edge of the bed.

My panting grew faster and faster as he explored every holy hill and valley. When the quivering of my legs got out of control and threatened to suffocate him, he stopped. I moaned in protest, and he pulled me off the bed before flipping me over. I gasped and then screamed into the covers when he stepped up behind me and set the world in motion. Pleasure built up inside me, filling every last inch, until I burst open, unable to contain it any longer. His lips grazed my neck as he sucked in his last lustful breaths before releasing them in a flurry of curses.

After a long and breathless period of quivering and gasping out obscenities, I crawled onto the bed and collapsed. The mattress dipped as Sam settled down beside me and pulled me to him. We lay there in a tangle of limbs and breaths and heartbeats until goosebumps crept across my skin. After a bathroom session to clean up, we slid under the covers together. I snuggled against him and sighed with contentment.

Thoughts of Olita and then Tom swam in the vague corners of my mind, and I pushed them away. I would deal with reality in the morning. Tonight was just for me.

27

IT WAS LATE morning when I woke to the sound of Sam whistling in the kitchen and the aroma of coffee brewing. A deep contentment wound its way through my core and unfurled itself into a luxurious, yawning stretch. The ghosts of last night's pleasurable pressures and releases still pulsed through my body and, like the best kind of drug, made me yearn for more. When I slipped out of bed, I found myself grounded yet floating, deliciously empty yet full at the same time. I smiled at my reflection in the bathroom mirror. My messy bedhead and remnants of mascara looked sexy, or maybe it was just the afterglow of a night of amazing sex. I finished my business and slid back into the warm bed, humming with pleasure as Sam's scent washed over me.

He walked in with two cups of coffee, and our mouths curved up in unison when our eyes met. I leaned against the pillows and took in his naked torso with delight. During our fuck sessions, I'd discovered his protruding stomach was packed with muscle—the strongman's answer to the bodybuilder's flat pack. Now, in the morning light, I could appreciate the contours of his muscles in their entirety as well as the tattoos covering his upper body. The twisting forms on his hands and arms were long, sinuous dragons that snaked along his shoulders and ended with their heads shooting flames across the back of his neck. Woven around them were motifs of skulls, daggers, and Celtic knots, leaving only bare glimpses of the skin underneath. A large faded tattoo in bold Celtic script arched across his chest.

He set my cup of coffee on the nightstand and brushed his thumb along my cheek before leaning down to kiss me.

"Good morning," he said.

"A great morning," I replied.

When he'd settled in beside me, I traced a finger down the neat rows of tiny skulls impaled with daggers on his side. "What do these mean?"

He glanced at me from the corner of his eye and didn't answer right away. "One for every divine I killed."

He took a careful sip of coffee when my eyebrows shot up. I'd seen more rows of the same skulls on his other side. There had to be hundreds.

I pointed to the letters on his chest. "What does that mean?"

"It means 'never forget' in Gaelic."

"Oh." We drank our coffees in silence for a while before I turned to him. "Do *you* regret last night?"

He smirked. "Fuck no."

"So you still want to hang out with me? I didn't ruin our friendship?"

He contemplated my features. "Maybe it's ruined cuz now I don't wanna be just friends." He put his hand on my leg and squeezed. "But, Jeanie, I'll do whatever you need. If you want me to go away, I'll go away. If you want me around, I'll be around. If you just wanna be friends..." he shrugged, "we'll be friends."

I searched his eyes. "But what do *you* need? Seems unfair that our relationship revolves around my needs only." (especially considering I couldn't even figure out what they were yet).

His eyebrows rose, and he hesitated, words waiting on the tip of his tongue. After a pause, he exhaled them away and gazed down at me, his mouth stretching into a suggestive smile. He set his coffee cup down on his nightstand and then took mine and did the same before lifting me onto his lap. I put my arms around his neck, and my eyes widened as he whispered his list of lustful needs into my ear. When my excited grin had reached peak fullness, he kissed my cheek. "And I need a fucking shower."

I laughed and wiggled against the wetness that bloomed between my legs. I whispered back, "I need all of those things, too." He slid out from under the covers and carried me with him to the bathroom.

The slippery lather made it difficult to stay focused on the task at hand, but the overall result was the same. The soapy bubbles were rubbed over every inch of our bodies as we stroked and slid against each other. If I'd been a scrub brush, the shower would've been sparkling by the time Sam finished pushing me up and fucking me against each surface. We went from smearing handprints on the steamy glass door to me shoving him down on the bed with barely a break to towel off in between. Sam went over the edge first, and all it took was watching the veins pop out along his tensed muscles before I followed, head thrown back and a flood of expletives gushing from my mouth.

When I'd recovered, I stroked the fingerprints he'd left on my thighs and hips and sighed. "I wish I felt a little bit of pain, just to balance out the pleasure."

He brushed his fingers over the red marks. "I'll have to rein it in when you lose that power."

I slid down his body until my head rested on his chest. My fingers traced lazy circles along his tattoos. "You mean in the unlikely event that Olita releases me?"

He stroked my hair. "I'm gonna make sure she does."

The rumble of his voice was soothing, and my thoughts drifted. What if my life wasn't bound to a psycho demon? Would I be able to open myself up again and have a relationship that went beyond the realm of simple physical pleasure? The thought put an uncomfortable lump in my throat.

I sat up and straddled him, staring down at his upper body and running my fingers along the contours of his muscles. "I'm going to have a full-time job trying to keep all the beautiful women away from you now."

He laughed. "Nah. I'm not interested in other women." I pursed my lips, and he shook his head. "Ah, Jeans, I wish you could see how beautiful you are."

He raised a hand and stroked my cheek, and I shook my head as a hot flush crept up my neck. It was mostly embarrassment but also disbelief and a tiny iota of delight (though I'd never admit it). He pushed himself up so his back was against the headboard and pulled me closer. My eyes had a hard time meeting his.

He sighed. "You're my type, even if you're not your own. I dunno what your ideal of beauty is, but I found mine." His hands drifted along my waist, and I looked away and chewed my lip, feeling too exposed and vulnerable. He sensed my discomfort and lifted my hand from his chest and kissed it before tipping me off him. I landed in a giggling heap at his side.

He propped his head on his hand. "I dunno how to explain it. It's like..." he paused and scanned the room, hoping to pull the right words from the air around us. "You know when there's a random pattern like in the leaves of a tree or the grain on wood?" I cocked an eyebrow—this was going somewhere interesting. "And when you really look at it, your eyes start to pick out shapes like an animal or a face and then when you look again, you can't unsee it? That's what you're like, Jeanie; once you popped out from the background noise, I knew I'd never see anything else."

I felt my cheeks turn an embarrassing shade of red, so I buried my face in his chest to hide them. He ran a gentle hand up and down my back, and I fought the urge to cry. Ugh, why did I want to cry? I couldn't bring myself to believe him. Stupid media, training me to think I'd never be pretty enough. Stupid me for thinking I'd never find another person who thought I was beautiful again.

After letting out a long, centering breath, I pulled away from his chest. "How did you know to come to the bar last night?"

He chuckled and reached for his phone. "My new best friend, Kaytee, texted. She musta got my number from your phone."

He pulled up the message and showed me:

> Sam, this is Kaytee. If you're into Jeanie, you
> better get your ass down to the karaoke bar and

tell her before she works you out of her system. If
you're not into her, then you're a fucking idiot.

He'd texted back:

See you soon.

I laughed and sat up. "Fucking Kaytee. I guess I owe her one."
He ruffled my hair. "Not as much as I owe her."
My pleased smile turned into a frown when I glanced down at my torn dress on the floor. "Shit, I forgot my phone at the bar last night."
Sam grinned and slipped out of bed to rifle through his pants. "Kaytee gave it to me when I showed up." He tossed it to me.
I shook my head. "That woman is a smooth operator." He pulled on some sweats, kissed my cheek, and grabbed our coffee cups before heading back to the kitchen.
I texted her:

Dearest Kaytee, thank you for instigating some
of the best fucking of my life, but also how dare
you. lol jk.

Kaytee texted back:

You're welcome! Also, change your phone
settings so it locks sooner. You never know
who's going to be getting into your business
when you're off doing your business.

I chuckled and sent her a thumbs-up emoji. The woman had a point, and I spent the next few minutes tightening up my phone's security before Sam walked back in. He tossed Jackson's knife on the bed.
"You recognize this knife? I found it in the driveway when I pulled up to your demon party."
"Oh yeah! I forgot about it. Thanks for grabbing it."
He stared at me, and I realized I hadn't told him about the accidental swapping of Olita's knife for Jackson's. I squirmed—this was going to get me in trouble. "Um, it's Jackson's knife."

His eyes widened, and his chest expanded more with each breath. "You mean you've been walking around with Jackson fucking Greene's knife?"

I winced. "Yeah, he took Olita's knife, and I thought I was getting it back, but it turned out to be his instead."

The color drained from his cheeks. "Do you know how much danger you're in with this?"

My body tensed, anticipating his anger, and I lowered my eyes. "Sorry. I kind of forgot about it with all the other stuff going on."

His head bobbed up and down in a slow nod, and he walked out of the bedroom and into the kitchen. Something shattered. Then something else. Uh oh. Unsure what to do, I slid out of bed and attempted to put on my torn-up dress. As I was reaching around to see if there was any way of closing the broken zipper, he walked in and saw me.

"What're you doing? You're not going anywhere til I can figure out how to keep you safe from that psychopath." His voice was even, but there was an edge to it.

"Um..." The straps slid off my shoulders, and I pulled them up again. "Just checking the extent of the damage."

He sighed before walking over and putting his arms around me. "We'll go to your place and grab whatever you need then come back here." He stiffened. "Fuck, it's probably not safe for you here, either. Jackson might have spies watching us."

The mention of Jackson's spies triggered a sharp inhale. "Do you think it's my fault that Rossi attacked Dram's family?"

Sam pulled away and looked me in the eye. "No. Jackson must be plotting to ascend to archangel level. He's tryna take out the competition and install angels that are weaker and loyal to him. But it means he's watching this area, and if he could find Dram's well-hidden family, then he can definitely figure out where you're living and what you get up to. Even if he doesn't know your real name."

"He doesn't know where I'm from, either."

"But he has Olita's knife. It's possible he traced it back to her. Or he could have pictures or video of you that he's shared with his network."

I contemplated the shadows of the trees as they danced across the wall. "I don't suppose he would leave me alone if I just gave it back to him?"

He shook his head. "I doubt he's the forgiving type." He walked over to the window and peeked behind the curtain. "He'll do whatever it takes to get it back and then punish you for taking it."

"But he probably has more than one, right? Like Olita does? So he doesn't *really* need this one."

"He probably does, but needing it for ascension isn't the issue. Another divine having any of your knives is dangerous. They could have you killed remotely and then ascend by claiming the second knife as their own."

"What, like a drone strike?" I raised my eyebrow and shot him a skeptical look.

He turned from the window. "You'd be surprised what the higher levels get up to. Human governments and their armies are nothing but pawns to 'em. They have no problem using drone strikes, elite forces, all-out wars even. They're ruthless and use every advantage they can."

"So...if we kill Jackson remotely, then you could ascend? Or Olita?"

"Sure, but we don't have that kinda stuff. Not even Olita does, and she's loaded."

I frowned and sat down on the bed. "Maybe I should send him the knife and disappear. Why would he waste time trying to find me if I don't pose a threat?"

Sam shook his head, unconvinced. "It might work for a bit, but he *will* come for you eventually. If for no other reason than to make an example of you for anyone else who might consider crossing him."

I flopped back on the bed in defeat and stared at the ceiling. "But...if Jackson traces Olita's knife back to her, then he'll assume she has his and go after her. We could even lie and tell him she has it."

"Yeah, but then he'll kill her, and I'm not gonna let that happen. Not til we lift the curse she put on you."

I lifted my head. "If we give Olita Jackson's knife, it would help her take him down, wouldn't it? If she wins, she'll lift the curse."

Sam watched me, unconvinced. "Maybe."

"We could help her."

He shook his head. "Still too risky." His gaze shifted away, and he paused. When he spoke again, his voice was tentative. "I've got an idea for how to deal with the curse, but I'm gonna need more power to do it."

I sat up. "How are you going to get incubi blood in Olita's territory?"

His blue eyes sparkled as he smiled. "Very carefully."

He stepped to the foot of the bed and pulled me up to standing. "First, we'll get your stuff and do our best to shake any tails, then we'll go scouting for incubi. After that, I'm gonna lock you down somewhere I can keep an eye on you."

I raised an eyebrow. "Lock me down? Sounds pretty exciting."

He gave me a lazy smile and wrapped a hand around my throat to pull me close before whispering into my ear, "You won't be going anywhere when I'm done with you."

28

SAM PARKED THE car in one of the sketchier neighborhoods south of Seattle and shifted into his wary street mode. We were on the hunt for Dimitri and a woman named Rani, the divine Sam had given Mara's knife to. We found Dimitri within ten minutes; he was threatening a scrappy goblin man behind a boarded-up building. When Sam started toward the pair, Dimitri whirled to face him, teeth bared, until he saw who it was. He released his grip, and the goblin promptly took off.

Dimitri sauntered over to us, shoulders square and menacing. "Hey, Shady, this ain't your territory." He stopped outside of arm's reach and looked Sam over. "The fuck? You a demon now? But Olita's still alive."

Sam stared back. "Yeah. I'm here to collect on that favor you owe me."

Dimitri shifted from foot to foot. "You know I would, but Olita will skin me alive."

Sam shrugged. "Won't be anything left to skin if you're already dead."

Dimitri considered his limited options before letting out a puff of defeat. With wary caution, he peered around before motioning us over to a beat-up dumpster enclosure. He pulled his arm out of his coat and offered it to Sam. "Make it quick."

I turned and studied the graffiti on the boarded-up windows and rotten siding of the adjacent building. It was all boring black, white, and blue scrawls of gang tags, names, and other random garbage. I shook my head; no one took pride in their work anymore.

When Sam was done, he put his hand on my shoulder and guided me away. Dimitri called out behind us, "Okay, Shady, it's open season on you now. No more favors." Sam gave him a thumbs-up without bothering to turn around.

We headed east to poke around in another of Seattle's slummy pockets, hoping to find Rani. It took a lot longer to track her down. After trudging up and down countless streets and questioning every goblin we came across, we finally found her. She was sitting on a sagging couch in a dark and dilapidated squatter house, surrounded by a group of five people in varying stages of inebriation. The assortment of liquor bottles, bongs, crack pipes, and pill containers on the coffee table made me itchy for a hit. Her drooping head lifted with a slow and lazy wobble when she noticed Sam's looming presence.

"Hey, Rani, time to pay me back."

Still in the depths of a drug daze, her deep-set brown eyes only blinked in confused acknowledgement. The two men sitting next to her sobered up enough to pull guns out of their jeans and hold them casually on their knees. I took a closer look at her companions and noticed the bandanas and face tattoos. During my stints in squats and sketchy apartments, I'd avoided going anywhere near gang members. Super unpredictable. Now, with no fear, the encounter felt no more dangerous than entering enemy territory in a video game.

I quietly hummed the Jeopardy song twice through before the rest of the group started to shift around and come to life. Sam ignored them and continued staring at Rani, pulling open his jacket to get easy access to his knife. She squinted at him—something was finally getting through to her.

"Shady?" She took a moment to examine him before drawing her head back in surprise. "Demon now? Does that mean Olita is…" She drew a finger across her throat.

Sam shook his head. "Not yet."

Her thick eyebrows furrowed. "What are you doing here, then?"

"Cashing in on the favor you owe me." He mimed slicing a knife across the inside of his elbow.

Rani's gaze darted around the room, taking in the increasingly menacing alertness of her friends. Her eyes narrowed in calculation before going vague again after studying Sam for several long breaths. She gestured for the others to lower their weapons before she stood and pointed us to the door.

We followed her outside to a backyard surrounded by chain link and huge brambles of blackberries. "I don't have much power yet, Shady. Bad start and not enough goblins in my area." She shrugged. "Take what you need and we're even, alright?"

Sam nodded and pulled out his knife. I turned to the adjacent house and admired the rendering of an enormous dick and balls done in colorful spray paint. Finally, some real art.

Two of Rani's companions watched us with narrowed eyes from the rotting front porch as we walked out of the backyard. "All good, Rani?" one of them asked.

She hesitated before responding, "All good, Hash."

The desire for violent retribution against trespassers hung heavy in the air as their gazes followed us down the street. I chuckled. Compared to Sam, they seemed like children.

We made our way back to the car, Sam deep in thought as he considered our next move. I contemplated the assortment of broken old houses squeezed between fancy new townhomes as we walked. The ridiculously high asking prices listed on the For Sale signs heralded the coming wave of gentrification. My brain switched over to expensive properties.

"Do you think anyone would look for us at Dram's place on Bainbridge?"

Sam's eyebrows drew up, and he tilted his head in thought before nodding. "That's a good idea." He squeezed my shoulder affectionately. "I can see why I keep you around. Let's get info from Kaytee first."

I put her on speakerphone once we were in the car. "Hey, Kaytee, I've got Sam here. We're hoping to ask you a few questions."

I could practically hear her eyebrow raise. "Okay, what's up?"

"It's about Dram's house on Bainbridge."

Sam chimed in, "Are there security cameras there? If so, have you been watching 'em?"

Kaytee's slow response was laced with curiosity. "Yes, there are, and yes, I have. Mind if I ask why you want to know?"

"We're hoping to stay there and lie low for a bit." My eyes met Sam's. "There's somebody I've pissed off and need to avoid until we figure out how to deal with the situation."

Her voice dripped with sarcasm. "You? piss someone off? Well, the cameras haven't caught anything, and the alarm system hasn't been tripped. I'm assuming whoever gave Antonio Rossi the intel knows the family is no longer there."

"Do you mind asking Dram if we can stay there?"

She laughed. "I don't need to ask him; he'll say yes."

Sam wrote down the key and alarm codes before thanking her and hanging up. "Want to take a trip to a beautiful island getaway?" I asked him.

"I'd take a trip to an ugly urban getaway if it means I get to ravage your beautiful body til you tell me to stop."

Heat flushed my cheeks. "Sounds like a date."

Dram had called when we were en route to Bainbridge Island and told us to make ourselves at home. As far as he was concerned, the place was ours since his family wouldn't be safe there for the foreseeable future. He apologized in advance for the mess they left behind in their rush to pack and flee to safety.

Once we were inside the house, I wanted to book myself into jail for all the privacy violations I was committing. My chest tightened in a physical manifestation of my mental discomfort. It didn't feel right to be there when the family wasn't around and be privy to the personal items and messes that make a house a home: piles of laundry on the floor, a collection of dirty shoes by the back door, framed family pictures on the walls, children's artwork on the fridge.

Sam unloaded the groceries while I investigated the bedroom situation. I glanced into the guest room where Dram had questioned Carlos. Spots of red stood out on the white pillowcase above the rumpled covers. Not there. I went upstairs next and closed the doors to the kids' rooms as I walked by—the hurricane aftermath of toys, books, and clothes strewn about put a lump in my throat. I vowed to pack things up and send them via Kaytee as a thank you.

The last room at the end of the hallway was the primary suite. More uncomfortable pangs shot through my chest when I took in the bits of clothing scattered on the floor and hanging out of open drawers. The Nguyens had left a whole life behind. Still, the king-size bed was the siren song I'd been waiting for.

As I finished tidying up the mess and changing the sheets, Sam brought our suitcases in and placed them by the dresser. He eyed the bed and then shifted his gaze to me. My heart pounded in response to his spreading smile. I skipped over and put my arms around his waist. "Want to fuck on an angel's bed?"

"Yeah. Then I wanna fuck all over an angel's house, an angel's yard, an angel's garage—"

"Don't forget the boat."

He grinned. "Definitely on an angel's boat and far enough out on the water to fuck in front of all the angel's neighbors." I giggled as he picked me up and heaved me onto the bed before taking off his shirt and rubbing his hands together. "Lots to do! Better get started."

29

AFTER CHECKING AN impressive number of items off our to-do list, we sat down to dinner. Thankfully, Sam had cooked. If I had, we would've been sitting down to a meal sourced exclusively from the canned goods and frozen-food aisles. Instead, we enjoyed a delicious salmon served alongside crispy potatoes and tender asparagus.

"Oh my god, Sam, this is amazing!" I exclaimed after a taste, my fork already loaded with the next bite. A soft blush crept up his cheeks, and he took a deliberate sip of wine so he wouldn't have to acknowledge the compliment. A tactic I was very familiar with.

After my last bite, I leaned back in my chair, hands rubbing my stomach, and let out a deep, satisfied breath. "Do you moonlight as a chef when you're not busy serving up pill cocktails?"

He shrugged. "I dabble. I've been alive for eighty-four years. You pick up stuff when you got the time."

My open jaw shifted from surprised to amused. "Eighty-four years old? You're over twice my age, you pervert."

He pointed his fork at me. "I'm not the only pervert in this house." He wiped his mouth and put his napkin down, expression thoughtful. "Does it bother you? That I'm that old?"

I pursed my lips and let my gaze drift unseeing along the framed photos of Dram's family on the wall. "No? I already assumed you were older than me." I shrugged. "As long as you don't talk down to me, and your you-know-what works, then I don't really give a shit." I stretched my foot under the table to poke him on the inside of his thigh for emphasis. Warmth flooded my cheeks at his hungry grin. "How old is that in human years?" I asked. "I don't get how you guys age."

"We just age slower. Once we hit puberty, our aging slows by about half. With each ascension, it slows down even more. Maeve told me the god rank ages backwards, in looks, anyway." He glanced up to do silent calculations in his head. "I guess I'm about low to mid-forties in human years."

"Perfect! Although, that means eventually I'll be the gross, old pervert." It was a joke, but as soon as I said it, my heart sank. I didn't know if it was because my subconscious slip revealed part of me wanted to be in a relationship with Sam for that long, or if it was because I'd reminded myself I might not live long enough to find out. Probably both. I gulped the rest of my wine before standing up to clear the dishes.

When I moved to take his plate, Sam placed a hand on my waist and drew me close. I tensed, waiting for him to say something too sweet or optimistic about my life's current projected outlook. He just gave me a gentle squeeze before letting go and didn't stop me when I stacked the rest of the dishes and carried them to the kitchen.

I stared at my reflection in the dark window over the sink for a long time. The shadows and highlights cast by the dim pendant light hid the details of my face—an accurate mirror of my current self: a couple of bright spots but mostly intangible darkness, a muddied past with only the barest glimpse of hope in my unknown future.

My melancholy had softened into a gentle ennui by the time I finished cleaning up. I found Sam at the table with the *Magia Deorum* in front of him, utterly engrossed in its pages. When I sat down, he tore his gaze away and looked up at me with a soft smile.

"What's up with this book?" I asked him.

He leaned back and tapped his finger on the page. "It's very rare. Maeve told me there are only a few copies left in the world. It has spells and shit that've been lost over the last millennia. The previous god wanted 'em destroyed cuz he was afraid the knowledge could be used to overthrow him. This might be the only copy outside a library of the top ranks."

I whistled. "Sounds pretty important; I can see why Olita would want it."

Sam nodded, eyes unfocused on the page in front of him. "Yeah."

Whoops. The uncomfortable tightness in my throat didn't go away after I cleared it. "So, um, have you found anything useful?"

"Some." He frowned as he flipped through the pages. "There's a lot here, and I'm pretty rusty with the language. It's taking longer to get through than I thought." He lifted his chin at me. "This is how I found out about the blood curse Olita put on you. Before that, I was looking for ways to weaken her so I could kill her."

"Did you find anything?"

He gave his face a dejected rub. "Most of the stuff in here is trickier than I'd hoped. It mentions a lotta old magic shit I've never heard of. Plus, Olita had the book for over seventy years and probably memorized the whole thing. Knowing her, even if I found a spell to weaken her, she'll already have something in place to block it." He shook his head. "Not that it matters right now. My biggest priority is to lift the curse she put on you." His eyes softened, and the corner of his mouth lifted in a half-smile. "That idea I mentioned? I think there's a good chance it'll work."

I raised an eyebrow. "Really? I thought we needed the blood vessel thing to do that." I noticed the phrasing of what I'd said and laughed. "You divines are terrible when it comes to naming things. Blood vessel." I shook my head.

He chuckled. "I know, right?" He paused and looked down at the page covered in flowing script and archaic symbols, brow furrowed. "I dunno if I'll have enough power, but I wanna try it in the morning, if that's okay with you?"

I shrugged. "Sure. It's not like you can make it any worse."

I went to bed early and lay in awkward silence while Sam slid in beside me. Despite my best efforts to dispel it, the gloom from earlier was still eating at me. I was unsure of both my present and my future, and couldn't figure out where Sam fit into the picture. I enjoyed spending time with him and loved having sex with him, but my emotions were starting to worry me. It didn't seem right to have feelings for someone else when I was still mourning my husband. If I loved Tom as much as I thought I did, then how could I ever be ready to move on? It felt like a betrayal.

My power did nothing to keep my heart from throbbing painfully when Sam's scent drifted over. I swallowed down the seemingly permanent lump in my throat again. I felt more vulnerable than I had in years. He slid his hand under the covers until it found mine, and more tears surfaced at the sweet gesture. I squeezed it before turning to curl up on my side. He gave my arm a hesitant stroke before shifting away and giving me space. I lay in the dampness of my pillow for a long time.

30

MY BREATH CAUGHT in my throat when I opened my eyes and saw the rumpled sheets where Sam had slept. I rubbed my face with rough strokes and groaned. Last night I shut him out with no explanation. There were no clothes on the floor or dresser, and no noises to indicate anyone was in the house. A frightened bird fluttered in my ribcage, and my common sense vacated the premises. What if he'd left? What if whatever brief fling we had was over? *We've been together for two days, Jeanie; get ahold of yourself.* I pushed my face into my hands. I hadn't even considered the possibility that I might hurt Sam in these untested waters; I should have been more careful.

The aroma of unfamiliar detergent and the ghost of Sam's scent wafted through the air when I threw the covers off and snatched a t-shirt and panties from my suitcase. I froze when a step creaked in the hallway, then let out a shaky sigh of relief when Sam walked in with a mug of coffee a moment later.

"Everything alright?" His eyes were uncertain as they scanned my face.

I nodded and gave him a tentative smile. "I thought you left."

He set the cup down and came over to wrap his arms around me. "Sorry, Jeans, it's gonna take more than a bout of depression to get rid of me." I sank into him, and he stroked my hair. "I've been there plenty of times."

The tense air from my lungs released, and I whispered, "I think I got a little scared." My smile was rueful when I pulled away. "I guess Olita didn't take all my fear." I met his eyes and let him see the uncertainties, hopes, and fears in mine. He dropped his careful mask, and I saw the same in his, too. In them was the lonely boy whose family had been taken from him far too soon. He'd lost everything and been forced into a cruel life of pain, anger, and fear. A sharp pang of sorrow cleaved my chest—had Sam felt loved since?

With tears prickling my eyelids, I reached up and stroked his cheek, following the line of his scar. He closed his eyes at the touch, and I guided his lips down to mine. The kiss was gentle, our fingers caressing each other's cheeks and necks, then more insistent as I tugged him toward the bed and tried to take his shirt off. He took my hungry hands in his and stopped me.

My eyebrows dipped in confusion, and he kissed my cheek. "Let me make you breakfast first."

Sam sat me down at the table next to him, the book open in front of us. He pulled his finger across a few lines of text, whispering under his breath, before turning to me. "Okay, Jeans, I just need you to sit still and relax." He took my wrist, closed his eyes, and chanted quiet words in the gravelly language of the divines.

At first nothing happened, but then a red glow shone through my skin beneath his fingers and brightened as it traveled into his hand. The light dispersed as it flowed up through his arm until it was no longer visible. I frowned.

When he opened his eyes, I peered into them. "What did you just do, exactly?"

He looked down at my hand cradled in his. "I replaced the cursed blood in you with my own." My body froze in shock, and my mouth gaped open. "I'm sorry. It was the only way I could think of to save you. I dunno exactly what'll happen to you if Olita dies. You might be in pain for a while, but you won't die with her."

My heart kicked into high gear, and I wrenched my hand from his, tears gathering on my lashes. "How could you?" It was a hoarse whisper. His eyebrows drew together, eyes pleading as I stood up, body trembling. "So now you'll die instead?" I shook my head and backed away. "It wasn't supposed to go like this,

Sam. I can't do this shit again. I can't be left behind again." I hated
the way my face crumpled into sob mode and my voice rose to an
annoying pitch as I yelled, "It's my fucking turn!" I threw my
hands up. "Fuck this. I'm done with all this shit." My feet guided
me to the foyer, and I snatched my purse off the floor. When
Sam's footsteps approached, I thrust a hand out. "I just want to be
alone," I croaked and slammed the door behind me. A more
dramatic touch than strictly necessary, but once the mind decides
to go extra, sometimes you have to let it play out.

The keys were in the center console of the little red convertible,
and it hummed to life before I lowered the top. I didn't bother
thinking it through before I opened the garage door and peeled
out of the driveway. It took a few stops and starts before I got the
feel of the car and started enjoying myself. There are very few
things in which I would consider myself an expert, but
dissociating in times of trouble happens to be one of my
specialties. Sudden tantrums that involve running away from
problems are another. A thrift shop in town caught my eye, and I
slammed on the brakes to make a U-turn. A dramatic drive
deserved dramatic attire.

Pleased with my purchases, I strolled to the car in a tight black
dress, enormous sunglasses, and a luxurious designer scarf to tie
around my hair. I cursed when I got a nasty paper cut from the
receipt and dripped blood onto the silk. Oh well, it just added to
the drama. I took to the road like an aging beauty queen on her
way to loot the property of her philandering husband's estate.

I turned back north, opting for the bridge to the mainland
rather than the ferry. It seemed a shame not to hit the open
highway and see what the lively little car could do. Taking the
bridge meant a long detour around the Puget Sound, dropping
south to Tacoma before heading north again to Seattle. I didn't
mind. It had been years since I'd done any serious driving, and
focusing on the road and scenery was working wonders for
clearing my head. I stopped for lunch along the way and grabbed
some necessary Jeanie-going-off-on-her-bullshit supplies. Alcohol
and cigarettes would have to suffice since opiates and LSD would

be nigh on impossible to come by on short notice. Especially after ditching my dealer to indulge myself in an unwarranted, over-the-top tantrum.

It was late afternoon by the time I made it to Seattle and found myself at the cemetery. I contemplated Tom's headstone until tears blurred my vision. Before they gathered enough momentum to fall, I blinked them away and unwrapped the scarf from my hair and spread it out on the ground to sit on. The brown paper bag crinkled around the neck of the wine bottle when I reached into my purse and pulled it out. It was no acid trip, but chugging rosé before pouring a stream onto my dead husband's grave seemed an appropriate way to end the day.

The stone was warm when I traced the lines of his name with my finger. "Well, Tommy, I'm back." I lit a cigarette and blew out a long plume of smoke. "Things are getting out of control and I have no idea what to do, What's new, right?"

I gazed out over the cemetery between swigs, watching the other mourners come and go with heavy steps. More people should bring booze and weed to graveyards. The funeral home would make a killing if they opened up a stand in the parking lot.

I stubbed out my first cigarette, lit a new one, and leaned back on my elbows, legs stretched out on the itchy grass. "Was I good for you, Tom? I mean, sometimes I wonder if we loved each other a little *too* much. Co-dependency and all that shit." I stared off at the hazy skyline until the long tail of ash fell from my forgotten cigarette. I dropped it and laced my hands behind my head. "What if it was just luck that we rode the ups and downs at the same time? Maybe we would've fallen out of sync eventually, or you would have gotten healthy enough to leave me behind." My shaking hand brushed away my tears as I whispered my biggest shame to the sky. "I held you back from who you could have been." I fished a tissue out of my purse and blew my nose before sitting up and finishing the bottle with one long string of gulps.

The glare of the midday sun softened into the golden rays of evening as I smoked cigarette after cigarette while my mind danced carefully around memories of the last years of my life with

Tom. Despite our deep love for each other, tiny cracks had appeared in the foundation of our relationship: unexplained bouts of silence, moments of uncertainty when we kept our thoughts from each other, the growing pile of unfulfilled promises to seek help for my mental illness and addictions. I had assumed there would be time to address the problems later—until later became irrelevant with Tom's diagnosis.

I tread most cautiously around the dark thought that lay like a sleeping dragon atop the pile of my pain and guilt. Would our marriage have come to a slow and painful end if fate hadn't intervened? Instead of bitter ashes, I was left with a perfect specimen of our love locked forever in amber, never changing, never dying—a bittersweet reminder of the beautiful gift I was given but never deserved.

When my pack of cigarettes was gone and sobriety had slunk back in, I pulled out my phone. There was a text from Sam, and another coin of guilt was tossed onto my towering pile:

> *I'm so sorry. I did what I thought was right.*
> *Can we talk about it?*

I put my head in my hands and wondered if Sam had felt the same impotent outrage when he figured out that Olita had cursed me. I wanted to be mad at him for what he'd done, but I couldn't —I would have done the same. The long drive had given me time to contemplate the source of my anger. I was ready to die. I'd been preparing myself for death ever since cancer took the one thing in my life worth living for, and then welcomed its inevitability once I found myself twisted up in the world of murderous divines. Now I was suddenly free of that fate, as though the universe was aching to see what new lows I'd sink to when I watched another person I cared about die. Because now there was nothing in the way of Sam killing Olita, and I wasn't sure I could stop him.

I replied:

> *Sorry I bailed. I needed to process a lot of stuff.*
> *Can we talk tomorrow?*

He texted back within a minute:

Absolutely. Whatever you need.

Ugh. Of course he would make it about *my* needs. My heart performed a painful flip when I thought back to the moment of open vulnerability that passed between us that morning. I tilted my head up to the sky and let out a long breath. So far, my midlife crisis was definitely playing out as a repeat of the tumultuous, hormone-addled affairs of my early years. For as old as I was, I felt a lot like a teenager trying to navigate the strange world of elation mixed with doubt that results when two people fall for each other.

My gaze drifted back to Tom's headstone. The petals from my previous bouquet twirled and danced across its surface in the gentle breeze. Their carefree beauty strummed a beautiful note from a long-lost string in my heart. "I was once like you," I whispered. Maybe I could be again. After all, stranger things have happened. Waking up to find I'd become a demon's assistant was proof enough of that concept.

31

IN THE REMNANTS of my receding dream, a young Tom stood, his grin dazzling in the sun, arms open wide as he gazed across the distant mountains from the rocky peak we used to hike. It hurt to remember the days at the beginning of our life together, when our love seemed like it would be enough to overcome anything, but it was a sweet kind of pain. With my eyes squeezed shut, I tried to hold on to the overwhelming emotion of the dream: openness. The memory of his beatific face was a reminder that life could be lived with an open heart or a closed one, a curious heart or a fearful one.

Goosebumps erupted on my skin. Another message from Tom from beyond the grave. I hadn't become the fearless woman I could've been when I was with him, but I'd felt her lurking in the shadows during my bouts of depression and then holding me steady through my manic phases. Now I was her, at least on a superficial level. It was time to embrace her fully and open myself up to the truth that was getting too loud to ignore: I wanted Sam, all of him. Fuck the specter of death that hung over us both—I was ready to let myself fall in love again.

Refreshed and rejuvenated, I checked out of the hotel and found a quiet cafe for breakfast. As I was finishing my pancakes, my phone chimed with a reminder that I had a video call with Olita in ten minutes. I groaned and threw cash on the table before heading to the car for privacy.

"Hello, Ms. Cummings, how are you?"

Her mouth didn't budge from its solid horizontal position. "I hope you have more to report today."

I took a deep breath. "Olita, I need out of this arrangement. I don't care how much pain you put me in or what you do to me, I'm not going to kill Dram."

Her eyes pierced through the small screen of my phone. "I'm sorry to hear that. Unfortunately, I can't release you. This is a do-or-die situation."

I knew the chance had been slim that she'd free me at my request, but it was worth a shot. "Okay, kill me, then."

Her mouth drew up a fraction, and she shook her head. "Perhaps someday, dear Jeanie, but lucky for you, it's not in the cards...yet." Her smile turned sickeningly sweet. "However, I have been keeping an eye on your beautiful sister-in-law and her charming son for you. It would be a shame if something unfortunate happened to them."

A jolt of icy hatred shot up my spine. Hatred and something like the clammy hand of fear. My nostrils flared, and I hissed through a tight jaw, "Don't you dare touch them or I'll kill you myself."

She laughed and wiped away an imaginary tear of amusement. "And sacrifice yourself? How noble. You would never manage it, but I would love to see you try."

As I stared at her vile face, a dim bulb flickered on in my head. "What if I captured Dram for you?" She cocked an eyebrow. "I won't kill him, but I can trap him so you can do it with your own evil hands. Would you release me then?"

Her eyes narrowed as she considered my offer. "If you can capture him, which I highly doubt you could, then I would consider it. There could be no room for error, though. No tricks, no surprises, and a guarantee that he will be in a condition where I can kill him easily."

I nodded slowly—time to extemporize. "I found out he's married." Olita's head pulled back in surprise. "And I know for a fact he'd do anything to save his husband. If I capture his husband, I can capture Dram." Her mouth fought against an amused smile as she stared at me through the screen. "Come on,

Olita, what kind of captivity situation would you need? You want him locked up in a room? In chains? Drugged?"

She snickered. "Oh, this is too good."

"Just tell me and I'll do it. You're a powerful demon and he's a weak angel, so I know you can kill him if he's immobilized. This is going to be the best chance I can give you."

Her eyes were narrow and calculating as she leaned away from the camera. She contemplated my offer for a solid minute before rubbing her temples with a sigh. "Fine. I'll prepare a space and send you an address. If you lock him up alone without his assistants, and I succeed in my ascension, then I will release you."

My shoulders sagged in relief. "Done. Once I've checked out the space, I'll need a day or two to set the trap and will contact you when I have him."

She gave me an uncanny stare that made it seem like she was right in front of me and not a small digital head in my hand. "Very well, Jeanie. But remember, if you blow this opportunity, I have no problem relieving you of the last remnants of family you have left."

The screen went black.

The afterimage of her smug face made me want to smash my phone into the steering wheel and then get out and smash every window in the car. I took deep breaths before closing my eyes and reviewing my situation. I had the barest beginnings of a plan that may or may not work and thus may or may not result in the death of my remaining family and the man I was beginning to love. Just another day in the life of Jeanine Bennett. C'est la fucking vie.

32

I'D BEEN SITTING on the bench in Cal Anderson Park for about fifteen minutes before a familiar figure ambled up the path toward me. He was looking pretty damn sexy in his bomber jacket and jeans. Several women turned to check him out as he walked past, and a pang of jealousy flared up, but also pride. Keep walking, ladies—this one was mine. Maybe. Sam draped his arm over the back of the bench as he sat down six inches away, face unreadable. He was waiting for my lead.

I met his eye before scooting closer and laying my head on his shoulder. "Everything is so completely fucked."

He gave my shoulder a reassuring squeeze. "This is some déjà vu shit right here. Wanna talk about it?"

The sky was a hazy blue when I looked up and took a deep breath. "I spoke with Olita this morning." He stiffened. "She's upped the ante. Now if I can't get her Dram's blood, she's threatening to kill my sister-in-law and nephew. And if I try to take her out in order to protect them, then I'll end up killing you." I groaned. "So lovely that I get to make a Sophie's Choice. Not exactly the exclusive club I dreamed of joining."

I leaned forward and put my head in my hands.

He ran a hand up and down my back and cleared his throat quietly. "If it's any consolation, I got the only woman I've really cared about in seventy years involved in some of the worst shit my kind has to offer. All while thinking I was helping you by ripping you outta the life you chose cuz I thought I could give you something better."

I peered up at him and matched his sardonic smile. "Well, I've been a moody and unpredictable lover who bungled things up with the only man I've cared about in the last two years. We're really good for each other, aren't we?"

"One of us," he tapped my back, "is good for the other, but it seems to be a one-way street. And you didn't bungle anything." He rubbed a hand over his face. "Jesus Christ, every time I tell you I'm not gonna let you get hurt, I end up hurting you more."

I sat up and met his eyes. "Sam, you haven't hurt me. Not any more than I've been hurting myself for the last few years, anyway. Yes, you ended up getting me involved in some serious shit, but I know you didn't do it intentionally, and I believe you did it because you wanted something better for me." My gaze shifted down to the hand in his lap, and I took it in my own, tracing the tattoos with my thumb. "I get why you did what you did yesterday. If I'd had the chance to take Tom's cancer away, even if it meant me dying instead, I would've in a heartbeat." I winced. "Uh, not that we're, like, together, or you lo—um, anyway…"

His arm came around my shoulders and hugged me to him, his breath soft against my temple. "Jeanie, You mean so much to me, and I'm gonna do everything I can to protect you and your family. I'm not sure my word means much anymore, but I'll do whatever it takes to redeem myself."

I pulled away and smiled up at him. "I'm going to do whatever it takes to protect you, too. I have some very tenuous strands of a plan coming together for how to get the vessel so we can destroy it and break the curse." He raised an eyebrow, and I laid out my idea of setting a trap for Olita by using Dram as bait. "She said if I lock him up in such a way that she can kill him herself, then she'll release me. I'm pretty sure she's lying, but it'll give us a chance to get the vessel from her, at least. I don't know how to do it without putting everyone in danger, but that seems to be the name of the game for you divines."

Sam scratched at the stubble on his chin. "It's not a bad plan, and it's something we can at least prepare for."

We sat in silence and watched the people go by. College students played frisbee on the lawn, tweakers hovered in the shade of the reservoir building, kids shouted as they waded through the shallow water. A breeze blew Sam's scent over to me, and my breath hitched with longing. I put my hand on his knee and slid it to the inside of his thigh as he ran playful fingers along my neck.

I stretched up to whisper in his ear, "I know Jackson might be watching your place, but do you want to go there and fuck like animals?"

A wide grin spread across his face as he lowered his eyes to my mouth. "You read my fucking mind."

We ended up breaking quite a few items in Sam's apartment. Coffee cups smashed into pieces when he swept them off the kitchen counter and set me in their place before dropping to his knees and spreading my legs apart. A vase wobbled off a shelf and shattered when he bent me over the table and proceeded to shake the entire room. Fractured glass from framed artworks glinted on the wood floor after he had me up against the wall. A lamp on the nightstand toppled over and snapped in half when the bed screeched along the floor and pinned it behind the headboard. We didn't go easy on each other, either. I left dark and angry fingernail marks down his back and neck, and he left bruises in the shape of handprints on my hips and thighs. With a final, rapturous release, I let go of the animal rage at being cornered and at the mercy of an evil woman.

More of the darkness dissipated when I splayed myself out next to him and pondered the ceiling. "You know what, Sam? I don't regret anything. I know where I'd be if you hadn't swept me up in all this, and it was a horrible, dark, and depressing place. You gave me the chance to see the light again, and I'm thankful." I turned my head and smiled at him.

He returned my smile. "You know what, Jeanie? Ditto."

My gaze roamed over his handsome face before settling on his lips, and a deep desire took my breath away. When I met his eyes, they radiated the same hunger and longing as my own. I pulled him on top of me, and we made slow and tender love this time, gazing into each other's eyes between passionate kisses. With a breathy crescendo, Sam found release, and I pulsed with pleasure along with him. After another long kiss, he settled in beside me, and I laid my head on his chest.

He stroked my hair and said, "I dunno what's gonna happen to us or where we're gonna end up, but I can't tell you how lucky I am to have met you."

I ran my fingers over his chest and stomach, trying to memorize every muscle. "You know what, Sam? Ditto." I sighed with contentment. "What are the odds that the man who sold me pills to bring me up could do the same thing without the chemical assist? I could've saved a lot of money."

He gently flicked my cheek. "No refunds."

After a break for dinner, we were back at Sam's place. He was poring over the *Magia Deorum* book while I sat across from him with a pen and pad, working on the plan for trapping Olita.

"Sam, what does the blood vessel thing look like?"

He glanced up and took a moment to focus before answering. "It can be anything. The actual vessel looks like a red pea, but most divines put it in something else to disguise it or make it hard to lose. Usually it's jewelry, since the closer it is to the divine, the more powerful the magic for the assistant. Maeve kept hers in a locket she wore round her neck."

"Maeve had an assistant?"

He smiled. "My sister, Bridget."

"Oh." I paused. "If you don't mind my asking, what was her power?"

His smile turned wistful. "She could make anyone laugh."

I stared at him in shock and stumbled through my words. "That's, um...beautiful."

He nodded in agreement. "Maeve said she did it cuz she wanted to spread joy instead of fear and anger."

My eyes teared up when I looked down at my notepad filled with sharp scribbles and angry doodles detailing all the ways I wanted Olita to die. "Maeve was a really incredible woman, wasn't she?"

His voice was soft. "She was. I wish you coulda met her; she woulda loved you." He put a hand over mine, and we smiled at each other. His thumb stroked across my knuckles. "You have any idea where Olita's keeping your vessel?"

I screwed my face up in thought, and the answer hit me. "Her ring. Her big-ass ruby ring. Its got to be." He nodded, and I inclined my head toward the book. "Any luck?"

He let out a dispirited breath. "Not really. But if I can get close enough and force her to stay still, I can transfer the cursed blood back into her. Like the opposite of what I did to you." He frowned down at the book. "There's a spell in here that says it can weaken a divine, but I'm having a hard time figuring it out."

My lips pursed as I mused over potential strategies. "Hmm. When Olita sends me the info on where she wants me to bring Dram, we'll check it out and look for ways to immobilize her so you can take the vessel or swap the blood." He nodded along while I stroked my chin. "And then, of course, we'll have to think through every possible way she might counter us so that we can come up with counter-counters and so on."

"Have you talked to Dram about it yet?"

I sighed down at my notepad. "No, I kind of want a more solid plan before I involve him and Marcus."

"Marcus? Is that Dram's other assistant?"

"Yeah, he can shield himself and others, according to Kaytee."

Sam's eyebrows rose. "A shield? That'll go a long way for us."

I nodded. "If nothing else, he can protect Dram from Olita while we get the vessel. Then Dram can lift the curse once we have it."

He leaned back in his chair and crossed his arms. "I'm gonna need more incubi blood to pull any of this off."

I grimaced. "I don't suppose there are any others that owe you favors around here?"

Sam shook his head. "No, and I'd rather not cross any demons in nearby territories, either. I'm not tryna start a war."

"Where was that Antonio guy from? Missoula? Can you go there and squeeze his guys?"

He chuckled. "I was thinking the same thing. It's risky to head into Jackson's territory, but there aren't a lotta other options. And it might be the last place he'd think to look for you."

I pulled up flights on my phone. "A nonstop from SeaTac to Missoula leaves in two hours. Should I book it for you?"

He stood and walked over to rub my shoulders. "Book it for *us*. I'm not letting you outta my sight again til this is over."

I leaned my head back against his stomach as I completed the transaction. "Done! Let's go mess with some divines in Missoula fucking Montana."

33

"FUCK, THIS IS gonna be a pain in the ass," Sam said as we turned down yet another alley. He seemed unsure of himself as we wandered the streets in one of the shadier parts of Missoula. It was just after midnight, and he wanted to find at least two incubi before heading back to Seattle, but refused to stay for more than a day in case Jackson got wind of me being in his territory.

Despite getting help from several goblins, it took two hours before we finally found an incubus. He was sleeping on a stack of pallets behind a Chinese restaurant near the freeway. When Sam shook him awake, he had the very understandable response of spitting out a string of violent curses and jumping up with his knife swiping at the air. After squinting at Sam, he stepped back out of arm's reach and paused, face shrewd.

"Who the hell are you?" He asked, his voice rasping like he'd been kicked in the neck. My throat cleared in a sympathetic response.

"I'm the new boss in town. Pay up."

Sam was in his element now; his bulky frame seemed to grow larger while his shoulders and stance remained casual. Not an invitation to fight, but a promise that you'd get what you asked for if you crossed him. I bit my lip with excitement when I pictured being on the receiving end of his intimidation act. I made a note to ask how he felt about role-play in the bedroom.

The incubus moved a fraction of an inch, and before I could blink, Sam had him on the ground with his blade to the man's throat. "I can bleed out all your blood, or I can take what I need and tuck you back in bed. Your choice."

The man considered his limited options before going limp. "Fine. You kill that asshole, Antonio, then?"

"Yeah," Sam said as he stood up and pointed his knife at the man's arm. The incubus sighed with resignation before straightening up to complete the deal. When Sam was done, he asked, "Where can I find another one? I'm heading back to where I'm from soon; you probably won't see me again." He grabbed the man's collar and lifted him until his toes skimmed the ground. "Unless you give me bad info. Then I'll find you and end you."

The incubus stuttered as he pointed his finger and gave us directions to a house on the edge of town. Sam dropped him and clapped him on the back. "Night night, don't let the goblins bite."

The next incubus was even easier. She didn't bother putting up a fight and barely registered Sam when she opened the door in rumpled pajamas, her hair a bushy mess around her broad forehead. When Sam asked for blood, she just grumbled and held out her arm. She kept up a string of curses and complaints while he drank. "Fucking no respect. Not like I don't have work tomorrow. Coulda woke my kids. Mother fuckers need some decency."

The sun was still inching its way above the horizon when we stopped by a coffee shop on the way to the airport. We took a seat overlooking the street, and I picked at my muffin and sipped my coffee between yawns. I would have preferred a diner and then bed, but Sam was antsy to leave.

When a perky blond woman walked by, I froze and leaned over to whisper, "I think that was Stacy, Jackson's assistant." I pointed at her petite figure disappearing around the corner.

Sam's voice had an uncharacteristically nervous edge to it. "Did she see you?"

"I don't know. I don't think so? Fuck! What is she doing here?"

He scanned the street. "She could be checking in on Rossi. Jackson mighta sent her if he missed his blood delivery." He grabbed our napkins and half-empty cups and slid off the stool to toss them in the garbage. "Time to get the fuck outta town."

As Sam was unlocking our rental car, I saw her again. This time she was across the street, talking on the phone and staring at us. Her mouth spread into a wicked grin when I met her gaze. She pointed two fingers at her eyes before twisting them around to point at me and mouthed, "I'm watching you."

I turned to Sam as we pulled out and passed her, her face alight with the promise of violence. "Well, I guess she saw me."

As Sam lifted our suitcase from the baggage carousel, a message popped up from Olita with an address and entry instructions for the place she'd prepared. I pulled the map up on my phone and showed it to Sam. It was in a suburb to the southwest of Seattle. The map listed the location as a restaurant, but a quick search revealed it had closed over a year ago. The street view showed a dark storefront in a rundown strip mall.

"Seems like a weird place for a divine showdown."

He shrugged. "It mighta been, or still is, a front for shady business. There could be a decent safe room or basement in there. We'll have to check it out."

My yawn nearly split my face in two. "Ugh. I'm going to need some sleep first. What do you think we should do? Head back to your place?" The encounter with Stacy still had me on edge.

Sam scratched the stubble on his cheek. "Let's go to Bainbridge, just to be safe."

By the time we walked through the front door, my feet were dragging and my jaw was sore from endless yawning. We peeled off our clothes and fell into bed.

It was late afternoon when I woke up. After rubbing my bleary eyes enough to make out basic shapes and colors, I noticed a small red blotch on the pillowcase where my hand had been. Confused, I examined my fingers and found the source. I felt around under the pillowcase for a secret sharp object, but stopped when I remembered my paper cut from the thrift store receipt. It must have snagged on something and reopened. It took a long moment for the realization to hit. I pulled the sheets down; the bruises from our passionate lovemaking were still there.

I turned to Sam and stroked his arm. He woke with a start and snatched the knife tucked under his pillow. When he saw it was me, he relaxed and smiled. "Hey, Jeans."

"Um, we may have a bit of a problem." I twisted and showed him the bruises on my hip. His fingers caressed them until his eyes went wide and he froze. "Maybe your blood doesn't have the same healing power as Olita's? Or it needs the curse to work?"

He shot up. "Fuck!" He pulled his knees in and leaned his elbows on them, head in hands. "How did I not thinka this? I swear to god there's a curse on me too cuz all I can do is hurt you."

I put a reassuring hand on his arm and scooted to face him when he wouldn't meet my eyes. When his fingers curled and dug into the sides of his head, I pulled them away. "Sam, it's going to be okay. Yes, this adds another layer of bullshit, but I'll just avoid torture chambers, knife fights, and getting thrown through glass doors. Easy peasy." He met my eyes with a sorrowful stare and shook his head, defeated. I stroked his cheeks and put my forehead against his. "Whatever happens, we're in this together, okay?"

His eyes were damp when they looked into mine. "Okay."

34

WE CALLED KAYTEE first to give her a rundown of the plan as it stood so far: use Marcus as pretend bait for Dram, use Dram as bait for Olita. She listened in silence and waited a long pause after I finished. She didn't sound surprised when she replied. "Dram expected something like this to come down the pipeline, eventually." The heaviness in her voice gave away that she had hoped it wouldn't. At least not so soon. "He's ready to help any way he can."

I winced at her tone. "I'm really sorry, Kaytee. I never wanted to call in the favor Dram promised. It's just that…" I took a deep breath to steady myself. "Olita is threatening to kill the only family I have left."

She gasped and replied, "Tell me what you need."

"You're good with computers and technology, right?"

"I'm pretty damn good, if I do say so myself."

"Is there a way to find hidden cameras with something other than your eyeballs? I'm sure Olita has this place under surveillance, and I want to get a good idea of all that before we tighten up the plan."

"Hmm, there's a phone app that can scan for devices like cameras or microphones. It's a general scan, though, so you'll need to put eyes on the camera in order to know exactly where it is. How tech savvy do you think Olita is?"

I frowned and looked at Sam. He shrugged and responded, "I dunno; I get the feeling tech isn't her thing, but she probably has a decent understanding. Especially about surveillance."

Kaytee's response was slow and thoughtful. "Well...finding cameras is a start. Based on your plan, I have an inkling the next step is trying to hack them. If we can trick Olita from the get-go, it'll be easier to trap her."

"Ugh, good point. Do you know how to do that?" The added layer of technology was making my head hurt. Whatever happened to the good old days when you could meet someone in a back room and not worry about being spied on by a voyeur across town? Or the entire globe, for that matter.

"It depends. I'll need to get close enough to pick up the Wi-Fi to know for sure." She paused. "It's possible she has them on a cell network, though. That would make this way more difficult." Another pause. "For now, just look for cameras and see if any Wi-Fi networks pop up when you're there."

I let out a breath of relief. "Ok, sounds like something I can handle. Also, thank you and sorry. I hope someday when I call, it'll be about dancing or makeup advice or whatever. Not this shit."

She laughed. "Me too, I'm getting too old for all this."

"Amen," I replied.

We did a slow drive-by of the strip mall before parking a few blocks away. A teriyaki restaurant and nail salon were the only places still in business. The rest of the shops were dark and empty, with hopeless For Lease signs hanging in the boarded-up windows.

When Sam opened his door, I put a hand on his arm. "Do you think Olita knows you're a demon now?"

He furrowed his brow. "Probably. Dimitri or Rani mighta told her, or others in her spy network."

"Maybe you shouldn't come inside with me. If she sees we're working together and you're already a demon, she'll be extra suspicious of the whole setup."

He nodded. "I'll keep an eye out from the street. You have the knife?" I pulled my jacket aside to reveal the ivory handle sticking out from the sheath on my belt. He put a gentle hand on my cheek. "Please be careful."

I smiled. "Always."

Olita's instructions said to enter through the back, so I walked by the shuttered storefront and circled around to the rear lot. The lock made a distinct click when I punched in the code, and the door swung open with a creak. The scent of rancid oil wafted out, and I fumbled along the wall until I found a switch. A buzzing fluorescent light flickered to life and revealed a narrow hallway leading to the front, with crates stacked to one side and two doors to the other. I crept to the end of the hall and peered into the dining area first. Peeling vinyl booths and chipped laminate tabletops gleamed dully in the dim light.

I checked out the two hallway doors next. The first revealed a bathroom with a cracked mirror, broken sink, and moldy toilet. My nose wrinkled when the fermented porta-potty smell wafted out. I quickly shut the door. The other led to the kitchen. Another switch turned on more humming fixtures, and their bluish light revealed dusty counters, scattered boxes, and empty oil jugs. Above one counter was a wide window into the restaurant for cooks to pass orders through. Next to the stove was what I'd been looking for: a large walk-in refrigerator with a metal door that sucked open with a whoosh of stale air when I peered inside. The shelves along the sides were empty, save for a few unlabeled cans. Two thick steel manacles hung from a hefty chain on the back wall.

The chain was strung through a heavy-duty U-bolt. Judging by the shiny metal filings scattered on the floor below, it had been recently installed. I tugged on it—solid. I turned slowly until I'd made a full circuit. There was room for three people inside, four if you packed them in like sardines, and even more with the shelves removed. I took out my phone for a surreptitious scan. The app dinged, and I swept my gaze across the ceiling until I saw the small black dome above the door. I assumed Olita was watching, so I avoided staring right into the thing as I looked around for more, checking the dusty shelves for any signs of recent activity but finding none. First camera logged.

Back in the kitchen, more secretive scanning revealed a camera above the vent hood over the old range. Even if Olita was watching, I decided being thorough couldn't hurt, so I opened up cabinets to look inside and poked around under the sink and anywhere else that might harbor hidden surprises. Empty. I walked into the restaurant and scanned for more. Nothing. There was another camera in the hall above the back door, but none in the bathroom. No pervy toilet peeking for Olita.

Next, I searched for Wi-Fi networks, and five popped up: TC738428, MyWireless34, Pho15-guest, BobSanders, and CumDiv143. I snickered at the last one before realizing it probably had something to do with Cummings and divine. It was password protected.

Back outside, I did a scan along the backside of the building for more cameras and found one under the eaves above the door. I retreated into the lot until the camera was no longer visible before scrutinizing the length of the exterior concrete wall. Halfway down, two threaded rods were sticking out and anchored in place with large galvanized nuts. They had to be the ends of the U-bolt. The sight coaxed a smile from my pursed lips. First big mistake, Olita.

Back on Bainbridge, we called Kaytee on video to go over my findings. "I found four cameras: one outside the back door, one in the hallway, one in the kitchen, and one in the walk-in. I also found the Wi-Fi network but couldn't log on."

She shrugged. "That's what I figured. There's a slight chance I'll be able to, but I wouldn't bet on it. We should come up with a Plan B that doesn't rely on any hacking, just in case the network is too protected."

I nodded and then frowned. "Another issue is that I have no way of getting Dram into the manacles if I pretend to knock him out. I need Sam to come in and help me, but we're assuming Olita knows he's a demon now, so it wouldn't make sense for him to do so."

Kaytee's brow furrowed as she considered it. "But she might also know that you're an item, in which case it *would* make sense, because he won't want you to be hurt."

The logic seemed sound after a moment's consideration, and I nodded then looked at Sam. He was scratching his chin. "I'll need to very obviously leave in order for her to come inside, though. I don't like the idea of leaving you with her, even with Dram and Marcus there."

Worry creased his brow, and I placed a reassuring hand on his knee. "I'll be fine." My gaze drifted up, and I squinted at the ceiling in thought. "What if I unlocked the front door so you can sneak back in?"

Sam and Kaytee's heads bobbed with slow nods, gazes distant as we all considered potential holes in the plan.

I spoke up first. "Does Marcus have to be touching Dram in order to shield him?"

"No, if he can see Dram he can shield him. But if he's further than ten feet away, the shield won't protect Marcus."

I hummed out a note while contemplating the sequence of events. "Okay. When Olita pulls up, Sam will sneak in through the front to hide somewhere and Marcus will stay close to Dram. After that, I'm not sure what to do. Hopefully, I can convince her to destroy the vessel, but I doubt she will. Our agreement was that she'd do it after she ascended. Maybe Sam or Dram can use swapping magic to get it away from her?"

Sam shook his head. "Swapping magic doesn't work on vessels. We'll have to weaken or cripple her then grab it. If we can't, I'll transfer the cursed blood back into her." His dour expression lightened. "And if she's weak enough for me to do it, it'll be easy to kill her after, especially with Dram around."

I perked up. "I have Jackson's knife. Maybe I can stab her when she goes into the cooler. That should weaken her, right??"

He shifted and frowned, uncomfortable with the idea. "That'll put you in a lot more danger than I'd like. If you're close enough to stab her, she'll be able to stab you back."

Kaytee raised an eyebrow. "I was under the impression that Jeanie could handle a little stabbing?"

"Not since Sam transferred Olita's cursed blood out of me."

Kaytee's head jerked back. "You can do that?" He nodded, and she whispered, "Oh shit."

He turned to me. "I'd like it better if you left before we take her on."

I sighed. "I know, but desperate times call for desperate measures." He shook his head and looked away, his objections logged.

Kaytee asked, "What's to stop Olita from running once she sees you're all working together?"

I frowned—another hole in our plan. "Maybe lock the place up from outside?"

Sam perked up. "That could be your job, Kaytee, if you're comfortable with it. Lock us in while we fight her and be ready to let us out if shit goes sideways."

Kaytee leaned back and crossed her arms. "There's a lot of loose ends in this plan."

I winced. "Yeah, that's a Jeanie plan for you."

She cleared her throat. "To recap, the primary goal is to get the vessel from Olita so Dram can break the curse. Then, if all goes well, you'll kill her afterwards. If that fails, you'll attempt to swap the blood?"

Sam nodded. "If we can't get the vessel or swap the blood, then I'll do whatever it takes to distract her so Dram, Marcus, and Jeanie can get away." I narrowed my eyes at him.

Kaytee took a deep breath and blew it all out. "This is some shit right here. I'll talk to Dram about it and see if he has any ideas. We can all meet or have another video call beforehand to go over everything. Do you have a rough timeline for this?"

Sam's eyes met mine, and we nodded in unspoken agreement.

"Preferably as soon as possible. I've got another angel pissed at me, and it'd be a good idea to get this over with and drop off the radar for a while." I looked into the camera and sighed. "Kaytee, I'm so sorry to get all of you wrapped up in this. We'll only do it if you're comfortable with the plan. Otherwise, Sam and I will find another way."

Another way that would likely end with me in a morgue and Sam floating away as a pile of dust. He gave my leg a reassuring squeeze.

"Alright, talk soon." Kaytee waved, and the video ended.

We leaned back on Dram's couch. "Do you think this is going to work?" I asked him.

"I'm gonna make it work."

With our hands clasped together on Sam's knee, I made a promise to myself. If Sam went down, then I was going down with him. It's what I would have done for Tom if a demon had taken his life instead of cancer. Now I could play the game out on the main field rather than watching helplessly from the sidelines. How often do you get the opportunity to literally fight for the ones you love? It was too sweet a chance to pass up.

35

"I'M GONNA READ a little more; I'm making some good progress," Sam said and kissed my forehead. He rolled out of bed and slipped on his sweats. I watched him with a soft smile on my lips before my cheeks slackened. The feel-good buzz of another breathtaking bedroom romp had quickly faded. I rose and pulled on his t-shirt, inhaling his scent, before walking out to join him.

Over the course of the day, I'd been trying to savor our time together and forget that it might be limited. It almost worked. After every kiss and touch, my heart rose, bright and soaring, before inevitably falling into darkness again. Another shit rollercoaster like the one I was forced to ride when Tom was dying: periods of hope with each new treatment followed by periods of despair when the cancer only got worse. It's a helpless feeling when you spot fate coming down the road and know there's nothing you can do to stop it. The healthy thing is to meet it; what I'd done was hide from it so that when it finally burst through my bubble of denial, it shocked me all the more. Now I was bouncing between the two.

I sensed Sam was doing the same: fluctuating between not being able to touch me enough, followed by periods where the uncertainty drove him to disappear into the *Magia Deorum*, hoping to uncover a miracle in its pages. After an especially lengthy study break, he leaned back and rubbed his face before letting out a long breath. "I figured out the spell that can weaken a divine." I straightened up and waited for him to continue, even though his expression was carefully blank. "A divine's knife has enough of their essence in it to allow the holder to drain off power."

I groaned and put my head in my hands. "Too bad Olita's is currently with the shit-king Jackson Greene."

He nodded and pushed the book away with a sigh. "Yeah. I don't think I'm gonna get much more outta this tonight." He gave me a look that made my heart skip a beat. "Maybe there's something else I can study instead?"

I pranced over and straddled him on the chair before running a finger down his chest. "I can think of a few things."

In the evening, we had a video call with Dram, Marcus, and Kaytee to go over the plan. Dram was surprisingly relaxed about the whole thing, while Kaytee and Marcus' tight smiles betrayed their concern.

After the initial greetings, Kaytee began. "I stopped by the restaurant this morning. I have good news and bad news."

Naturally, we opted for the bad news first.

"I found a camera outside the front door." I smacked my forehead—of course I'd forgotten to check an area crucial to our plan. "The good news is I was able to log on to her Wi-Fi. Whoever set the system up didn't do a great job creating a secure network."

After a small, relieved smile, I frowned again. "Maybe I'm being paranoid, but what if it's intentional? What if she wants to see if someone logged on? It might mean she's already onto us."

Kaytee tilted her head and pursed her lips. "I suppose that's a possibility. I guess it depends on how paranoid Olita is and how much she knows about setting up an alert when an unauthorized device logs on."

Sam scratched his chin while he considered it. "Olita's paranoid, but she also thinks she's better than everyone, especially humans. It's her blind spot. Plus, there's no reason for her to think Jeanie is working with Dram and would mess with the cameras."

I shook my head. "She knows I don't want him dead, though, since this whole venture is about me handing him over so I don't have to kill him myself. She's already suspicious."

Dram held up a hand. "I think we're all getting a little paranoid. We can't assume anything other than Olita is smart and highly motivated to ascend. If she's suspicious, the most likely thing to happen is she won't take the bait. Also, as Sam said, if she believes herself to be superior to others, then she'll ignore the minor details because she assumes neither of you are smart enough to take advantage of them."

I relaxed my tense shoulders and allowed myself a thin hope that Dram was right. I turned to Kaytee. "Since you can log on to the Wi-Fi, does that mean you can hack the cameras or something? Can we loop some video?"

She rolled her eyes. "The movies have ruined people when it comes to hacking. Is it possible? Maybe. But not for me. What I *can* do is reset the router so the system has to reboot, which will make the cameras go dark until it's back on again. That usually takes about a minute, enough time to get someone in, but she'll notice if she's actively watching the feed."

Marcus chimed in. "Are there any low-tech ways to blind a camera?"

Kaytee tilted her head up and tapped a finger on her lips. "You can shine a laser at them, but you'd have to aim it just right, and most cameras have multiple sensors. Glass can fool the motion detector, too, but if the camera's on, then she'd see you install it."

I sat up. "What if we blocked the sensor while you reboot the system?"

Kaytee's eyebrows dipped in thought as she nodded. "That might work."

Sam's expression was a shade less morose as I got us back on track. "Okay, let's talk timeline. We reboot the system at night when she's least likely to notice. Once it's down, I'll unlock the front door and cover the motion sensor on the camera. The next day, we can start."

Marcus cleared his throat and asked, "What if she watches Jeanie bring me in, then attacks Dram before he gets inside?"

Sam shook his head. "I doubt she'd try it unless she was absolutely certain she could take him." Sam's frown changed into a hungry grin. "And I won't let that happen."

Marcus smiled in relief.

Next, we discussed what we'd do if she took the bait. Dram was confident he'd be safe as long as Marcus was with him. Kaytee suggested we all wear hidden microphones so she could monitor what was happening inside. Sam and Dram talked through ways to get the ring from Olita.

When the discussion shifted into negative territory, with Kaytee and me pointing out all the things that could go wrong, Dram interrupted. "There's no such thing as a perfect plan when it comes to dealing with divines. Risk is a part of our existence. I dislike involving humans in our affairs, but I owe Jeanie everything. Marcus and Kaytee, if you have any doubts or concerns, then you don't have to take part. I'm sure Jeanie and Sam feel the same."

Sam and I nodded as he looked from Kaytee to Marcus.

"I'm all in," Kaytee said.

"Me too," said Marcus.

I smiled in relief. "Last question. When?"

Sam pulled me to him and kissed my forehead. "I'd like to say never, but we should do this as soon as possible before we overthink everything too much."

"Agreed," said Dram.

I looked into Sam's eyes. "So...tonight?"

His eyes didn't leave mine. "Tonight."

Kaytee cursed at her laptop before turning to me. "Okay, Jeanie, hop out and get ready. I'm going to hit the reset; wait until my signal before you go in. Got everything?"

I nodded and stepped out of the car, hands shaking from nerves and the 2 a.m. chill. Kaytee had done more research online and discovered that a silicone-based spray would also work to trick the camera's motion sensor and be much easier than trying to attach a piece of glass. I gripped the can like a baton in a relay race and crouched, ready to sprint. She flashed me a thumbs up, and I dashed to the door and punched in the code.

My flashlight carved a dull beam through the dust particles in the air as I ran to the front, grabbing a crate on my way. The door had two simple deadbolts that slid open with shuddering screeches. I let myself out, set the crate down, climbed onto it, and sprayed the bejeezus out of the camera. Back inside, I did another quick scan of the place, even rushing to peek into the cooler to make sure Olita hadn't changed anything. Forty-five seconds later, I was outside and locking the door behind me.

In the car, Kaytee and I exchanged smiles of relief. "Phase one accomplished," she said.

I bumped my fist against hers. "The badass babes strike again!"

Dram, Marcus, and Sam met us at the hotel an hour later. Marcus gave us his patented shy smile while Dram wrapped both Sam and me in a big hug. He seemed calm and relaxed, as if the day would be no more exceptional than his usual nine-to-five and not potentially his last. There was worry in his eyes when he looked at Kaytee and Marcus, though; it was obvious he'd rather not have them involved. I felt the same way, but they would be the ones in the least danger. Hopefully.

We'd decided that bringing Marcus to the restaurant around 10 a.m. was as good a time as any. The two adjacent businesses were closed on Sunday, so the number of random passersby would be minimal. The midmorning start would also give us a reasonable amount of time to rest, if rest was possible. After we said our goodnights to the Dram crew, Sam and I collapsed onto our bed. We pondered the air above us, hands behind our heads, before I turned to him. "What chance of success do you think we have?"

He shrugged. "As good a chance as we'll get."

"Yeah." My eyes barely registered the dark ceiling as I stared at it. "I confirmed a weird quirk about the power Olita gave me." He turned to me with a raised eyebrow. "I still feel fear for other people's safety. Like, a lot of fear." He opened his arm, and I moved over to snuggle up against him.

He ran a reassuring hand through my hair. "It's not a fun feeling, is it?"

I shook my head against his chest. "No, it is not."

We lay in silence until my annoyance at wearing clothes overrode my dark thoughts, and I rose to brush my teeth. As I watched Sam take his shirt off, my breath hitched in my throat. What if this was the last time we shared a bed together? I tried to swallow, but it felt like drowning. He heard me bite back a sob and walked over to wrap me in his arms. I clung to him, and we swayed to silent music, not wanting the moment to end.

I pulled away and met his gaze. "Sam, for what it's worth, and probably to your own detriment, I love you."

His glistening eyes and ecstatic grin were enough to raise my spirits up and out of the black pit they were sinking into. He lifted me off my feet, burying his face in my neck for a long moment before setting me down and putting his hands on my cheeks. His gaze roamed over me like he couldn't believe I was real, like I was a lost treasure he'd been searching a lifetime for.

"Jeanie, I love you so much. These last few weeks have made me a happier man than I've been in a very long time, even with all the dangerous bullshit."

Before he kissed me, I put a firm hand on his chest, my mouth set and eyes serious. "I need to be perfectly honest with you. I have no intention of leaving you to deal with Olita alone. I am one hundred percent in on this. It's ride or die time, Sammy."

He nodded, and I watched the conflicting emotions wash over his face before his shoulders relaxed and he met my eyes honestly and openly, accepting that our fates were now entwined.

"Okay." He put his hands on my cheeks. "Ride or die, Jeans."

He kissed me, and I melted into him.

A happy spark lit up my heart when our eyes met again and reminded me that life should be lived to the fullest, most chances are worth taking, and loving someone is the bravest thing you can do because nothing lasts forever and everyone dies in the end.

With an open-hearted joy that shone like a beacon despite the surrounding darkness, I pulled him to the bed. We took our time kissing and stroking each other until I drifted off into a deeper sleep than I'd thought possible.

The next morning, Sam and I woke up to the alarm chiming on my phone. We curled toward each other, our smiles widening as we gazed into each other's eyes.

I waggled my eyebrows. "Are you ready to do some fucked-up shit today?"

He grinned. "I'm ready to do anything if I get to do it with you."

My gaze lowered to his mouth, and a lustful heat spread throughout my body. In response, his eyes softened into a drowsy look of desire, and my heart thudded wild and demanding in my ears. He climbed on top of me, and my lips and tongue met his as we moved in sync. His breath was heavy against my neck, and I sank my nails into his back, frantic and urgent, begging for more. This was no time for long and languid lovemaking. This was the time for spitting in the face of fate, for fierce and feral fucking, for giving darkness the middle finger.

We sprawled out beside each other, panting and sweating, after our frenzy came to its climax. Moments or days passed before my mind swam back to the present and remembered where we were. The normalcy of the setting surprised me; I'd almost forgotten the world still existed outside of our bodies.

In unspoken agreement, we rose and took a shower together. My fingers traced the streams of soapy water as they ran down his torso, and a pang of need stabbed through me so sharply it stopped my breath. The same desperation was in his eyes, and we kissed the warm water away from each other's lips. But there wasn't enough time.

There is never enough time.

36

KAYTEE AND MARCUS both had dark circles under their eyes when we met them in their hotel suite, but Dram seemed refreshed and ready for anything. Kaytee's tired smile turned into a smirk when she looked me over. I blushed, wondering how obvious my post-coital glow was.

She gestured for Sam and me to sit on the small couch while Dram took a chair and Marcus hovered behind him. "Alright everyone, let's get our tech together and set up." She pulled five small boxes out of a bag and handed one to each of us. "These are earpieces we can use to communicate with each other during this whole thing."

I lifted the tiny flesh-colored blob out and examined it. "How the hell did you get ahold of these?"

Kaytee smiled. "You know, from a local online shopping and delivery company with a logo that looks like a dick print." Marcus and I let out synchronized snorts. "I ordered them after you told me about the plan. Figured they might come in handy," she said in response to my questioning look.

I shook my head in awed admiration. The woman was a goddamn genius.

"Okay, you all need to connect these to your phone's bluetooth and then set them to the same frequency." When she saw me poking with hopeless fingers at my screen, she sighed, and I put the phone into her waiting palm. After several minutes of focused silence, everyone tapped their final clicks and held up their phones for her inspection. She examined them each and nodded. "Perfect. Let's do a sound check."

Interference noises crackled when I pushed the earpiece into my ear. Kaytee left the room and walked farther and farther away with periodic check-ins to confirm whether we could still hear her until there was only static.

She came back. "It looks like we have maybe fifty feet of range on these things, probably less through thicker walls...and metal boxes." She looked pointedly at Dram, and he nodded. "They have limited battery life, so keep them off if you're not in the building." She took a deep breath and let it out. "That's all I had to go over before we begin. Anything else?"

"Does your power work if you see a face on a video rather than in person?" I asked.

She nodded. "Yes, as long as the face is visible, I can tell."

"Can we set up a live stream on my phone so you can see if Olita's lying while I talk to her?" I shrugged. "It probably won't matter, but it could help."

Kaytee nodded, and we spent a moment setting up the video communication. When we were done, she asked again if anyone else had something to discuss. Everyone's face held the same anticipatory blankness as my own. We stood up.

Dram put his hands on Kaytee's and my shoulders and cleared his throat. "Well, team, let's do our best to stay safe and give it all we've got. I have faith that things will work out."

I suppressed a grin. Coach Nguyen had entered the building. He looked at each of us, and we all returned his genuine smile. Just another day in the life of divines and their assistants.

Marcus and I sat in tense silence on the car ride to the restaurant. He clenched his trembling hands in his lap, and the silver play-handcuffs glinted when they caught the light. Kaytee had bought them at a local sex shop. I shook my head and smiled; Dram struck gold when he found her.

I turned to him. "First time being cuffed?" He nodded, and I flashed him a wide grin. "Congratulations! How lucky are you it was a beautiful woman who did it and not a cop?"

He blushed and gave me a shy smile. "Pretty lucky, I guess."

"Kaytee is an incredible woman, isn't she? I don't think there's anything she can't do."

He nodded again, and his blush deepened. I smiled to myself. I knew it. The way they'd hugged before Marcus got in the car revealed a lot more about their relationship than Kaytee had been willing to share. It was the embrace of two people who adored each other and loathed being apart. Sweet and heartbreaking at the same time.

Before we got out of the car, Marcus and I took a deep breath and turned our earpieces on.

I winked at him. "Let's do this."

We put on quite the show for Olita. He staggered drunkenly while I shoved him through the parking lot and into the back door before manhandling him into the cooler. As a finishing move, I opened up a pill bottle and mimed shoving them down his throat. He pretended to go limp, and I drug him over to the corner. I dusted my hands off and reminded myself not to look at the camera, even though I was itching to take a bow. For a drama class dropout, I'd pulled off a pretty decent performance.

Back outside, I stood below the eaves and called Dram. In my most menacing voice, I told him I had his husband and if he ever wanted to see him again, then he better come and get him. I gave him the address, made up a deadline, and told him to come alone. After a few more violent threats, I hung up and texted Sam. I paced until he showed up and then ran into his arms and kissed him passionately in case Olita still wasn't aware of our relationship. I'm sure she appreciated the show, and I smiled as I pictured her nose wrinkled in disgust. Inside the restaurant, I had him pull a shelf unit out from the cooler to make room for him to wait inside.

Next, I went out to the car and retrieved the threaded PVC pipe we had spray-painted silver to serve as our prop for bashing Dram on the head. There had been some debate about the most believable way to knock out a divine until Sam chimed in that a head injury from a heavy object would do the trick. No one asked how he'd found that out, and he didn't offer. I handed the pipe to him and sat on the kitchen counter while he paced, stopping every once in a while to squeeze my leg in reassurance. I winced in sympathy when I thought of Marcus having to lie still on the cold floor.

Twenty minutes later, Dram arrived, and the light fixtures rattled when his violent kick slammed the door against the wall. Sam scrambled into the cooler, and I closed it behind him, crossed my arms, and put my meanest face on. Dram skidded to a stop when he saw me.

His voice was believably frantic. "Where is he? What have you done to him?" The feedback from the earpiece was disorienting, and I flinched as I gestured him over and opened the door of the dark cooler to shine my flashlight onto Marcus's prone form.

Dram sucked in a breath, and I took the moment to step behind him and shove him in. Sam's pipe came down on his head, and I prayed the hollow bonk of the plastic tube didn't sound as fake on video as it did in real life. He swooned and sank down, one joint at a time, to the floor. Sam prodded him with his toe before dragging him over to the wall and holding him up while I put the manacles on. Another masterful performance.

In full view of the outside camera, I thanked Sam and told him I'd call him when everything was over with. He kissed me and walked off to wait for my signal before sneaking in through the front.

I messaged Olita:

It's done. He's in the cooler and chained up.

Out of surveillance range, I started the live stream and put my phone in the breast pocket of my jacket with the camera just peeking out. Olita didn't message back but pulled up in a black sedan fifteen minutes later.

"Go time, everyone," I whispered as she opened the door.

Dram's reassuring voice came through the earpiece, telling all of us to stay calm and that everything was going to be okay.

I didn't bother plastering on a fake smile. "Hello, Olita."

She was wearing a long black jacket a la The Matrix and pulled her dark sunglasses off as she slid out of the car. "Hello, Jeanie, let's see how you did, shall we?"

Beads of sweat broke out on my forehead when I pictured Dram and Marcus cornered in a small box as she prowled closer. She unbuttoned her coat, and I caught a glimpse of the ornate golden dagger strapped to her belt as I opened the door for her. Once inside, she gave me a long, calculating stare and made a point of locking the door behind us. When we reached the cooler, I cracked it open just enough to flash my light over Marcus and Dram before quickly closing it again. She raised an amused eyebrow.

"See, I got him for you. Now let me go."

Kaytee's smooth voice spoke in my ear. She had blocked the doors and was working on the nuts holding Dram's chains in place while watching my video stream.

Olita laughed as she pulled her coat off, adjusting her dagger to be within easy reach. There was no hint of a ruby sparkling on her finger. My gaze roamed all over her—she wasn't wearing a single piece of jewelry. A cold lump of fear settled in my stomach, causing my thoughts to swirl in confusion until I remembered what Sam had said: the vessel needed to be close to the divine in order for their assistant to receive the maximum amount of power. My heart thundered in my ears. She didn't have the vessel at all.

37

THE HAMSTER POWERING the wheel of my mind screeched to a halt. What was Plan B again? Did we have a Plan B? I had to talk so the others knew what was going on. "Where is it, Olita?"

There was confusion in her careful expression. "Where is what?"

"The vessel. You didn't even bring it, did you? You never had any intention of releasing me."

Her lips curved up into a cruel arc. "Aw, yes, been chatting with your demon lover? Did he tell you how all of this works? Because I know you didn't learn it from *The Assistant's Handbook*, since it is still in my library." She pulled her knife from its sheath and admired its shining blade. "I look forward to punishing him for his treachery."

A welcome anger pushed back against my dread. "How far away is it? You could at least have kept it close long enough for you to finish this so I don't have to feel fear as well as revulsion."

Her smile didn't change. "Oh, a little fear is good for you sometimes." Her expression hardened. "And if you're hoping Sam will fetch it for you, rest assured it is too far away for him to retrieve before we've finished our business here." She laughed at my surprised face. "I know he's listening in." She gestured to the phone in my pocket and waved at it. "Sam, I will kill her and then you if I hear that door open." She pointed toward the back with her knife before fixing me with a glare. "Now, turn it off and put it over there." Her knife swung around to indicate the back counter, and I did as she asked.

Kaytee's voice piped up. "Jeanie, she's lying about it being far."

I narrowed my eyes at Olita. "Why not just kill me now?"

She looked me up and down. "Well, in the face of all odds, you *have* proven to be quite effective. You've helped Sam ascend for one." She nodded toward the cooler. "And this is the closest I've ever been to Dram, if the man in there *is* him." She tapped her lip. "If it is, then perhaps I'll keep you as a little pet. Make you do horrendous things, torture you, watch your heart break when you realize Sam was just using you, too." Her teeth gleamed white through the red lips of her villainous grin. "But first, let's confirm that you delivered what you promised."

Heart pounding, I opened the door and gestured her in with a raised middle finger. "Be my guest, you lying bitch."

Her pupils flashed red, and she motioned for me to enter. "After you, sweet Jeanie. I wouldn't want you to miss out on any traps you set for me."

I rolled my eyes. "Fine."

My gaze darted to Sam as I walked in; he was squeezed up against the corner with his knife at the ready. I stepped close enough to Dram to shine the flashlight onto his face while avoiding Marcus on the floor. Dram raised his head, dazed, and saw Olita. His eyes went cold, and he let out a humorless chuckle. "Aw, Olita. I can't believe you finally got to me. How long have you been trying? Twenty years? Funny how a mediocre human accomplished what you could not."

I turned back to leave room in the cooler for her. Her hungry red eyes gleamed in the glow of my flashlight. She stopped me and pointed to Marcus. "Remove him."

I hesitated, and her eyes narrowed. "Any reason you don't want to separate them? Could he be one of Dram's assistants waiting to spring on me?" She jabbed her finger at Marcus. "Take him out of there. Now."

I threw up my hands. "Okay, Jesus!"

My eyes flicked up to Dram, eyebrows dipped in apology as I stepped back to grab Marcus. Once I had a good grip on his wrists, I dragged him out, keeping my body between him and

Olita as I did so. I propped him up against the cabinets opposite the cooler door.

"Don't you dare hurt him!" Dram's voice was sharp but frantic.

Olita hovered near the cooler and watched me, her eyes shrewd and calculating. "Cover his eyes and put him over there." She pointed to the far wall of the kitchen. My heart thudded, and a fearful weight settled in my stomach.

I covered my shaky breath with an annoyed groan and did as she asked. After turning an empty box over and placing it on Marcus's head, I swept my arm toward the cooler in a wide, sarcastic gesture. "Anything else, queen bitch? Want me to get a palanquin and carry you in there myself?"

Still skeptical, she narrowed her eyes and scrutinized my face. There was no reason to disguise the hatred I was feeling, so I crossed my arms and returned the glare.

Kaytee's voice came through the earpiece. "Dram, the bolts are free. I'm going to look in Olita's car for the vessel."

Olita looked back and forth between me and the cooler door before pointing to Marcus. "Actually, bring him over here to prop this open. Wouldn't want you to lock me inside." Her evil smile was wearing thin; I wasn't the only one getting sick of this. I grumbled as I drug him over and leaned him against the door. "Okay, now you stand over there." She gestured toward the doorway to the hall.

"Fine by me. I don't want to watch this shit."

I stood where she told me, and after another long sweep of her gaze up and down my body, she turned to the cooler. As slyly as possible, I reached under my jacket and pulled the cord keeping Jackson's knife from falling out of the upturned sheath taped to my back. My heartbeat sounded like a speed bag in a boxing gym as she crept closer to the door. Once the dagger was free of its restraints, I slid it out and held it behind me. I was ready, willing, and able to stab the bitch if I got the chance.

Knife in front of her, she stepped inside and immediately saw Sam. She recoiled as he rushed out, pinning her against the counter and stabbing her in the gut. He deflected her knife as it plunged toward his heart, and it found its way into his shoulder instead. He grunted, and an icy wave of fear froze me in place. Olita's superior strength became terrifyingly apparent as she shoved Sam away with ease and pinned him against the stove, her knife now finding his gut while his only grazed her neck.

Her chuckle was low and cold. "Can't kill me without killing Jeanie, can you? Poor Sam, surely you don't care about a pathetic little human? Look at her, she's not worth dying for."

She pushed her knife in deeper and twisted it. Sam's face went pale, and his body slackened.

As they fought, Marcus freed himself from the handcuffs and was now crouched, gaze darting back and forth between the dark interior of the cooler and Olita. When she moved to strike Sam's heart, I rushed forward, but an invisible barrier deflected the blow. Sam's grin widened at Olita's confused face. She narrowed her eyes at Marcus then bared her teeth and lunged at him. Before she'd gone two steps, Dram leapt out and tackled her to the ground. He wrapped the chains of his manacles around her neck as she struggled against the surprise attack.

Her breath hissing, she swung her knife in wild slashes at Dram, but her dagger bounced away at every attempt. Sam dropped to his knees and was about to stab her through the heart until I cried out, voice trembling with fear, "Sam, don't!" His hand stopped, and he looked up at me, his red eyes deep in a pit of hate, bloodlust, and retribution. He glared down at Olita. "Please, Sam." My voice broke, and he pulled his knife back a fraction.

My hands shook when I tucked my knife into my belt and knelt next to Dram to unlock the manacles. I forced myself to take deep, measured breaths as I took them off. "Can you transfer the cursed blood from Sam to Olita?" I asked him. He nodded and gave my shoulder a reassuring pat. Olita spat, snarled, and thrashed until Sam slammed her head against the floor, temporarily stunning her. Dram handed the manacles to him, and he squeezed the chain tighter around her neck.

As Dram reached for Olita's wrist, Sam said, "I'll do it. I need you to find and break the vessel. Please." There was a note of pleading in his tone, and his gaze flicked to me and then back. "If Olita dies before it's broken, Jeanie could get hurt."

Dram nodded solemnly at Sam and shifted to stand up. Sam jiggled the chains. "Might as well bleed her before you go. You'll need the power."

Dram took the knife Marcus offered him and slashed it across her inner elbow and then leaned forward to drink. Sam stared down at Olita, the hatred naked on his face, the point of his knife twitching above her heart. I touched his shoulder, and the loathing melted away when he looked into my shining eyes.

"We're going to win, Sam," I whispered, and he nodded, a dribble of hope trickling into his weak smile.

As Dram wiped the blood from his mouth and stood, Kaytee's sharp voice startled us. "Who are you?" Mumbling. "What do you want? Stay away from me!" Her fear vibrated through the earpiece.

Dram glanced at me, eyes wide and wild, before he and Marcus rushed to the back door. While Dram rammed his shoulder against the blocked exit, Marcus ran to the front. I sucked in a shallow breath—it seemed locking us in with Olita was a bad call.

The mumbling in my ear grew clearer, and a man's voice asked, "Is there a Jeanine Bennett in there, by any chance?"

My blood froze at the jeering tone. Sam's wide eyes met mine, and his shocked expression matched my own.

"It's Jackson. He's an angel!" Sam winced, and I remembered I didn't have to yell for everyone to hear me. Whoops.

Kaytee was wheezing and gasping—Jackson was using his powers on her.

"Y-yes," she whimpered.

"Good, very good. Who else is in there? Sounds like they want out."

She was panting and growling, trying to resist Jackson's mind control. "D-d-demonnnn..." Dram was ramming furiously at the door, Marcus back beside him. "And...angel" A speck of hope filtered in through my fear.

"A demon and an angel. Interesting. How about human slaves? I imagine you're one. Jeanine is one. Is there another inside?"

Kaytee was sobbing. Jackson told someone to hold her tighter. "One...more."

"What is their power?" Her whimpers turned into a snarling scream, her mic cutting in and out like she was thrashing against something.

Jackson laughed. "You can't resist me, pretty one. You *will* tell me."

"Sh...sh...shield."

"A shield you say? Excellent." His voice was muffled, as if he'd turned his head to speak to someone. "Go for the shield first and trap them. Leave Jeanine to me."

More murmuring.

"No, knock her out."

Dram stopped ramming against the door. My voice was calmer than I'd expected. "He's after me, Dram. Try the front again, break a window, do whatever you need to get to Kaytee."

He and Marcus ran to the front of the restaurant. "His assistants!" I grimaced and dialed my volume back down. "The man can knock you out with a touch and the woman can zap things with her nails."

Dram's breathless voice thanked me, and the sound of a window shattering followed by the frantic banging of feet kicking nailed-up plywood thudded through the restaurant. I looked at Sam and then down at Olita. Her eyes were almost back to their usual sharpness. She was confused, but mostly pissed. Sam was still kneeling on her, but her thrashing arms and legs were threatening to throw him off.

As the battering thumps from the front stopped, a loud scraping noise came from the back. I squeezed Sam's shoulder. "Come on, let's get out of here."

He paused for a moment then bashed Olita's head against the floor again and stabbed her in her lung before rising and putting a hand on my waist to follow me out of the kitchen.

The back door burst open, and Jackson sauntered in with a toothy grin. "Oh, hello, Jeanine. Fancy meeting you here."

38

SAM AND I froze, and Jackson chuckled. "Surprised to see me? Well, you shouldn't have taken blood from the territory of a demon whose last known whereabouts happened to be the Seattle area. It was almost too easy to track you. Especially with Stacy's contacts at the airport and my spy network here."

Sam stepped in front of me, shoulders tense and arms braced.

Jackson smirked. "Is this your master, Jeanine? Is this the demon who sent you to take *me* out?" He shook his head and waggled a finger. "Tsk, tsk, demon. A word of advice: don't send a weak human to challenge the most powerful angel in the region."

I swung my head around to glance at the dining area. Sunlight was slanting through the opening where Dram and Marcus had broken through. I pulled Sam's shirt to get him to move backwards with me. If we could just make it outside...

Jackson chuckled. "Not that way, sweetheart." I spun around. Jim was standing in the doorway, arms crossed, with a deranged grin on his face.

"Dram, what's going on out there?" Nothing. "Marcus? Anyone?" No response—my earpiece battery was dead. My heart constricted with a painful throb. Oh good, both fear *and* pain were back on the menu.

Jackson cocked his head and tapped his lip. "What were you all up to in here, I wonder? Trying to get your master to ascend? Shame you won't complete that mission, either. Dram and his assistant took off like cowards, but don't worry, I'll hunt them down. I found his family before and I'll do it again." His bland realtor's smile shifted to a psycho serial killer's grin. "That beautiful human woman, though?" He pointed his thumb over his shoulder to the back lot. "She is now mine."

My eyes widened.

"Do you care so much about other humans? That's a serious shortcoming for an assistant, you know." He tutted at me and shook his head. "Don't worry, I won't kill her...yet. I'll make sure to do it in front of you. It would make a nice addition to my revenge plan." He winked at me before shifting his focus to Sam. "Let's see your knife, demon; I'm assuming your little pet there gave you mine?" His gaze traveled down to Sam's hand, and his eyes narrowed.

When Jackson reached for the knife in his belt, I reflexively reached for the one tucked into mine. He caught the movement, and his smile returned. "Ah, Jeanine, so nice of you to hold on to it for me. Give it back, please."

The buzzing began in my ears and spread inwards, drowning out all other sounds. I gasped and backed away, clutching the hilt in my fist, forcing it farther down. Jackson told me to stop and then asked for the knife again. I froze in place, and my hand slid the blade out, slowly and steadily. Without Olita's cursed blood, I couldn't withstand his magic. Sam leapt forward, and something hit him with a dull thud before he grunted and dropped to a knee. A hilt stuck out beneath his collarbone.

Jackson shrugged, amused. "It's a shame you can't hit a divine's heart with a throw. I could have ended it quickly and painlessly for you. No matter."

He walked forward, grabbed the hilt, then yanked it out and plunged it into Sam's neck. Helpless tears streamed down my trembling jaw as I stood paralyzed, unable to help. Jackson kicked him over, and Sam slumped to the floor, clutching his throat, blood leaking through his fingers as he wheezed for air. "Don't go anywhere," Jackson jeered. "I'll finish you soon."

He turned to glare at me through lowered eyelids, his voice deep and commanding. "Give me my fucking knife, Jeanine."

My powers still numbed the pain of Jackson's control magic, but my ability to fight his command was fading fast. A movement flashed in my peripheral vision, and I flicked my gaze over to the window between the restaurant and the kitchen. Olita was there, half crouched and listening. My arm was lifting and preparing to toss the knife to Jackson. Using every ounce of willpower I had left, I turned myself to throw it toward Olita instead. Sound ceased to exist as it arced through the air with my last remnants of hope pulled along in its spinning wake. I winced as it bounced and clattered against the side of the opening. She threw herself forward and grabbed it before it spun away, and time resumed with a sudden violent assault on my senses.

Jackson instantly doubled the buzzing in my head. "Who's in there, Jeanine? Another friend for me to kill?"

Between coughs and gasps, Olita's name came out of my mouth as I sank down beside Sam; he was still wheezing, but his breath was steady. I crouched over him, ready to defend him any way I could—which only made Jackson laugh. He grabbed my hair in his fist and wrenched my head up before drawing the tip of his knife down my cheek like a caress. A thin line of pain followed. He paused and hovered the blade above my neck before sighing and lowering it, a benevolent smile on his face.

"Wouldn't want to end you too soon, sweetheart. Now, stay."

My breath rushed out with a soft oof when he kicked me in the gut before turning to the kitchen. A low, guttural chanting had begun. With a dramatic groan, he took a step and froze. When he tried to move again, the motion was slow, like he was wading through deep water. The tight knot of terror in my airways released, and I sucked in a shaky breath of hope. Olita was using the spell that sapped a divine's power. If I could have reached my back, I would have patted it. Thank god that gambit paid off. Jackson slumped against the wall, and the buzzing in my head finally stopped. I was free to move.

He hissed through clenched teeth, "Jim, kill them all."

39

JIM INTERLACED HIS fingers and pushed them out in front of him, getting a good stretch in before strolling toward me. His eyes grew wilder and hungrier with every step. Jackson should have given the guy offensive powers; he was obviously underutilizing Jim's bloodthirstiness. My frantic gaze swept the room, hoping to find something to help fend him off. I lunged at the tables and started pulling them over, making a barricade to buy us time before we were within reach of his paralyzing touch. With a maniacal grin on his face, he yanked them away one by one as he closed in, sliding them across the floor hard enough to slam into the wall behind him.

I scrambled backwards to crouch by Sam, but he wasn't there. I hazarded a glance. He was crawling toward Jackson, who was bent over and leaning against the hallway wall like he was experiencing the world's worst stomachache. I whipped my head back around—Jim was almost through. My brain shrugged when I asked it for ideas, so I ran behind the counter, hands scrabbling in the shelves underneath for something to throw. A half-empty package of napkins bounced off his chest, followed by a box of straws that missed his head by a foot. A plastic squeeze bottle hit his hip and spun away before a stack of cardboard coasters pelted his torso. Unsurprisingly, he didn't slow his advance, and his savage grin widened further in anticipation.

My hand finally encountered something round and hard. I picked it up, said a brief prayer, and flung it at Jim's face. The jar of old chili paste smacked the middle of his forehead and splattered its contents everywhere, the spicy red oil leaking into his eyes and blinding him. His hands shot up to clear it away, but only rubbed it in farther. He growled in pain, and I kicked him in the crotch. He doubled over and sucked in a rasping breath.

"Sorry about your nuts, again," I said as I kneed him in the face before vaulting over the counter.

When I got back to Sam, he was chanting hoarsely and gripping Jackson's leg while Jackson struggled in vain to kick him away. The glow of the cursed blood was moving up Sam's arm and disappearing. I leaned against the wall in relief—things were looking up. But before the last glimmer left his hand, he collapsed, his face slack and colorless. I slumped down beside him and struggled to roll him over. When I finally got him onto his back, I stroked and patted his cheek, but he didn't respond. I forced myself to take measured breaths. He wasn't dust, he would recover—if I could keep the psycho angel away from him.

Jackson was straightening up, his face twisted in a murderous rage. "Too bad your power is running out, you fucking bitch," he snarled.

I lifted my head, and my last ember of hope went out. Olita was in the kitchen doorway, Jackson's knife shaking in her hand, her face creased and gray. Before Jackson straightened all the way up, she rushed him, his own blade aiming for his heart. He laughed as his hand darted out in a blur and caught her wrist, twisting it so the knife dropped into his waiting palm.

"Did you really think you could overpower *me*?" He grabbed her by the throat and lifted her off the ground. "Know your place, demon."

Still clutching Sam, I watched with horrid anticipation as he pushed the knife into Olita's heart, his face contorted into a grotesque mask, and his eyes red and savage. She spat at him as he did it. Helpless, my gaze darted between Olita, Jackson, and Sam as I waited to see what effect the cursed blood would have. He buried the blade to the hilt, and she sneered at him before her struggling limbs gave out and she fell into a pile of dust.

Three things happened at once. Sam stiffened; Jackson sank to the ground, clutching at his heart; and an explosion of pain erupted in my body. I screamed and then choked as I fought to take air into my lungs. My fists gripped Sam's shirt. I was struggling to string two thoughts together, but the overwhelming urge to save him kept me from giving in to the inferno of torture that was ripping its way through me.

Sam's bloodied chest wasn't moving. I sucked in a breath, gasped, then doubled up and toppled over. My hand landed on Sam's knife. *Grab it, Jeanie!* My fingers slipped on the blade as I fumbled for the hilt. I barely registered the sting; there was too much pain everywhere else to bother logging yet another hurt. I cursed and crawled forward, pausing each time a fresh wave of torment washed over me. When I found Jackson's leg, I stabbed the knife in to help pull me closer. His breath came in short pants as he tried pushing me away with limp and useless arms. I stabbed his gut and pulled myself forward again, both of us moaning in agony.

Jackson hissed, and a sharp stab of pain bloomed in my side. Just another layer of torment—I could do this. Tunnel vision narrowed my sight to a pinprick, so my hand scrabbled up his chest to his neck and fumbled around until it got a grip on his throat. I lifted the knife up and pressed it in, using all my meager strength until it sank into the skin. I didn't acknowledge the new throb in my side and kept pushing the blade until it reached the hilt.

When I pulled it out, Jackson's blood bubbled up in its wake. I dropped the knife. My shaky breath wheezed in and out as I raised a hand to the gruesome fountain. With the warm blood pooled in my palm, I slid on my knees to Sam. *Save him, save him!* I chanted the words over and over in my head to fight back against the unending flood of agony racking my body. One knee forward, gasp, the other knee forward. My own blood was spilling out and spreading its warmth down my side, weakening me more with each passing second.

In the back of my mind, I appreciated the irony that I'd missed the opportunity to die without pain and fear, and now I would get to die with an overabundance of both. Classic Jeanie karma. When

I reached Sam, I stretched my arm toward his mouth, hand shaking, blood spilling down the sides. I screamed in defiance. The blackout was coming, and with it, the finality of death.

"No!" I cried and pitched forward, my hand reaching for his lips.

If I could get just one drop of blood in, he might survive. Squinting through the halos of the relentless migraine, I smeared my fingers against his mouth, hoping against hope that some would find its way inside and save him.

I collapsed next to him, my consciousness fading in and out. This was it. Maybe I saved him, maybe I didn't, but it was time to go. I did what I could—I fought for love.

40

IT WAS LIKE swimming up from the bottom of a lake. A muddied haze turned to a murky brown before the sparkling beams of sun danced down from the surface, and suddenly I could breathe. My eyes squeezed shut; the light was too brilliant. Then I didn't want to open them. What if this was death? I wanted to prepare myself for the mystery that awaited us all, excitement and anticipation building...until a gentle snoring reached my ears. My eyes flickered open.

Squinting through my blurry eyelashes, I saw...a ceiling? This couldn't be right. I turned my head. Sam was in a chair by my bedside, his head and arms resting on the mattress, shoulders rising and falling with steady breaths. My feeble arm shook when I reached toward him, not quite convinced he was real.

He jerked at my touch and his head snapped up, hair flattened on one side and creases running down his cheek from the rumpled sheets.

"Jeanie?" His eyes were wide, worried, and wondrous.

"Am I dead?" My voice was dry and raspy.

His concerned brow softened in relief. "Nah. Sorry to disappoint you."

I blinked rapidly to clear my bleary eyes and squinted at him. His pupils were an unbelievable glacier blue, and the scar on his cheek was now a thin white line, barely visible in the soft light.

I whispered, "Are you an angel?" The way the question sounded after assuming I was dead made me laugh and then cough. Sam held my head up and helped me drink a few mouthfuls of water. The cool wetness on my parched throat perked me up like a desert bloom after the rain.

He lifted my hand and kissed it. "Yeah. Thanks to you."

My gaze roamed over his handsome face. "Shit. Now you're definitely out of my league."

He sighed and shook his head. "If you're back on your bullshit already, then things are looking up for a speedy recovery."

A weird, itchy ache tickled my side as I moved to sit up.

He pushed me back down. "Take it easy. You'll fuck up the wound glue."

"What the hell are you talking about?"

I tore my gaze away from his face and scanned the room. Sunlight filtered in through the half-drawn shades of the large window and revealed white, subtly patterned walls. Wires snaked out from beneath my cotton gown to monitoring equipment next to the bed, but I was definitely not in a hospital. Not in any type of hospital I'd ever seen, anyway. When my gaze settled back on Sam, memories trickled in, and a hollow dread settled in my stomach. I tried to sit up, but he pushed me down again.

"Are they okay?"

His beautiful blue eyes lit up even more when he smiled. "I assume you mean Kaytee, Dram, and Marcus, and yeah, they're okay. Kaytee is still recovering, but Marcus and Dram are fine."

My breath left me in a long and relieved exhale. "What about Jackson?"

"He's now living with the other pieces of shit in his new home in the sewers." His pleased tone carried a note of smugness as he placed his warm hand over mine.

My tense shoulders relaxed back onto the pillow. "Thank god. Fuck that asshole." I squinted at him. "So...everything actually worked out?"

"Mostly." I raised an eyebrow and he shrugged. "I didn't get to kill Olita myself, and the police came before Dram and I finished cleaning. We might have to charm some officers and do a little forgery later. We also had to leave Jackson's assistant there. We wiped his memory so he won't remember anything, but that's two times in the last week you left a mess and an injured man behind. You're a dangerous woman, Jeanie." He squeezed my hand and winked.

I returned the wink and scanned the room. "How long was I out? Where are we?"

"You've been out for two days, and we're at Olita's place."

My body wanted to jerk itself up again, but I stopped myself in time. With every movement, my side got itchier and more annoying. When I attempted to scratch it, the thick bandages covering my fingers got in the way.

"Why are we here?"

He rubbed the stubble on his chin. "Technically, it's your place now." I squinted in confusion. "I forged a death certificate and a will for Olita. She was very generous to her assistant and many local charities."

I snorted. "Good for her, but I hope the market for penthouses in Bellevue is solid because this place gives me the creeps."

He chuckled. "I'll put it up for sale." His eyes softened as he stroked my face. "You saved my life, you know."

A shy smile accompanied my shrug. "That's just the ride part of ride or die. I'm glad we didn't make it to stage two."

He clasped my hand in both of his and kissed it. "Me too." Tears shone in his eyes, and my own responded in kind.

When I shifted to get more comfortable, the irritating prickle started up in my side again. I pointed to it and waggled my bandaged fingers. "What's going on with all this?"

He shook his head, eyes distant with regret. "While I was out cold and useless, you sliced your hand and got yourself stabbed twice. Once in the gut and once in the kidney."

I cast my mind back and remembered the laughably feeble knife tussle with Jackson. "Oh yeah." I paused. "Then...how am I alive?"

There was a soft knock on the door before Dram poked his head in. "Ah! I thought I heard voices." He stepped inside. "Hello, Jeanie, how are you feeling?"

I grinned. "Great now that I know you're all still with us. I guess I owe *you* one now, don't I?"

He smiled as he patted my shin. "Nope, not by a long shot, but I'm happy we were able to help check off all the boxes on your To-Do list." He walked over to examine the screen on the monitoring equipment. "Everything looks great!"

I raised an amused eyebrow. "Are you a doctor, too?"

He folded the blanket back and peeked under the bandages on my side. "Not licensed, but I have studied extensively throughout my life. It comes in handy for situations like this."

My smile turned to a frown. "Sam said Kaytee is recovering. Will she be okay?"

Dram's mouth tensed as he nodded, and his eyes grew distant before his soft smile returned. I knew he'd never forgive himself for letting her get hurt. "Yes, she'll make a full recovery. The strain on her mind from Jackson's magic is still healing, but she should be up and back to her normal self in a day or two."

A lump caught in my throat, and I swallowed. "Dram, I'm really sorry I put her in danger. I thought she'd be the safest out of all of us, but I was obviously wrong about that."

His smile was gentle. "It's not your fault, Jeanie. If I'd had any doubts, I wouldn't have let her participate. It was a fluke Jackson found you when he did." He sighed as he shook his head. "I love my assistants, but sometimes I think I should let them go. No matter how hard I try, being part of a divine's life will never be one hundred percent safe."

"Well, being alive isn't a hundred percent safe, either." I pointed to my chest. "And hanging out with yours truly drops those safety stats considerably."

He chuckled and patted my shin again. "Get some rest, Jeanie. I'll check in on you this evening, and we'll all catch up soon."

After he left, I turned to Sam. "Did you guys use magic divine powers to stop me from dying? I thought I was a goner there."

"Well...yes and no." He scratched the back of his neck. "Dram destroyed the vessel and helped stop the bleeding with a charm. But also..." He winced, eyes apologetic. "To keep you from going into shock and getting worse, I made you my assistant and gave you a power. Sorry, I know I shoulda asked first. I'll release you whenever you want, I promise." He held up a hand, face solemn and serious.

My eyebrows drew together. "I thought you couldn't give humans healing abilities?"

"We can't, not without tying our life force to yours with the blood curse. Hence the bandages and bed rest."

"Okay, so what power did you give me?"

Sam's smile was cautious, but hopeful. "Nothing can hurt you."

41

DRAM DROPPED BY again in the evening to check on my wounds before re-bandaging them. He smiled and nodded, pleased with the progress, and recommended I take a week of bed rest to give my body time to heal. He let his serious eyes rest on mine for a long moment, then Sam's, when he told me to avoid strenuous activities. I sighed—this was going to suck. I hated the idea of spending a week at Olita's condo, but it had everything we needed, and Sam was excited about going through the library.

The power Sam had given me prevented my condition from worsening, but it would still take time to fully heal. Thanks to his careful wording, I felt no pain again, though the itching from my healing wounds nearly drove me to distraction. I tested my new power by trying to stab a fork into my arm and grinned in amusement when an invisible force repelled every attempt. It was like Marcus's shield, but was active all the time and protected only me. I was annoyed with Sam about that aspect and told him so when he stretched out on the bed beside me.

"Maybe you should give me a power that will let me actually defend you, you know, like a good assistant should."

He grinned. "Nah. I like the one I gave you. And if I need to, I'll just toss you at an attacker and run away."

I laughed louder and longer than I had in three years. "But why run when you can have someone else piggyback you from the scene?" He snorted and shook his head at me, his eyes sparkling. I nudged him with my elbow. "But seriously, you should get another assistant to help protect you from all those bloodthirsty demons out there."

He shrugged. "I'm pretty happy with just the one." He winked at me. "We'll cross that bridge when we get there."

My eyes scanned from his head down to his feet. "Where'd you put the vessel?" His mouth widened into a self-satisfied smirk when he pointed to a round bump in the hollow above his clavicles. It looked like a BB lodged under the skin of a careless teenager. I poked at it. "You're such an adorable dork."

He grinned and carefully took my hand in his and kissed it.

My gaze drifted down to our entwined fingers. My amusement drained away as I stared at my fresh bandages and thought of Dram.

"What do you think Dram will do when his wife gets old?"

Sam's brow turned thoughtful, and he shrugged. "I dunno. Each divine handles the aging thing different. Some go on til they're ready to find someone new, some only have relationships with other divines. Some refuse to have relationships altogether." He scratched his chin. "Dram'll probably do what very few of our kind do." I raised an eyebrow, and the corners of his mouth lifted into a soft smile. "He'll retire." I tilted my head in confusion. "He'll give up his powers and die along with her," he clarified.

"Oh."

The tears welled up in my eyes, and I looked away. Our relationship was too new and untested to be thinking about the distant future, but the issue had been on my mind ever since Sam explained the different rates of aging.

He kissed my hand again. "That's another bridge to cross when we get there."

Sam cared for me throughout my entire recuperation period. The attention made me uncomfortable, but somehow he knew when to leave me alone and when to be around. At first, I was nervous that after an intense week of danger and wild sex, a slow week of boring and celibate house arrest would reveal there was nothing to hold us together beyond physical attraction. After two days, I put the worries to rest. Tom and I had fit each other like gloves: providing warmth and protection from the outside world but having no form or purpose if we didn't have the other inside to fill the void. Sam and I were more like two different puzzles cut from the same jig; we each had our own individual pictures, but fit together to create new and interesting combinations that neither of us could've predicted.

Sam had a long past that I begged him to share with me, and he started with the easy stuff: old relationships with other goblins and incubi, tales of his life on the streets of Dublin, moving to Seattle to carve out a new territory. During the dark nights, when it's easier to talk about secret things, he told me about his childhood. It was idyllic: long days exploring the Irish countryside, gentle tutoring from Maeve, playing silly made-up games with Bridget. He didn't tell me about the day they were murdered, and I didn't push him. It's risky to break down someone else's door, because there's probably a good reason they locked it in the first place. Years of trauma might spill out and take ages to clean up again. I wasn't going to be responsible for destroying the work done by decades of coping mechanisms. Besides, I had time now to wait for an invitation.

I filled him in on my younger days too, although my stories were decidedly less interesting. Still, the tales of being raised in white, middle-class America captivated him, like he was an anthropologist studying the customs of a distant civilization. Explaining the family dynamics that shaped my childhood proved more of a challenge. Growing up with a mother who's the textbook definition of narcissistic personality disorder, and a father who dealt with tension at home by disappearing behind a bottle was as alien to him as divines were to me. A lot of things seemed to click into place for him after learning about that part of my upbringing. I told him a little about my life with Tom, too. I kept most of it to myself, though—my own locked door I wasn't ready to open for anyone.

Sam and I watched our favorite movies together and read each other's favorite books. He called it a crash course in understanding one another's psyches. The more I learned about him, the more I fell in love, and pieces of my old self started returning. It was a strange reunion; sometimes I had moments of vertigo where I would forget what year it was and couldn't be sure if the person I heard in the other room was Sam or Tom. My heart would pound in confusion until he came in with a cup of tea or a book, his beautiful smile lighting up his face when our eyes met.

As the new me took shape, I made it a point to kiss and touch Sam as often as he would let me, my capacity for love growing with each caress. I desperately wanted to help make up for all the years he'd spent alone. He struggled with the attention, but I knew it would take time to convince him he deserved to be loved. It took me longer than I cared to admit before I realized he was trying to do the same for me, too. I just hoped we'd both have enough time to get there before the end.

On the last day of our week in seclusion, I was reading on the couch when Sam came in with a thin box in his hand. I frowned when he handed it to me.

"It's not a birthday present," he said quickly.

I'd told him that birthdays and gifts weren't my thing and that chocolate and a solid screw were more than enough to celebrate. With a weary eyebrow raised, I opened it. Inside was the knife Olita had given me.

"We found it on Dram's assistant," he explained. I peered up at him, brow furrowed in confusion. "I've made it mine, and I want you to have it."

I lifted it out of the box. "Why Olita's knife?"

His gaze lingered on the shining blade. "Because it was Maeve's."

42

KAYTEE LEAPT UP to give me a hug when Sam and I met her, Marcus, and Dram at the office. I squeezed her back, tears in my eyes and a thousand thank yous on my lips. She just laughed me off. "Now we're even."

Marcus and Dram took turns giving me hugs and Sam handshakes before we sat down for lunch. Between bites, I asked them about what had happened outside the restaurant.

Kaytee started off. "The first part went to plan. I was able to get the doors blocked and release the bolts with no trouble. I also found Olita's ring, but then that asshole and his people showed up." She hesitated for a moment. "The angel did his mind control on me. It was...awful." My chest tightened in sympathy. She took a deep breath before continuing. "After he made me tell him about you all, his assistant touched me, and I guess I passed out. The next thing I remember was seeing Marcus." They shared a soft smile. My gaze darted back and forth between the two.

When Dram finished chewing, he told his bit. "There's not much to Marcus's and my story. As you know, we broke out through the front and must have passed Jackson's assistant without realizing it. When we got to the back, Jackson was already inside, and Kaytee was on the ground with the woman standing guard. I charmed the woman, but I couldn't wake Kaytee." His brow drooped, and his habitual smile dimmed when he looked at her—his inability to help her had obviously shaken him. "We found Olita's ring next to her, but it took several tries before I was able to destroy the vessel. I'm so sorry I wasn't able to prevent your pain, Jeanie." His eyebrows dipped in apology. "By the time we got back inside, everything was over. Olita and Jackson were dead and Sam was trying to stop you from bleeding out. I did what I could to help, and the rest is history!" His dimples reappeared as he ended on the successful note.

I shook my head and let out a slow breath. "I hope we're all done fighting divines. I've had enough in the past month to last me a lifetime. Now that I have my fear back, I'm going to be running from them every chance I get." I smiled at Dram and then Sam. "Except for you two, of course." Sam gave my shoulder an affectionate squeeze. "What's next for you all?"

"Well..." Dram's eyes meet Sam's. "There's been some talk about relocating to Montana. I hear there's an opening for an angel in the area." Dram winked at my surprised face. "Lupita and I have discussed it; it might be a good move for us. Cleaner air, more space for the kids to roam, and the opportunity for me to use a new alias."

I turned to Kaytee and Marcus. "What about you two? Would you also go to Montana?"

Kaytee shrugged. "I've never been, but I'm curious to see what it's like." She exchanged a look with Dram. "I've decided to resign from my position as Dram's assistant." She laughed at the shock on my face. "I'm not ready to leave the Nguyen family yet, though. I'm going to help with the kids while I finish my degree."

Marcus's smile didn't change. "I'm staying on. I like keeping the family safe." His gaze flickered to Kaytee.

Yep, definitely something there.

The obvious implication of who would stay in Seattle remained unsaid as we finished our lunch. Instead, the discussion shifted to Dram's family: their upcoming vacation to Italy, what kinds of sports the kids were into, and Lupita's next fundraising event she was organizing.

I asked Kaytee about her plans for a degree.

"I'd like to become a licensed therapist and work with men and women who are recovering from abusive relationships." She smiled at Dram. "Dram already has a business plan drawn up for a nonprofit to provide counseling services to disadvantaged youth and adults. I haven't even graduated, and I already have a job lined up!"

After lunch, Sam and I took an unhurried stroll along the waterfront until we found an unoccupied bench overlooking Elliot Bay. The seagulls wheeled and dove among the tourists, and the scent of fried fish, creosote, and saltwater filled the air. I leaned my head on his shoulder and sighed with pleasure as he ran his fingers up and down my neck with gentle strokes.

"What now, Sam? Any grand plans for your new territory?"

He gazed out over the water and blew out a long breath. "Not really. I never expected I'd make it to angel rank. I think I'll take a page out of Maeve and Dram's book and do good where I can..." He glanced at me from the corner of his eye. "But I'm also gonna keep fucking up any divine that hurts a human." He looked down at his lap and shook his head. "All I ever wanted was to kill Olita, and then all I wanted was to be with you. All this other shit is kinda overwhelming." He met my eyes. "Listen, Jeanie, I dunno what you wanna do and where you want to end up, but I'll go wherever you go. If you're okay with that?"

"But don't you need to stay here if you're taking over from Dram?"

He shrugged. "Nah. The territory covers the entire state. There's plenty of places to go." He saw my look and added quickly, "You don't have to decide now. Just something to think about."

I screwed up my face and nodded my head while I pretended to consider it. "Well...I think I'm going to go wherever you are." I winked at him and stretched my neck up to whisper in his ear. "Ride or die, Sammy."

He whispered back, "Ride or die, Jeans."

When he kissed me, sunlight touched the shimmering water and bathed my world in light.

EPILOGUE

THE CLOUDS WERE a patchwork of mottled grays when I gazed up from Tom's grave. The grass tickled my arms in the chilly autumn breeze as I lay there, sober, trying to conjure up a vision of his face. It was growing faint around the edges, and I blinked back the tears collecting on my lashes.

"Well, Tom, I got to see Isaac and Jenny yesterday. Isaac's so big now, but he's still got your goofy grin. It was kind of awkward when he first saw me, like he couldn't quite remember who I was, but then we played soccer and it was like I'd never left. It's crazy how kids can roll with the punches; I could've learned a lot from him if I'd stayed." I sighed and closed my eyes. "I started therapy. I hate it, just like I knew I would, but you were right, Tom. I should have started a long time ago. I could've been a better person for you…and been there for you in a more meaningful way at the end. I'm so sorry."

Eyes unfocused, I watched the sky, wondering where I'd be if I'd chosen the healthy path: gone to grief counseling with Jenny, gotten help for my mental illness and addictions, confronted my demons instead of spiraling downward. I shook my head at the absurdity of life and smiled. "You know, it's funny how the wrong choice ended up leading me in a new and wonderful direction. I never imagined being where I am now. I didn't think I'd ever fall in love again, but somehow it happened despite myself. You'd like Sam. He takes care of me and he loves me. I love him, too, but not the same way I loved you. I'll never love someone the way I loved you. That's always going to be just ours, forever."

I paused my thoughts to watch the clouds as they swirled and broke apart into wispy tendrils to reveal the pale blue sky beyond. There was probably a metaphor in there somewhere.

I sat up and fumbled in my purse for the small silver box Sam had given me. Inside were two rings that gleamed dull gold in the overcast light. "Look! Jenny had our wedding bands. She's a much better person than I am, and I'm lucky to still have a piece of you in my life. I won't screw that up again." My fingers caught my tears before they fell, and I took a deep breath. "I'm finally fulfilling the promise I made to you, Tommy. Sorry it's taken so long." I kissed my teary fingers and touched the epitaph. "I will always carry you in my heart and so we'll never be apart. I love you forever."

With a lighter step, I headed down the hill to the van laden with camping and traveling supplies.

Sam stroked a hand down my back and kissed me when I walked up. "All good?" I nodded, and he opened the door for me. "Ready for a new adventure?"

I smiled up at him. "I think I finally am."

ACKNOWLEDGMENTS

I would like to thank my amazing husband for his support as I pursue the dream of becoming an author. I hope one day I can return the favor so he chase his own dream of riding tigers in circuses.

Thanks also to my beta readers and editors for their feedback and encouragement. You're awesome!